Praise for the novels of Julie Kenner

"Julie Kenner always takes you on a wild, funny ride!" —Stephanie Bond

"Fast-paced suspense and sparkling, snappy dialogue . . . action that literally doesn't let up till the last page should keep readers returning for more."
—*Publishers Weekly*

"Julie Kenner just might well be the most enchanting author in today's market."
—The Romance Reader's Connection

"What fun! The characters were well developed, sympathetic and lovable, while the supporting cast was fabulous. . . . [A] wonderful read."
—Scribes World (5 Stars)

"Amusing fantasy romance . . . a fabulous tale."
—BookBrowser

"Witty and fun . . . [a] wonderful book by a fabulous author." —Huntress Reviews

First Love

The Bridesmaid Chronicles

JULIE KENNER

A SIGNET BOOK

SIGNET
Published by New American Library, a division of
Penguin Group (USA) Inc., 375 Hudson Street,
New York, New York 10014, USA
Penguin Group (Canada), 90 Eglinton Avenue East, Suite 700, Toronto,
Ontario M4P 2Y3, Canada (a division of Pearson Penguin Canada Inc.)
Penguin Books Ltd., 80 Strand, London WC2R 0RL, England
Penguin Ireland, 25 St. Stephen's Green, Dublin 2,
Ireland (a division of Penguin Books Ltd.)
Penguin Group (Australia), 250 Camberwell Road, Camberwell, Victoria 3124,
Australia (a division of Pearson Australia Group Pty. Ltd.)
Penguin Books India Pvt. Ltd., 11 Community Centre, Panchsheel Park,
New Delhi - 110 017, India
Penguin Group (NZ), cnr Airborne and Rosedale Roads, Albany,
Auckland 1310, New Zealand (a division of Pearson New Zealand Ltd.)
Penguin Books (South Africa) (Pty.) Ltd., 24 Sturdee Avenue,
Rosebank, Johannesburg 2196, South Africa

Penguin Books Ltd., Registered Offices:
80 Strand, London WC2R 0RL, England

First published by Signet, an imprint of New American Library,
a division of Penguin Group (USA) Inc.

First Printing, September 2005
10   9   8   7   6   5   4   3   2   1

Chapter One

Don't rush your wedding . . . savor it. Overcome the cliché of the stressed-out bride by focusing on your secret weapons—time and planning. Pick a date that will allow you to blossom along with your plans, each step in the planning process bringing you one calm, smooth and organized step closer to that final, wonderful day.

—from The Guide to the Perfect Texas Hill Country Wedding, *Summer 2005 Edition*

"I'm screwed," Julia Spinelli said miserably. "Absolutely, totally and completely screwed."

Across the table, Sydney stabbed some sauerkraut onto the end of her fork, then looked at it dubiously. "Maybe it would have been smart not to fire your wedding planner."

Julia shot her sister a scathing glare, then rocked forward, banging her head rhythmically on the picnic table and the bridal magazine she had open in front of her.

Maybe if she banged hard enough, she'd wake up and realize this was all a dream. It wasn't really five days to the wedding—it was five months. And instead of a laundry list of details still to attend to, she'd awake to discover that everything was ready and in place, and all she had to do was have a facial, shave her legs, buy something sexy for the wedding night and then go marry the man she loved.

She opened her eyes, clinging to the hope that this was a bad dream and she had more than five days, five hours and thirty-two minutes to pull together the ultimate wedding. But instead of a reprieve, all she saw across the table was an amused pair of brown eyes. The sauerkraut, she noted, was back in the dish, having never made it past her sister's lips.

"Damn it, Syd," she said. "This isn't funny."

Syd's mouth curved up into a smile, but she was smart enough not to laugh. As Julia's big sister, she knew well enough that any misplaced chortle could easily earn her a kick in the shin. "You're right," she said. "Not funny at all."

Behind them, children frolicked on the playscape that dominated this corner of Market Square, a lovely little park with a small museum, a charming garden with an arbor, and lots of covered picnic tables. After a morning of prowling through the Main Street shops for welcome-basket goodies, Julia and Syd had grabbed takeout bratwurst from Auslander Biergarten and walked the short distance to the park. She didn't really have time for a break, but Julia knew that if she didn't eat, she'd probably pass out. Of course, if she continued to eat bratwurst—a wonderful sausage that had never crossed her lips back home—she'd have to add finding a new wedding dress to her list, because the one currently scheduled for delivery tomorrow would rip to shreds the second she tugged it over her ever-widening hips.

Since the dress was the one part of her wedding plans that had yet to dissolve into disaster, Julia didn't intend to tempt fate. She'd eaten just two bites, then pushed the sausage away to pick at the garden salad—without dressing—that she'd bought as an afterthought.

Syd, Julia noticed, didn't try to talk her little sister into consuming anything more nourishing than wilted leaves of iceberg lettuce. In fact, once it was clear that Julia was done with the salad, she'd reached across the table, nailed the sausage with her fork and started to chow down.

Julia scowled, ignoring the blatant food theft. She pushed the magazine across the table, her manicured nail tapping on the article that had plunged her into this bout of misery. "Right there." She tapped the page. "See? I'm supposed to be savoring." She repeated the word for emphasis: "*Sa-vor-ing*. Instead, I'm suffering."

Syd took another bite, then closed her eyes, doing a good impression of someone entering nirvana. "*I'm* savoring," she said.

Julia rolled up the magazine and smacked her sister.

"Hey! Don't take it out on me! I'm not the one who got engaged and set the wedding date for just barely a month later. And I'm not the one who set you up with a wedding planner with an agenda."

"It wasn't his agenda—it was Kiki's."

"Exactly. Too bad your future sister-in-law is a little overexuberant."

Julia raised an eyebrow. "Overexuberant? She had Breckin wasting hours researching destination weddings instead of following up on *my* list. It took him ages just to rent the tables and chairs, and he was absolutely no help at all with the photographer or with finding me a morning-of makeup artist and hair designer."

"You're going to design your hair?" Syd looked completely baffled by the concept. "You've spent the last twenty-some-odd years putting your hair into every possible style. What could anyone do better than you can manage yourself?"

"Syd . . ."

Her sister held up her hands in surrender. "Whatever."

"My point is that Breckin was spending so much time doing Kiki's bidding, he wasn't focusing on me." At first, Julia had been patient because she did need the help. Putting together a wedding with over three hundred guests required a ton of planning—especially a whirlwind wedding. But she'd reached the end of her rope when Breckin admitted that he hadn't confirmed the photographer because Kiki'd had him running interference for *her* wedding. If Kiki hadn't already stepped up to the plate and arranged for Vera Wang gowns for the bridesmaids, Julia might have had to throttle Roman's little sister.

"Despite all her trouble, though," Julia had to admit, "Kiki did come through in the end." In fact, at the moment, Julia considered Keeks a goddess, since she hadn't been blowing smoke about the Vera

Wang thing. The dresses had already arrived at the same shop in Austin that Julia was using for the groomsmen's tuxes, and Syd and Viv had already been fitted, and Kiki was bringing her dress with her. Fabulous, sleek gowns in peacock blue silk with spaghetti straps and plunging necklines. If Julia hadn't already fallen madly in love with another dress in a San Antonio shop, she would have snagged a Vera Wang gown, too.

"She did good by the gowns," Syd agreed. "But overall, you have to admit that by comparison, I've been the voice of reason from the beginning."

"Voice of reason? Have you gone mental? You wanted me to call off the wedding!"

Syd looked only slightly abashed. "Well, yeah, but I thought that was reasonable at the time."

"You thought Roman was some sort of con artist! You thought I was being flighty and naïve." She tried for a light tone, really she did, but her voice held more accusation than good humor. She'd forgiven her sister for trying to sabotage her engagement, but the incident still stung.

"I had justification," Syd said, getting her back up and slipping into her know-it-all persona. "You hadn't even known the guy a month, and suddenly you were making wedding plans? Of course I was concerned. How could you fall in love so fast? Be so sure that he was the one?"

"You did," Julia pointed out, thinking of her sister's recent tumble into *l'amoure*. And her sister's fall had given Julia such pleasure. Not only was it poetic justice after the way Syd had doubted the strength of Julia's feelings for Roman, but Julia was genuinely happy for her big sister. Syd might be a real pain at times, but Julia loved her anyway.

She flashed a grin. "Yes, indeed. I'd have to say that the ever-stalwart and reasonable Sydney Spinelli fell hard and fast."

It was Syd's turn to scowl, but the sour expression was marred by the light shining in her eyes. "Yeah, I did. But," she added, sitting up straighter and sliding easily into big-sister mode, "*I* don't have a history of collecting men."

"*Collecting men?*" Julia repeated. "God, Syd, you make me sound like Hannibal Lecter. And for the record, I never 'collected.' I dated. And also for the record, Roman's the first man I've been in love with. If you'd put any thought into it before you rushed from Jersey to Texas to save your poor helpless little sister, you would have realized that I'd never been engaged before. Roman's the first and the only and we're getting married with or without your approval or Pop's approval or anyone else's for that matter."

"Touchy much?" Syd countered, without a hint of remorse.

Julia huffed, feeling a little martyred, but, damn it, ever since she'd told her bridesmaids about the wedding, everyone seemed to be planning sabotage. First Syd, then Kiki, then most recently Julia's best friend Vivien. It was enough to give a girl a complex.

"At least tell me you understand," she finally said. "And that you approve."

"I do, and I do," Syd said, and despite her lousy temper, Julia smiled.

"Practicing?" she asked.

"I take the Fifth," Syd answered, but her eyes told another story, and Julia wondered if Alex had popped the question yet.

Across the table, Syd leaned forward and took Julia's hands. "Seriously, Jules, I do understand how you fell so hard so fast. I didn't when I came, but I do now. You know that, right? That I only wish you the best?"

"I know." It had been a little rocky when Syd had first barreled into town. But after a few missteps, they'd finally come to terms, and now Julia was genuinely grateful her sister was in town to help with the wedding details and, well, to just be a big sister.

"Then don't take this the wrong way." Syd took a deep breath. "But maybe you should postpone the wedding. Get married at Christmas instead of next Saturday."

"Are you insane? Kiki already tried to manhandle us into a winter wedding, and we are *so* not doing that." A fresh jolt of anger cut through her. "Damn it, Syd, every time I think you're on my side—"

"I *am* on your side, sweetie. You're the one who said you're stressing out. You're the one who said there's no way you can get everything done in a week—"

"Less than a week," Julia cut in morosely.

"And you're the one who's going to have to deal with Marv when he gets here."

Julia sighed heavily. She loved her father, really she did, but Marv Spinelli was Jersey born and bred, living proof that all clichés and stereotypes had some basis in fact. If Julia didn't know better, she would have easily believed that Joe Pesci had used her father as a case study when he'd boned up on his character for *My Cousin Vinny*. And Julia knew with absolute certainty that Marv's brash, bull-in-a-china-closet manners weren't going to blend seamlessly with the Southern charm of the small Texas town. Left unattended, Marv would clear a path through Fredericksburg as wide as Sherman had cleared through Atlanta.

"If you think you're going to be able to focus on wedding details with our father stomping around town, then the Texas sun has seriously fried your brain."

Obviously, Julia didn't intend to leave her father to his own devices—which meant she had to add "Babysit Pop" to the top of her list of last-minute wedding tasks.

"I almost wish I hadn't told him. Or that his memory wasn't so long." Marv hadn't been thrilled when she'd called yesterday to finally tell him about the whirlwind wedding. But what had really smoked his goose wasn't the short engagement, but the identity of the groom.

Marv had never met Roman, but he'd butted heads with Robert Sonntag, Roman's father, over a real estate deal some fifteen-odd years ago. That wouldn't have been a problem if Marv had won the battle, but he hadn't. Not only had Sonntag managed to hold on to his property, but he'd also won in court. Always a sore loser, Marv had bought a neighboring parcel of land and plunked a Marv's Motor Inn at the corner of Main and Orange, a reminder to everyone in the town that what Marv Spinelli wanted, he got.

The irony, of course, was that if he hadn't later shipped his youngest daughter off to manage that very motel, Julia would never have met and fallen in love with the enemy. Fate's twist amused Julia, but her father hadn't seen the humor. As soon as he'd heard the Sonntag name, he'd barked into the phone that he'd be out there soon to "smash some sense into that dreamy-eyed blond brain of yours." Nice, Pop.

His plane was scheduled to land in Austin the next morning, which meant that Hurricane Marv would be arriving before lunch. One more day of sanity, and Julia intended to savor it. Of course, she'd considered expanding that to two days by spending tomorrow at Rivercenter Mall in San Antonio for a little credit-card therapy, but she'd talked herself out of it. She was a grown-up now. And grown-ups stayed for the fight.

"You *had* to tell him," Syd pointed out reasonably. "You want the big wedding, right? That means that the father gives away the bride."

"The Elvis chapel in Vegas is looking better and better," Julia muttered.

"Would to me, too," Syd said—then added, "Seriously, why *don't* you just postpone? Roman's the one, right? It's not like you have to get married before the love wears off."

"No, it's not like that," Julia admitted. "But I'm not going to France as Roman's girlfriend." Roman's business was wine, and he'd recently scheduled a long trip to the south of France to meet with a group of vintners. The trip was important to Roman, and that made it important to Julia. "I'm going on the trip, and I'm going as his wife. And that's all there is to it."

As Julia lifted her chin defiantly, Syd nodded, resigned. The one truth throughout their childhood had been that what Julia wanted, Julia got. This wedding wouldn't be any different. She might suffer a few bumps and bruises along the way, but in the end, Julia would be exactly where she wanted to be: smack-dab in the middle of a fairy-tale wedding with several hundred guests admiring the efficiency, grace and classy elegance of what would surely be the most fabulous social event in the history of Fredericksburg, Texas. Or South River, New Jersey, for that matter.

"So you'll help me?" Julia asked.

"You know I will," Syd said. "But maybe you would have been smart not to fire Breckin."

Julia grimaced. "He tried to move the wedding to Disney World! And he *insisted* on snapdragons, when I made it perfectly clear that I wanted birds-of-paradise and South African orchids."

"Yes, but now that A Floral Affair's gone out of business, you don't have snapdragons or orchids *or* birds-of-paradise, or even daisies. You've got—as they so charmingly say down here in the South—bubkes."

"The florist didn't close its doors because I fired my wedding planner," Julia said.

"No," Syd agreed. "But Breckin might know another florist that can pull together exotics in less than a week. As it is now, you're stuck. Unless you want to just forget about flowers altogether."

"You're kidding, right? Without flowers, the ceremony, the reception, *everything* will look totally naked."

"Or natural. You know, back to nature. Rah-rah the environment?"

"Are you insane? What would I carry down the aisle? Grass clippings? And if I wanted au naturel, I'd get married in the buff. This is an *event*. And flowers symbolize everything I want in a marriage. A thing of beauty and endurance. Something with inherent beauty that blossoms over time."

Syd blinked. "You say the weirdest shit."

"Damn it, Syd. This is my wedding. I've been fantasizing about this day since I was nine years old. I think I know what I want. And since I'm the bride, what I want is what matters."

"Julia, honey, you've never been a bride before, but you've *always* gotten what you want."

Julia frowned a little at that, but she had to concede the point. Of course, she hadn't wanted her father to ship her off to Texas, but at least the end result had turned out to be fabulous.

"At any rate," she continued, "what I want now are flowers. I'm not worried about the birds-of-paradise; those are easy. But they were only for accents, anyway. The orchids are the real focal flower." She started to tick items off on her fingers. "I need bouquets for me and the bridesmaids. Some sort of spray for my hair. Roman's boutonniere and the same for all the groomsmen. Mom's and Sarah's corsages. We don't need anything for the arbor since it's already so lovely, but I need floral centerpieces for the tables at the reception and something with flowers and ribbons decorating the chairs that line the aisle." She pressed a finger to her lips as she closed her eyes, picturing the ceremony and the reception. "Yeah. I think that about does it."

"And you're telling me this why?"

Julia didn't answer. Instead, she just rested her chin on her hand and smiled, waiting for the light of realization to shine in her sister's eyes.

"What?" Syd said. Then her eyes narrowed. "Oh, no . . ."

"Oh, yes," Julia said. "You just promised to help me. First thing you can do is call every florist in Austin and San Antonio until you find one that can step up to the plate."

"Julia . . ."

But Julia just shook her head, ignoring all protests. "Don't even try, Syd. I'm not listening."

"But—"

"*No.*" She held out her hand, and Syd closed her mouth. "The one thing I did right was get my invitations out first thing. Now I have a box full of over two hundred RSVP cards confirming over three hundred and fifty guests. If you think I'm going to walk down the aisle holding a spray of carnations and baby's breath, you are sorely mistaken."

"Sweetie," Syd said, taking Julia's hand between her own, "the flowers really aren't your major problem here. Marv is coming. *Tomorrow.* If you want to focus on a crisis, focus on that."

"I'd rather not," Julia mumbled, then shut her eyes as if that could block out the knowledge that her tacky—and tactless—parents were about to descend on and tarnish her shiny new life.

That her parents would show up for her wedding had, of course, been inevitable. In fact, knowing that Marv and Myrna would fly to Texas for the nuptials had been the only reason that Julia had truly considered—however briefly—eloping to Mexico or Monte Carlo or anyplace else exotic and far away.

But, no. Julia wanted the fairy-tale wedding too badly to make that kind of sacrifice. Had wanted it all her life, in fact. And she had to acknowledge that her father had been the one who'd firmly planted that dream in her head.

At the same time, she deeply resented that Marv had always seen—and treated—her as "the pretty one" while Syd had been "the smart one." He'd never failed to tell her how pretty she was, or how dear, or how easily she'd snag a rich and worthy husband. Depending on her mood, she'd been alternately flattered and irritated. Over time, irritation had settled in as the primary emotion, coupled with a desperate need to prove to her myopic father that she had more than a model's face and a debutante's knowledge of all things fashion.

That frustration with her father, however, had never edged out Julia's gut-deep desire for the pageantry of matrimony. She wanted it, needed it. She wanted to be a bride and walk down the aisle. She'd been treated like a princess for much of her life, and she wasn't about to turn her back on what she considered the ultimate royal treatment simply because her father exasperated her.

She and Roman had made the decision to have a big, Texas-sized wedding the weekend after he'd proposed to her. She'd seen in his eyes that he would have been just as satisfied with a quick visit to the justice of the peace, but in the generous way she'd come so quickly to love, Roman had insisted that she plan the wedding of her dreams. And—bless the man—he hadn't even flinched when she'd laid out for him the vast expanse of those dreams.

From the beginning, Roman believed Julia could pull off anything she set her mind to, whether it was making a success of the tacky Marv's Motor Inn her father had banished her to or pulling off a dream wedding.

Roman supported and helped her. More important, he had faith in her, while her own father had never once believed that Julia could do anything more than be a pretty bauble. Well, this time, Julia intended to show her father what she was made of. She'd not only convince Marv that Roman wasn't the spawn of Satan, but she'd throw the wedding of the century. Seamless, perfect and dripping with class. No tacky blue tuxedo for her father; she'd clothe him in Armani even if she had to fly the designer here herself.

And in the end, she'd prove to her father that she was capable, confident and worthy.

She only hoped that she could prove it before he drove her absolutely and completely crazy.

"Location locked in?"

"Check," Julia said. The ceremony was being held on the Sonntag estate, which overlooked the winery and vineyard. Afterward, guests could drive or walk the short distance to the centuries-old limestone building that housed the winery itself. Before she'd fired him, Breckin had arranged for tent and flooring rental, along with hundreds of folding chairs and matching linens to cover both chairs and tables. The harvest was almost on them, and the air was filled with the scent of plump, juicy grapes. The aroma would be heady, and the wine would flow freely.

"Tables and chairs?" Syd continued, her gaze drifting down her list.

"Check," Julia said. She stopped to look over Syd's shoulder. "See? Breckin marked it off." She frowned. "What about place-setting cards?"

Syd consulted the list. "Nothing marked. But do you really want assigned seating?"

Julia pondered. She'd always pictured a formal wedding with calligraphy place-setting cards and waiters in tuxes. About that one detail, though, maybe she could compromise. "Maybe not. People will want to mingle, right?"

"Absolutely," Syd said, agreeably.

Julia nodded, pleased that at least *that* little detail had been easily tackled. As they walked, she swung her single shopping bag, which held an absolutely darling T-shirt with a beaded neckline that she'd been unable to resist when they'd passed it in the window three blocks ago. "Okay, let's move on to the rehearsal dinner preparations. Did Breckin make the reservations?"

"It's marked off the list," Syd confirmed.

Julia exhaled in relief. Maybe Breckin had done more than she'd believed. "Sonntag vintage supplied to the restaurant?"

Syd scowled as she scanned the items under the "Rehearsal Dinner" heading, then flipped to the pages covering the other categories of wedding prep. The list had been typed, then each page laminated so that notations could be made for each task with a dry erase marker. Less than a week to go before the wedding, and too many of the line items had no mark beside them whatsoever. "Nothing here."

"As in, it's not on the list? Or as in, it hasn't been done?"

"Both, I'd assume," Syd said. "And when did you get to be such a high-powered taskmaster, anyway?"

Julia ignored the dig, turning instead to hurry toward the crosswalk.

"Uh, Jules? Where are you going? I thought we

were going to see if there was anything cool for the welcome baskets at Rustlin' Rob's." Syd pointed in the direction they'd been heading.

"Yeah, but Der Lindenbaum is this way." Julia nodded across the street toward the restaurant. "When Breckin gave me this list, he *assured* me everything had been included." She made a face. "Not that everything had been done, but that it had at least made it onto the list, so I knew what I was up against. I can't believe he left off stocking the family wine. If he left that off, what else did he forget?"

"At least you've got the list," Syd said. "And this laminate idea is pretty cool. I may start keeping my to-do lists like this. Breckin may have flaked out on you, but he was clever about that."

"That was my idea," Julia said offhandedly. "I've used a laminated list to organize my wardrobe since forever. That way I can tell what I've worn recently, what's at the laundry, all kinds of stuff."

Syd just stared at her.

"What?"

"That's both entirely neurotic and completely brilliant."

Julia made a face, not entirely sure whether she'd been insulted or praised by her elder sister. In the end, she decided it didn't matter which. The to-do list itself wasn't important. All that mattered was making sure it filled up fast with check marks.

As she marched across the street with Syd at her heels, she wished that Vivien had stayed in town. Until a few days ago, her best friend had been a high-powered divorce lawyer—the Ball-Busting Bitch of Manhattan, according to the *Post*. And the woman was as organized as a butler's cutlery drawer. With Viv's help, Julia could get through the to-do list in no time.

Vivien had showed up on Julia's doorstep not too long ago, the latest participant on the Sabotage Julia's Wedding bandwagon. Fortunately, Vivien had finally seen the error of her ways. Even more, she'd fallen in love and decided to do a complete one-eighty with her life. But before she could move part and parcel to Fredericksburg and settle onto her ranch for rescued greyhounds, she had to wrap things up in New York. She'd promised she'd be back by the bachelorette party.

Julia didn't begrudge Viv's good news, not at all. But she sure did wish she had another shoulder to lean on.

Thinking about Vivien's determination to protect her made Julia smile, even more so since Vivien had—finally—admitted that Roman was a great guy and that he and Julia were perfect for each other. Considering Vivien's hard-ass reputation, Julia considered her friend's change of heart a major victory.

If she could change Viv's mind, surely she could change Marv's, too. Right?

She shook off thoughts of her dad, forcing herself to concentrate. Confirm the wine for the rehearsal dinner first, then—

She stopped in front of Bling, a relatively new store on Main Street. "Oh, wow," she said, eyeing the exquisite lace and pearl teddy so prominently displayed in the window. "Wouldn't Roman just die if he saw me in that?"

"Is that the goal of a wedding night? To kill off the groom?"

"Very funny." She hitched her purse higher on her arm and adjusted her shopping bag. "I'm going in."

"Just like an admiral readying for battle," Syd murmured.

"What?"

"I said great," Syd sang. "Let's get into the air-conditioning and out of this blasted heat."

With a grin, Julia pushed inside, pretending she hadn't heard her sister's snark.

The cold air hit them immediately, and Syd made a show of lifting her hair and standing near the air vent. "Thank you, God," she said, "for inventing Freon. And I take back every nice thing I ever said about Texas. Who knew that it could actually keep getting hotter? At this rate, the earth is going to be boiling by Christmas."

"Maybe if you wore something more suited for the climate," Julia suggested, eyeing Syd's outfit with disdain. Jeans, socks, loafers and a white button-down—each piece perfectly fine on its own, but entirely lacking in interest and comfort when worn as an ensemble. "You knew we'd be walking all over the place today," she said. "Why on earth didn't you dress for the occasion?"

Syd held up her foot, displaying one Rockport loafer. "I did. These are walking shoes." She aimed a pointed gaze at Julia's feet, and the pedicured toes peeking out from Jimmy Choo sandals.

"Don't give me any grief, sweetie," Julia said. "*I'm* not the one collapsing from discomfort." She did a little pirouette for her sister's benefit, showing off the flirty Juicy Couture skirt she'd coupled with a stretchy D&G halter top. "Fashion *and* comfort."

"Not with those heels," Syd muttered. "And you're going to get a sunburn."

"I'm used to the heels, and I've invested in a little miracle called SPF." Julia studied her sister's outfit once again, and couldn't help shaking her head. "You look so cute when you let me pick out your clothes. And comfortable, too. I don't know why you insist on—"

"I'm not five," Syd snapped.

"Couldn't prove it by me," Julia said mildly. She expected Syd to rally with another comeback, but instead she just waved Jules farther inside the store.

"Go. Shop. Buy the teddy. I'll be right here. Fighting the urge to melt."

"You should get one, too," Julia said. "Alex seems like the kind of man who'd appreciate fine lace."

Color rose on Syd's cheeks, and Julia stifled a laugh. Syd might be older and have more business finesse, but in certain areas, there was no question but that Julia had the upper hand.

She left Syd with her cheeks burning and went to seek out Darla, the owner. She found the woman stocking shoes in the back. Nice shoes, too, actually.

Julia frowned and told herself to focus. This was a surgical-strike shopping spree. Lingerie and *only* lingerie.

"Julia!" Darla sang. "I'm so glad you came in. I've been meaning to call you. We've got some new stock and I think—" She leaned closer, then lowered her voice. "Well, let's just say that I'm sure Roman will have no objections."

"I saw," Julia said. "In the window, right?"

"Don't you just love it?" Darla asked. "I knew right away you would. I took the liberty of setting one aside for you. Fire-engine red."

Julia cocked her head, then shook it. "That sounds hot," she conceded, because she didn't want to hurt Darla's feelings. "But for a wedding night I was thinking something more traditional. Ivory, maybe. Or dusty pink?" She leaned forward conspiratorially. "I need a muted color because I want to wear it under my wedding gown and under my traveling outfit. We're staying at the Four Seasons in Austin before we fly out on Sunday for the honeymoon. I thought it would make a nice little entrée into the wedding night festivities, you know?"

"I do indeed. And we've got both colors. Size six, right?"

Julia nodded, then happily followed Darla to the back, imagining the look in Roman's eyes when he unbuttoned the silk blouse she'd picked out as part of her traveling outfit.

She ended up buying two—wedding-night ivory

along with honeymoon red—and was happily browsing her way back to the front of the store when she realized that she'd lost Syd.

"Darla? Have you seen Sydney?"

Darla called an answer from the back, indicating that Syd hadn't collapsed on the small sofa near the dressing rooms.

"Well, hell," Julia muttered. Didn't Syd realize they were on a schedule?

Since she really didn't have any time to waste, she told Darla where she was going, then headed out the door, determined to deal with the wine problem and then track down her MIA sister.

She was pulling open the door to the restaurant just as Syd was pushing in from the other side. "Syd!"

"All taken care of," Syd said, looking smug. "While you were luxuriating in silk and satin, I braved the heat and talked with the owner. She's going to call Roman today and have a few cases of Sonntag Special Reserve brought over."

"You're the best," Julia said, giving her sister a hug. Her mood—already improved by her recent purchases—brightened even more. "I'm beginning to believe that maybe—just maybe—we really can pull everything together before Saturday."

"Of course we can," Syd said. "We're two efficient women. We can handle any task. Face any crisis. Overcome any—"

The sharp ringtones of Julia's cell phone interrupted Sydney's barrage of praise. They both eyed Julia's tiny pink purse.

"Why do I have a feeling this isn't good news?" Julia asked as she pulled out the phone and saw that she didn't recognize the number on caller ID.

"Answer it," Syd said. "Maybe one of the billions of florists you've contacted has managed to come through with the flowers."

Julia doubted it, fearing yet another disaster, but she answered anyway. Her wariness changed to pleasure when she realized the caller wasn't Marv, but someone from the Bridal Boutique in San Antonio.

"Hi!" she said brightly. "Are you calling to confirm tomorrow's delivery?"

The man on the other end cleared his throat. "Not exactly," he said. "I'm afraid I have some bad news for you, ma'am." And as he explained why he called, Julia realized that she'd been right all along—she was screwed. Totally screwed.

"I see," she said when the man finished his spiel. She wanted to argue, but she was too numb, so she simply said goodbye like an automaton, then slid her phone back into her purse.

In front of her, Syd bounced on one foot. "What?" she demanded. "What did he say?"

"The boutique filed bankruptcy. That was the receiver. Everything's been frozen. And they're not delivering my dress." A single tear streamed down her cheek, and she wiped it away.

Syd just stared at her, clearly shell-shocked.

"Syd?"

"Your dress. Your *wedding dress?*"

Julia nodded, miserable. "God," she finally said. "It is so *very* Monday."

"They can't do that. We'll call Viv. There's got to be some loophole, some catch. You *paid* for it!"

"He said I'm a creditor now. And I only put down a deposit. I was supposed to pay the balance tomorrow." She closed her eyes and counted to ten, determined not to fall apart. Gossip traveled fast in a small town, and she wasn't going to have rumors flying about why Roman's fiancée burst into tears in the middle of Main Street.

Beside her, Syd still looked ready for a fight.

Julia put a hand out to still her sister, then took a deep breath. "It's okay."

"Okay?" Syd repeated. "Jules, I may not be the fashionista you are, but even I know that losing your wedding dress five days before the wedding is not *okay.*"

"Don't rub it in. I was trying to be optimistic. I mean, at the very least I know that nothing else can go wrong."

The sharp *ah-OOO-ga* of a horn blasted through the thick, humid air, followed by a tinny rendition of "The Yellow Rose of Texas." As one, Julia and Syd turned and looked down Main Street, facing roughly east toward Austin. There, barreling toward them, was a pink stretch limo with the broad horns of a longhorn mounted in place of a hood ornament.

Julia's stomach roiled, and she gripped Syd's hand. "It can't be," she said.

"No," Syd agreed, her voice just as low, just as desperate. "They aren't supposed to get here until tomorrow."

But even though Julia couldn't see through the tinted glass windows, she knew with absolute certainty who was in that limo. *Marv.* No one else could possibly have commissioned such a tacky, tacky ride.

"I was wrong," she said, fervently wishing that the Texas sun would just melt her into the pavement. "Things just got a whole heck of a lot worse."

Chapter Two

Remember that your family members are more than just guests; they're vital participants in the wedding process. Even more, they can be your biggest asset! So get your parents, siblings, aunts, uncles and other relatives involved. Make memories that will last a lifetime.
 —from How to Throw an Intimate Wedding for
Over Two Hundred Guests

"Please tell me that I've died and gone to hell," Julia said. She wanted to look away from the approaching limo—actually, she wanted to *run* away—but she couldn't seem to stop staring. It was like watching a car wreck. Only worse, since she was the one about to go down in flames.

"You must have," Syd said, shaking her head. "It's hot enough. And even Marv isn't so tacky that he'd come all the way to Fredericksburg in a pink longhorn limo. That's got to be Satan in there. It's just got to."

The limo pulled to a stop in front of them, and as the rear window started to roll smoothly down, Julia saw Thelma Lynn Grafton and Delores Rosenbaum across the street, staring and pointing. *Great*. The High Priestess of Gossip and her lady-in-waiting were witnessing the entire scene. How perfect was that?

After a rocky start as That Jersey Girl, Julia had moved on to the equally unattractive title of Roman's Little Fling. It had taken her weeks of mingling, socializing and generally being friendly, but she'd won over the locals. And now that she was known as simply "Julia" or "Roman's lovely fiancée," she really, really, *really* didn't want to be demoted to "that obnoxious Jersey businessman's daughter."

"Well-ah, lookey what I found takin' a little stroll through the heart of Texas." Marv's fleshy face and Doughboy shoulders pretty much filled the window. Even so, Julia could see her mother, Myrna, curled up in a corner, her hand in front of her as she inspected her nails. *No help from Mom,* she thought. *Nothing new there.*

"Come on, youse two." He swung the door open, revealing a puke green polyester suit. "Get in."

Without thinking, Julia took a step backward. "Um, hi, Daddy."

Beside her, Syd's eyebrows rose. Julia shrugged. All the local girls—even grown women—referred to their fathers as "daddy." Apparently it was a Southern thing. And though it rolled awkwardly off her tongue, the moniker was kind of sweet. And Julia wasn't above blatantly borrowing the term if it would win her any points with her own father.

"Don't 'hi' me, young lady. We gots things to talk about. Serious things. Now get your tush in the car, and your sister, too."

A quick burst of a horn sounded from behind them, and Julia turned to see Alex Kimball pull his dusty Suburban to a stop on the opposite side of the road. Beside her, Syd practically quivered with delight. And though Julia was certain Syd was thrilled to see Alex, she had a feeling that the depth of her sister's happiness stemmed primarily from the possibility of ducking Marv. "Coward," she hissed, but Syd just smiled at Julia and waved at Alex.

"I've got a conference call set with the owner of a California spa," he called from his truck. "Can you spare Syd for a few hours? I'd really like her in on this."

For a moment, Julia considered saying no. But she knew how important Alex's current business venture—marketing a variety of products derived from bizarre, gangly birds called emus—was to him and his uncle Ted. More, she knew that Syd had been helping him with packaging and other aspects of the business. Her sister had even had the nerve to ask Julia if she'd serve emu at the wedding, but while Julia might be a little amenable to stretching the bounds of tradition, she wasn't *that* generous. The wedding was going to be held sans ugly-ass birds.

Still, as much as Julia found the idea of emu meat completely unappetizing, she found the body lotion to be an absolute dream. And if Alex had a meeting with a California spa, that must mean he'd had some serious interest in Emulsion. Julia hoped the product found a niche in the market. She dreaded the day that Ted quit selling the stuff. Her hands and elbows were *so* much softer when she used it.

For something as important as negotiations with a

spa, Syd should definitely be involved—even if that meant Julia had to face Marv alone.

She swallowed, then nodded. "Go," she said. "But you owe me. Big-time."

Syd's eyes lit and she signaled to Alex that she was coming. Then she turned to the limo. "Sorry, Pop. I'm totally booked. But I'll catch you at the motel later." She blew him a kiss, then started across the street before Marv had time to argue.

"Syd!" Julia yelled, then slid into a whisper when her sister turned around. "Warn Roman that I've been captured by the infidels from Jersey. Tell him that if he loves me, he'll rescue me. But that if he wants to run away and hide, I'll understand."

Syd smirked. "Roman's not the running away type. Of course, he's also not Pop's type . . ."

And on that happy note she dashed across the street, leaving Julia to deal with Marv and Myrna all by herself.

"Yo! Hey, Princess? Am I your pop or a street lamp? Get your keister into the car."

"Coming, Pop," she said, dropping the Daddy pretense. Marv just wasn't a "Daddy." Too rough around the edges. Too *Jersey*.

She trotted to the side of the limo and climbed in, certain that within the hour, Thelma would report to everyone at the local beauty parlor that Julia Spinelli had climbed into a hideous beast of a limousine. Maybe if she was lucky, the gossips would opine that she was having a wild affair with a cowboy. That would be preferable to having everyone in town believe that someone who shared Julia's genes would actually, on purpose, rent a beast like this.

"Going native, Pop?" she asked, taking the seat across from her mother—which also happened to be the seat farthest away from her father.

His brows—two bushy caterpillars—crawled into a "V." Julia didn't bother to explain herself. Maybe she didn't really want an answer. After all, the day that he'd shipped her off to Fredericksburg, Marv had made perfectly clear that it was a punishment and that he reviled all things Texan. So if the man was now riding around in a limo with longhorns and, she noted in horror, wearing cowboy boots, then maybe there was a chink in his armor.

A chink would be good. Because at the end of the day, Julia was marrying Roman Sonntag. And the less of a battle it was to get to the altar, the better.

Across from her, Myrna beamed. "Doll-baby, you are just positively glowing. Now let me see that rock."

Julia extended a hand, a smile coming automatically to her lips. "It belonged to Roman's great-grandmother. There's a story there, but I'll tell you later."

"Not too shabby," her mother said, with just the right amount of awe. If she could tell that the three-carat stone was glass, she didn't let on.

"I'm totally harried with details," Julia said, tucking her hand back in her lap, "but I'm also completely over the moon."

"Out of your head, you mean," Marv cut in, shooting daggers at Myrna. She pursed her lips and settled back in her seat. Julia stifled a sigh. She loved her mom—heck, she even loved her dad—but she couldn't count on Myrna to help drag Marv into Julia's court. In their family, no one ever won a battle with Marv except, maybe, Syd. And Syd, unfortunately, had decided to sit this round out.

Julia could only hope that, for once, *she'd* find the guts to stand up to her dad. She closed her eyes, pictured Roman, and knew that, one way or another, she had to.

Roman hung up the phone, satisfied that he'd negotiated a good price for old man Hubert's fifteen acres. The land was adjacent to the Sonntag vineyard, and the family needed room to plant more vines. Since Hubert wasn't up to working the land anymore, it had been natural for Roman to approach him about selling to the Sonntags. After three days of on-and-off negotiations, they'd just agreed to terms— which brought the total Sonntag acreage up to forty-two on-site and another three hundred fifty acres they were leasing across the Lone Star State. Not too shabby for a winery that used to be barely a blip on the radar. And it would be even better when the winery could afford to buy those additional acres, rather than siphoning rent monies off every quarter.

Still, Roman couldn't help but grin, feeling oddly satisfied. Odd, because the price he'd offered Hubert was undeniably fair. Five years ago—hell, even two years ago—he would have started negotiations with an obscenely low price, fighting Hubert for every dime added to the bottom line until the elderly gent finally settled on a price at least twenty percent below market.

Funny the way things changed. Ironic, too, considering that five years ago, Roman could have afforded the higher price that he would have fought so desperately against. Now that he was strapped for cash, though, he was willingly incurring more debt than was comfortable. And all in the name of community pride and fairness.

Not that he'd lost his edge, he reminded himself. He still fully intended to do whatever it took to get the Sonntag label recognized as one of Texas's finest wines. Hell, one of the world's finest. But he'd do it without stepping on the toes of the citizens of Fredericksburg. The little Texas town had been his family's home for generations, and he respected that even more than he respected a finely tuned entrepreneurial spirit. Considering he'd given up a six-figure salary to come back and help his father expand the little winery, he figured he was definitely practicing what he preached. And, he knew, the townsfolk respected him for that.

This was, in fact, a town that respected both history and wine. The Sonntags had come to the Hill Country in the 1840s, along with many other German immigrants. Texas had been a republic back then, still a few years away from statehood. The German settlers, like the state, were proud and independent, and very resourceful. When Ercel Sonntag had discovered mustang grapes in the area, he'd experimented with old-world winemaking techniques until he'd developed a wonderfully drinkable wine. In fact, the Sonntag label still produced the wine, albeit in much smaller quantities.

The winery had always been small, originally making drink only for the family, and then for travelers through the Hill Country. When Prohibition came along, wine production ostensibly shut down, but everyone in the family knew better. And after repeal, production started up again. By that time, Roman's great-grandfather was involved, and he was determined to make a great wine—maybe not get rich off it, but at least produce it.

He'd started cultivating the vines, bringing in a limited number of varietals to complement the hardier and more traditional grapes like the Cabernet Sauvignon, Chenin Blanc, and Merlot. The Chardonnay was popular, of course, but so difficult to grow in Texas that the Sonntags had never troubled with it.

Roman had grown up among the vines, but he'd never actually expected to work them. That he'd come back, though, had never been a disappointment to him. He'd gotten tired of the pounding drive of a purely business life. Here, he was involved in every aspect of the wine, from the growing of the grape to the final bottling of the finished elixir.

Winemaking was only about a quarter science, and the rest was art or love or whatever you wanted to call it. All Roman knew was that wine was in his blood, and he was going to do whatever was necessary to make the vineyard a success. So far, his efforts were paying off. Since he'd come home, production and sales had increased, and currently, the winery was producing approximately fifteen varieties of wines. Not a bad showing, but Roman intended to double that figure within the next three years.

Idly, he flipped through the stack of bills that littered his office desktop. Unfortunately, good intentions didn't pay the bills, and his creditors weren't local. Instead, they were from Dallas, Austin, California, even France. It cost money to make money, and expansion had necessitated taking on some serious debt. Not an easy thing to deal with, considering that the entire reason he'd come back to Texas in the first place was to help his father *out* of his financial bind.

Eventually, though, Roman knew that the investment in time and money would pay off. In the meantime, he'd pay the winery's creditors slowly, holding off until the last minute so as to earn every possible bit of interest on the meager funds left in the winery's accounts.

Paying the creditors earlier was an option, of course, but one that would require bringing cash from investors into the mix, and that was something Roman didn't want to do. This was a family business, and he intended to keep it in the family. No outside money, especially outside money that came with restrictions and conditions and firm opinions on how the winery should be run. Cash flow might be tight right now—"tight" being a huge understatement—

but Roman knew what he was doing, and he was confident that the winery would soon be in the black. Until then, the winery could survive on a shoe-string budget.

At least, he hoped it could. Because if things got much tighter, Roman knew his father was going to be lobbying for the family to sell out to one of the California wineries that had been sniffing around, looking to get a foot in the door in the still nascent Texas wine country. Robert Sonntag had spent his entire life with money in his pocket, able to pay cash for anything he wanted, from cars to houses to acre-age. Even though the family was hardly destitute, they were no longer flying high, Texas royalty with oil money flowing from their veins.

The lack of cash made the family patriarch uncom-fortable, and Roman understood that. But if they sold out, they'd lose everything that had been built up over generations. And Roman was doing his damnedest to ensure that the winery was never in such dire straits that he couldn't keep his father's fears at bay. From Roman's perspective, selling out simply wasn't an option.

He was doing everything in his power to keep the winery going, even traveling to France in a few weeks to interview possible enologs, wine experts skilled in their ability to mix a variety of grapes grown at a particular vineyard into a bottle of stun-ning quality. Though the Sonntag label was already well-respected, he hoped that engaging the services of a French enolog would give the winery an extra edge, perhaps pushing the label up into the realm of spectacular.

And, of course, he was looking forward to the trip itself, particularly since it wasn't just a working trip. It was also part honeymoon, and he couldn't wait to show Julia Bordeaux and the Luberon. And, of course, Paris.

She'd never been to France, and Roman was thrilled to be the one to show her around. He'd seen the sights several times, but this trip, he was mostly looking forward to seeing her face when she saw the mountains, the oceans, the landmarks and, of course, the shopping.

Julia Spinelli was absurdly beautiful. Flawless skin, eyes the color of Caribbean seas, a mane of blond hair that put whatever starlet was in fashion to shame, and an adorable dent in the end of her chin that Roman had claimed as his own personal kissing spot. She was also the youngest daughter of a man who'd probably make the *Forbes* list in the not-too-distant future. As a result, Roman had expected her to be icy and distant. To his surprise, she was anything but. Julia Spinelli was earnest and clever and had a genuine interest in the people around her. Best of all, she was his, something that still astounded Roman and made him wake up every morning thanking God for bringing him this amazing woman who'd fallen just as hard and fast for him.

He checked his watch, saw that it was almost noon, and wondered if Julia and Syd were still working through Julia's list of pre-wedding errands. Almost without thinking, he picked up the phone. He'd see her at dinner tonight, but that didn't mean he couldn't hear her voice now, did it? Get an update on her day?

He was just about to dial when the intercom buzzed. "Roman? Your father's on line three."

"Thanks, Amy." He punched the line, then listened to his father's worried spiel.

"They're in breach, Roman," his dad said, wrapping up his diatribe. "But what can we do? We can't force them to take the cases. And if we sue them they'll just file bankruptcy."

"Don't worry, Dad. I'll handle it." He hoped his voice sounded calmer than he felt. Gristali Markets had been their biggest account of the year, with stores in twenty-seven states. If they were now reneging on their commitment to purchase, that would seriously affect the Sonntag Winery's bottom line.

"How? How are you handling it?"

"I've got to go, Dad," Roman said. "But I've got it under control. We'll talk about it later." He hung up the phone before his father could protest further, then ran his hands through his hair before settling back in his desk chair and exhaling.

Not an auspicious moment, he thought. For the first time that he could remember, he'd flat-out lied to his father. He wasn't in control. And that fact bothered him almost as much as the lie.

Frustrated, he headed out of his office toward the front sales floor and tasting room. The vineyard was

located just off of Highway 290. Ercel Sonntag had
built the limestone building that nestled at the end
of a tree-lined caliche drive. Once the family home,
it had been converted to guest and servant quarters
after the big house had been built, then later turned
into the base of operations for the winery. Now the
building housed the administrative offices and sales
floor for the winery, and Roman had ensured that it
looked the part.

He'd brought in professional landscapers to trim
and shape the bushes that complemented the acres
of vineyard surrounding the building. Flower beds
overflowed near the front and back porch, their fra-
grance mingling enticingly with the heady scent of
the ripening grapes.

Inside, the place was kept cool by the thick limestone walls, the well-worn oak floors inviting strang-
ers and friends alike. Amy and two others worked
there full time, manning the phones to take orders
from out-of-area customers, and overseeing wine
tastings for the many tourists who came through,
eager to try a local wine. The store also sold wine-
related paraphernalia such as glasses, openers, deco-
rative bottle stoppers and books dedicated to the art
of wine.

And, if a guest made arrangements in advance,
Roman was happy to give a complete tour of the
facilities.

A long tasting bar filled one end of the room, and
a set of French doors beyond that opened onto an

outdoor area with wrought iron tables and chairs where guests could sit and sip wine, enjoying the scenery and the company.

The employees-only area began to the right of the tasting bar, marked by a long thin corridor off of which were Roman's office and a smaller office for Roman's father. The door at the end of the hallway accessed the outside, where a sidewalk led to the back building that housed the fermentation tanks and other equipment. A set of narrow stairs just off the back door led down into the basement wine cellar.

Those areas weren't the only places off-limits to the public. Roman was currently living in the upstairs apartment, a twelve-hundred-square-foot suite that Julia swore they should turn into an elegant bed-and-breakfast retreat once the couple moved into Sonntag House. That the stately mansion he was currently remodeling would eventually be their home was a bit ironic, especially considering it was the flash point for their families' feud.

Roman wasn't currently worrying about his present or future living quarters, however. At the moment, he had plenty of other things to occupy his mind.

As Roman moved from his office into the public area, he saw that Amy was busy with a harried-looking couple bickering over whether to purchase a bottle of port or Riesling. He considered suggesting they compromise and buy both, but he could see easily enough that this couple would only say no.

That far apart with regard to their wine, and it was likely they were far apart on everything else important in their relationship.

He was about to say something anyway, just to test his own theory, when the bell above the door jingled. He turned, expecting new customers, and was delighted when Alex and Syd walked in. His heart stuttered a bit, and he held his breath, expecting Julia to traipse in after her sister. When the door merely banged shut, he frowned, and Syd laughed.

"Roman, I'm sorry I ever doubted you. You're so in love with my sister it's almost pathetic."

Roman raised his brows. "I'm not sure if I've just been insulted or complimented."

"Just stating a fact," she said, looking absurdly pleased with herself.

"Jersey's in a mood," Alex said, lifting her hand for a soft kiss to lighten the sting of the nickname.

"I am," she admitted. "But that doesn't change the fact that Roman's smitten." She grinned, broad and wide. "You should've seen the look on your face when you realized Julia wasn't behind me. Like a little boy who just found out there's no Santa Claus."

He didn't bother to deny it, especially since he had a feeling she wasn't exaggerating in the slightest. "Rather than stand there and tell me how disappointed I am that Julia's not with you, why don't you tell me where she is? For that matter, why are you with Alex and not her? I thought this was supposed to be a shopping day. Julia even left Carter at the front desk. Alone. For the entire day. She woke up twice last night afraid she'd made a terrible mistake, certain he'd accidentally rekey all of the guest rooms or somehow manage to drain the pool."

"That was our plan," Syd agreed. "Something came up."

"Carter crashed the system? All the reservations and accounts have been erased?"

"No, that would be an inconvenience. This qualifies as a disaster." She paused, looked Roman in the eye. "Our father came into town a day early."

Roman didn't waste any time. He headed for the door, reaching into his pocket as he walked to make sure he had his car keys.

"She wanted me to tell you she could use some rescuing," Syd said, even though it was wholly unnecessary. Roman was already in full-fledged rescue mode. "Just so you know, Pop seemed, um, less than excited about the wedding."

"I can't say I'm terribly surprised. If she calls you, tell her I'm on my way." He'd rescue Julia; that was a given. But the bonus was that at long last he'd get to give Marv Spinelli a piece of his mind.

And as he pushed through the door into the thick Texas heat, he realized that his earlier despondency had lifted. Amazing what the possibility of confrontation could do for a man's mood.

Chapter Three

Don't skimp on transportation. Do you really want to be the bride who left her wedding in a Ford Fiesta with tennis shoes tied to the back and "Getting Laid Tonight" written in shaving cream on the window? Not for you, darling. You go in style—a black limo, a driver in livery, and rose petals strewn along the walkway to the Rolls. Trust us. It's not an expense. It's a necessity.

—from *The Bad Girls' Guide to a Very Good Wedding*

Julia looked wistfully out the limo's window as they passed by the motel for the third time. She'd kept quiet during the ride, even though she knew Marv had ordered the driver to cruise through the town for no more reason than to show the locals that Marv Spinelli had arrived. Thank God the windows were tinted; she could postpone crawling under a rock for at least one more day.

Marv pointed one thick finger at her as he shook his head. "I don't know, Princess. I just don't know about you. I thought I knew my baby girl, but I ain't never imagined you'd pull a stunt like this."

"I'm getting married, Pop. I'm not swinging on a trapeze."

"Married?" he barked, his face blotching a deep red. "You're not getting married. You're stabbin' the family in the back. You're ripping my guts out and spilling them all over the floor of this here limousine. *That's* what you're doing." He crossed his arms and rocked a bit as if he were trying to burrow back into the leather seat.

Julia kept her mouth firmly closed, prepared to wait him out. She didn't doubt Marv's emotion—the man was definitely in a full-blown snit. But she also knew that her father tended to let any injury, real or imagined, build up in his head until it became so big and all-consuming that it had no choice but to explode out of him. For days now, Marv had been stewing, the pressure building and building without Julia there to lay into. But she was there now, and Marv was letting her have it in typical Marv fashion.

"Never thought you'd be a traitor, Princess. Your hardheaded sister, maybe, but not my baby girl."

"Marv . . ." Myrna pressed her hand against Marv's thigh. "Your blood pressure."

Marv scowled, drew in a deep breath, then smiled. Or tried to, anyway. He looked more like a pudgy three-year-old trussed up in his holiday best and trying desperately to smile for the camera.

After a moment, he held out his arms and wiggled his fingers. The explosion, apparently, was over. "I'm sorry, Princess. Come give your old man a hug."

She wanted to stay mad at him, to keep her ire up and keep him at a distance. But he was her pop, and although he could be a clueless pain in the ass at times, she still loved him. Most of all, though, she wanted his approval. She always had, even though she'd never really gotten it. And so now she moved across the small space to give him a hug. She closed her eyes and squeezed tight, breathing in the unpleasant but familiar scent of tobacco mixed with Old Spice, a scent he continued to apply even though she bought him new colognes and aftershaves for every birthday and Christmas. Marv, being Marv, never seemed to take the hint.

"That's my princess," he said, wrapping his arms around her and squeezing her tight. "Shouldn't never have sent you down here. Too much pressure. Not the way you were built, you know? Shoulda known better than to dump all that responsibility on you."

She frowned, and wormed her way free as the limo pulled to a stop in front of the Motor Inn. "It's not too much pressure, Pop. I like it here."

"You like it here? Yeah, well, I guess so, if you're banging a cowboy. But what about my motel?"

She stiffened, then counted to ten as she pushed open the limo door and stepped into the parking lot. She was *not* going to cry. "*My* motel is doing just fine. Our receivables have increased by *over* twenty percent, which is what you wanted, right? In fact, we've been at ninety-six percent occupancy for the last six weeks."

"Oh-ho! Listen to you. Your brainiac sister been giving you word power lessons?"

She lifted her chin, ignoring his dig. "I intend to get that up to ninety-eight percent by the end of summer."

Marv barreled out of the limo, then held his hand

out for Myrna. "You hear that, babydoll? Our little princess is a motel mogul."

"Damn it, Pop. I've been working my tail off here. Did you know there were fleas in some of the rooms? *Fleas!* And rats. And mattresses that streetwalkers would have refused to do business on. The place was a wreck, Pop. And look at it now. I'm doing a good job. A damn good job, actually."

"You're doing a good job," he repeated, deadpan. "You listen to me, Princess, and don't forget who you're talking to. *I'm* the one who built an empire starting with one broken-down little motel in South River. And *I'm* the one who worked my tail off making sure you and your sister never have to worry about having money. And *I'm* the one who knows damn well that you can't be doing a good job on my motel *and* banging your cowboy—"

"*Pop!*"

"—and planning a wedding *and* reading all them damn fashion magazines *and* burning a hole in your credit cards. I've seen the statements, Princess, and it ain't like you gave up shopping when you moved to the Lone Star State."

She looked down, dragged the toe of her Jimmy Choo sandal in the thin layer of dust on the driveway. "There are nice malls in Austin and San Antonio. I had to check them out."

"And what's all this?" he asked, swinging his arm wide to indicate the giant clay pots overflowing with colorful flowers. They didn't completely camouflage the brown and mustard building, but at least they gave it some flair. If Marv wouldn't pony up the money for new paint, she was going to get the high school shop kids to build a trellis. And then she was going to try to hide the façade under blooming flowers.

She wished she had money of her own to use to make the Inn prettier, but she had only the measly salary her pop paid her and the miniscule budget Marv had allotted for the Texas-based Inn.

She and Syd both had trust funds, of course, but Marv had set those up so that she had no access to the money for several more years. It was just too depressing, really. All those dollars that she could be spending on shoes and handbags and paint and flowers, just sitting in a brokerage account doing nothing. But since she couldn't get at the money except under some really obscure circumstances—like emergency surgery—she'd trained herself to not even think about it.

"Yo! I'm asking you a question, Princess."

She licked her lips. "Um, they're flowers, Pop."

"No? Ya think? I couldn't see that with my own two eyes, I need you to tell me they're flowers?" He waved a hand. "You wanna tell me why all this frou-frou crap is mucking up the place?"

"Ambiance, Pop," Julia said. She pressed her fingertips to her temple and rubbed, hoping to forestall the migraine that was about to hammer its way into her brain.

"Ambiance, my ass. Colossal waste of money, that's what it is."

"I got the flowers at a ninety-five percent discount, Pop." That had been one of her first tasks when he'd banished her to the Motor Inn—making the place look more attractive. Someplace a traveler might *want* to stay, not someplace they were stuck because all the darling bed-and-breakfasts were full up. She'd gone to a local nursery, chatted up the owner, and made a deal for all of their near-death flowers. Julia hadn't been able to resuscitate every posy she'd bought, but she had a track record that a trauma surgeon would envy, *that* was for sure. "They make the place look prettier. Syd agrees," she added weakly, when he just stared at her. Syd and Pop might go at it like bar brawlers on occasion, but Marv never questioned his eldest daughter's good sense. No, those kinds of criticisms were reserved for his pretty little princess.

Marv *harrumphed* a bit, then headed for the door. "Maybe you got a good deal on the plants," he said, "but for the money you spent on the pots, you coulda stocked a year's supply of toilet paper."

"The pots weren't expensive, Pop. Texas is pretty close to Mexico, remember? We just took a weekend and went over the border."

Even with the very minimal investment, though, Julia had to admit that Marv was probably right. The off-brand of toilet paper he'd earmarked for the motels cost next to nothing—and you could tell. Last week the supply room had finally gone empty and she'd had Carter, her part-time front desk clerk, order a fluffier brand from the wholesaler. There were some things, she thought with a shudder, that simply shouldn't be scrimped on.

Marv grunted in response, holding the door open for her and Myrna. "That was smart," he admitted grudgingly as the door shut behind him. "Don't need to be spending hard-earned capital on sprucing the place up, but if you can do it on the cheap, you're sure to get a return on your investment."

Julia stared, not quite willing to believe her father had paid her a compliment. Amazing. And since Julia wasn't in the habit of carrying a tape recorder on her person, entirely unprovable. Syd would never in a million years believe it.

"Don't go getting a big head," he said. "I'll eat my shorts if you were as smart with the rest of the operations as you were with prettying up the place."

Bizarrely, Julia relaxed slightly with the dressing-down. *That* was the father she recognized. Marv the ass she knew how to handle. Warm and fuzzy Marv was a mystery.

He grunted again, this time at Carter, who was staring at him from behind the front desk, his mouth hanging open as he goggled at the short, Jersey-fied Napoleon.

"Uh," Carter said, "it's, uh, been real quiet, Ms. Spinelli, ma'am."

"Thanks, Carter. You got a room ready for my parents, right?"

The kid sprang to action. "Oh, yeah. Absolutely. 143. So, uh, can I do anything for you now? Vacuum the halls? Restock the vending machines?"

With great effort, Julia managed not to smile. Carter wasn't a bad employee, but he was hardly a self-starter, and now his motive was perfectly clear: He wanted the hell away from Marv.

She decided to toss him a bone, both because she felt sorry for him and because if Marv decided to rail on her some more, she really didn't want her employee watching it. "Actually, that would be great. And if you could take my parents' luggage back, too, I'd appreciate it."

"No problem," Carter said, gratitude practically dripping off him.

She waited, watching as he shoved two bags under his arms and grabbed two others by the handles. As he trundled off, she reluctantly turned back to her father. "So, um, do you want to look at the books? Everything's in order. I had Syd go over them last weekend and everything."

Since Syd was also a CPA, Julia hoped that the fact that she'd enlisted her sister to do a mini-audit of the motel's records would score points with Marv. Especially since she'd passed the audit with flying colors.

Marv took off his polyester jacket, revealing dark sweat stains as he lifted his arm to toss the hideous garment over one of the lobby chairs. "Do I look like I'm in the mood to go over your records? Of course they're in order, because I'd have to fire your pretty ass if they weren't, wouldn't I?"

"Oh." Julia tried not to look too disappointed. The truth was, Julia had spent her first week at the motel teaching herself the basics of bookkeeping. She'd even cancelled plans to attend a trunk show in San Antonio, which was evidence of how important making a success of this motel was to her. At the time, she hadn't yet met Roman, nor had she been seduced by Fredericksburg's charm. No, in her first week all she'd wanted to do was nail the job to the wall and prove to her father that she had some brains under her naturally blond (albeit chemically enhanced) hair.

Last weekend, her efforts had paid off. Syd had taken two entire days away from Alex, locked herself up in the motel office, then had been unable to hide her grin when she emerged, exhausted but wired on coffee. She'd given Julia a big hug and congratulated her on having all the books in order. Roman, bless him, had taken the four of them to dinner to celebrate, and they'd all got stinking drunk on champagne. The victory, Julia thought, was even sweeter than the time Syd had relentlessly beaten basic algebra into Julia's head so that she could—with a heck of a lot of effort—move from ninth to tenth grade.

But while Julia might have been giddy from Syd's praise of her accounting efforts, Marv didn't even care, and that pissed her off. If she hadn't gotten engaged to his old nemesis's son, would he have even bothered to check on the daughter he'd shipped off to Siberia? Did he care how hard she'd been working or how much she'd increased the motel's occupancy? How much she'd managed to get the townspeople to support the ugly eyesore instead of shun it?

No, he didn't. And although Julia opened her mouth to tell him, somehow the words didn't come out. Somehow, the words never managed to come out when she was around Marv.

She shot a quick glance toward her mom, whom she'd always considered a doormat, and felt a quick twinge of guilt. Apparently, Julia and Myrna's family resemblance ran deeper than just blond hair and big boobs. Julia, it seemed, was a doormat, too.

Damn.

In front of her, Marv was pacing in circles, clearly agitated, his arms flapping in front of the fan as he tried to dry the damp moons under the arms of his wrinkled blue shirt. "It's hotter than hell out there," he said. "Just walking from the damn car to here. And it's a damn sauna in here, too. You think you can keep guests when the lobby's an oven?"

"You set out a pretty strict utility budget, Pop. And Texas is hot during the summer."

"You keep the rooms this hot, it's a wonder you get any business at all."

"The rooms are much cooler, and we let the guests adjust the temperature themselves. Since I had limited funds, I thought it made more sense to focus on the comfort of the rooms rather than the lobby."

Marv snorted, then walked deliberately to the thermostat and slid the lever down so low that Julia anticipated needing a coat within the hour.

Once again her gaze darted to Myrna, and, upon seeing her mother looking so frail and quiet, Julia was determined to widen the gap. She took a deep breath for courage, then said, "I'm doing a good job, Pop. Why can't you admit that? Tell me I'm doing good?"

His eyes narrowed until they were almost lost in the folds of his face. "Doing good? You want to hear you're doing good? All right, Princess. I'll say it." He puffed out his chest. "Sounds like you're doing a damn fine job running things in Texas, Julia." His voice was hearty, his tone almost jolly. Not at all like Marv, and she winced. He never called her by her given name. Not unless she was in trouble.

"But?" she demanded, even though her instinct was to turn tail and run. Or start in with a barrage of apologies.

"But I'm a little surprised, is all."

"What are you talking about?"

"I thought you was at least a little bit smart, is all. I guess maybe your sister really is the only girl got brains in the family."

Her mind whirled; he'd never called her smart before. "I . . . I don't understand."

"You and this Sonntag a-hole. You gotta know he's only using you."

"No, he's—"

"See? That's exactly what I'm talking about. Naïve. You really think your cowboy fell in love at first sight? Just had to have you? That it was just a coincidence that his father and I had it out all them years ago? And that I got the better of Robert Sonntag in the end? That cowboy don't love you, baby girl. He's using you. For payback." He gestured between them. "To mess up what you and me got."

Her eyes flooded, and she forced herself not to blink, determined not to leak tears down her cheeks. "You're wrong, Pop. The Sonntags aren't still obsessed with the past. It's not eating them up inside. They're not throwing temper tantrums."

At that, Marv bristled, but she hurried on. "They've moved on. This isn't about the Inn or Sonntag House or even you or Robert Sonntag. This is about me and Roman and that's all. Nothing else. *Nothing*."

Marv made a snorting gesture and shot her a pitying look.

Julia stood straighter, anger making her bold. "Roman loves me, Pop. And I love him. And you're just going to have to get used to that."

"Love him? You hardly know him. He's just one more in a long string of boyfriends. You've had your fun, had your fling. Okay, fine. I get it. But you ain't gonna let this punk-nose cowboy ruin our family, are ya?"

"It's not like that—"

He spread his hands wide, a big smile on his face. "You wanna get married, Princess. I get that. You, you were *made* to get married. And you find the right guy, and I'll pay for the biggest wedding you ever saw. One'll make them royal weddings in England look like some white trash in Vegas gettin' hitched. But you come back home. You marry a guy who gets you. Who *loves* you. One who ain't just trying to use you."

"Bart was nice," Myrna put in, her voice small. Julia turned to her mom, her eyes narrowed. "And he adored you," Myrna added. "Oh, that would be so nice. You could get married in the backyard. By the fountain. Maybe even arrange to have doves released from the roof. You like doves, don't you, Julia?"

Doves? She loved doves. For that matter, doves were on her to-do list, with butterflies in the fallback position. But she wanted Texas doves. In a Texas wedding. With a Texas groom.

She opened her mouth, not sure if she wanted to point that out to her mom or simply scream. No, what she *wanted* was to calmly and rationally tell her parents they were full of it. She wanted to explain to them that she and Roman didn't give a fig about some stupid business battle their parents had more than fifteen years ago. They were in love and they were getting married. She loved *Roman*. She didn't love Bart. Hell, she barely even remembered Bart.

Just a nice, simple, civilized conversation. They'd sit down, talk it all out—then Marv and Myrna would nod and kiss her and tell her they understood and of course she and Roman had their blessing, and wasn't it wonderful, and could they have the honor of renting white horses and carriages so that Julia and Roman could ride off into the sunset together?

Such a wonderful, wonderful scenario . . .

Braawwwp!

Marv's loud belch made Julia jump, and she closed her eyes, thrust as she was back into such an unpleasant reality. Her fantasy might be nice, but it was just that: fantasy.

In front of her, Marv had plunked himself down in the puke green lobby sofa that Julia swore she'd slipcover if she could just learn to sew. Marv had bought three hundred and fifty of the things for about as many dollars from a bankrupt furniture supply company, then had shipped one to most of his Inns across the country. Considering how hideous the sofa was in both comfort and visual appeal, Julia had no doubt why the company went bankrupt in the first place. Ethan Allen it wasn't. "That guy you got working the desk. He good?"

Julia blinked at the change in subject. "Well, yeah. He's not as seasoned as Hector," she said, referring to the part-time clerk who had been working at the Inn since before Julia came on. "But he's learning. He's a quick study."

"Good. He's the interim manager."

"Excuse me?"

"You're out of a job, Princess."

"*What?*" She shot a glance toward her mother, but Myrna, as usual, was hiding in her own little world. No help at all. "You can't!"

"I can and I did," Marv said. "It ain't your motel to run anymore. So why doncha pack your bags and come back home with us. This cowboy really loves you, he'll come after you."

"No."

"What?"

She shrank a little under Marv's evil glare, then dug deep to find her courage. "I said, no. I'm staying here."

"Then you're staying unemployed. And you're moving outta my motel."

"*My* motel. And no, I'm not." She whirled on her heel and slid behind the counter. She'd given up things she loved before because of her dad's ridiculous temper. Well, she wasn't giving the Inn up without a fight. Not after all the work she'd put into it.

She stopped in front of the computer, put her hand on the mouse, and called up the registration log. "Fire me, and I call every single one of these people and cancel their reservations. I'll say we've got a rattlesnake infestation. They'll never book again, and our ninety-six percent occupancy rate will just fly out the window."

"You wouldn't."

She picked up the phone, her heart pounding with terror in her chest, but anger fueling her courage. "Watch me."

His eyes narrowed to slits. "You're making a mistake, Princess. No one plays hardball with Marv Spinelli and wins. I'm the best there is."

Her chin lifted automatically. "Yeah? Well, I'm a Spinelli and I can play hardball, too. Believe me, I learned from the best."

He snorted, his face turning so red she almost expected steam to come out of those ears. She clenched her fists, fingernails biting into her palms. She'd never stood up against her father this hard and fast—never had him this angry at her. And she feared that if he didn't cave soon, she would. So help her, she didn't want to, but this was her pop. And she was his little girl. And maybe that made her a sap, but she didn't want her father mad at her.

Seconds ticked by, and then she watched in relief as the color drained from his face. His mouth was firm, his eyes narrow, but he nodded. "All right, Princess. You can stay on as manager. For now."

She nodded, not quite trusting her mouth to form words.

"But you're making a mistake. The cowboy doesn't love you. He's using you. And you'll figure it out soon enough."

"I assure you," Roman said, his voice, low and dangerous, coming from behind her, "that the cowboy loves her very much."

The cowboy in question had come in quietly through the back door, and had stood in the doorway, his temper flaring as he listened to Marv Spinelli browbeat his daughter. Now he stepped forward, sliding his arm around Julia's shoulders and pulling her close. He wanted to give her his strength, and as he held her, he felt her body relax against his.

He kissed the top of her head, then looked up to meet Marv's stormy brown eyes. "If anyone is making a mistake here, Mr. Spinelli," he continued, "it's you."

* * *

Roman had a lot of things in his life to be proud of. Being named high school valedictorian. Making Eagle Scout. Negotiating successful business deals. Winning the love of a beautiful woman.

At the moment, though, he was most proud of *not* strangling his fiancée's father. And, frankly, he wasn't entirely sure if he was clinging to Julia to lend his support, or because if he let go, he'd flatten her pig of a father.

He'd watched as Marv Spinelli had fired his daughter, for no other reason than that she was engaged to the enemy, and then proceeded to insult both Julia *and* Roman. All because of some damn dispute over a building that should have been forgotten years ago.

A wave of cold shame washed over him because he *hadn't* forgotten. He'd come here not only to support Julia, but also itching for a fight because some fifteen-odd years ago, Marv had bought this plot of land, slapped up an oversized COUNT SHEEP FOR CHEAP sign, and made Robert Sonntag look like a fool. Marv Spinelli had gotten the last word, but he was still carrying a chip on his shoulder. And Roman had come here intending to knock it off.

But no more. He'd seen the hurt in Julia's eyes when her father'd lashed out from the past. Roman wasn't about to add to her pain.

Gently, he pressed a kiss to her forehead, then took his arm from around her shoulders. He stepped forward, hand extended. "Mr. Spinelli, sir. It's good to meet you. I'm Roman Sonntag."

"I figured as much," Marv said, ignoring Roman's hand.

Roman slipped his arm smoothly back around Julia, purposefully not reacting to Marv's slight and also subtly reinforcing the simple fact that Julia belonged with him. "You're going to have to refresh my memory, sir," he said, keeping his voice even and his eyes on Marv. "Have we ever met?"

Marv's eyes narrowed, as if he was looking for an angle. Smart man, since that's exactly what Roman was doing. "No, cowboy," he finally said. "We haven't. But that doesn't mean I don't know you. Know what you did. What all of you did. And," he added with a pointed look toward Julia, "what you're doing now."

Roman nodded. So much for civility, but at least the cards were on the table. "What I'm doing is marrying your daughter. *Now*. Not fifteen years ago. And we'd like your blessing."

Beside him, Julia stiffened. Roman felt a twinge of guilt, wondering if he'd taken it too far, but there was no turning back now.

Marv took a step forward, his expression belligerent. "Don't play games with me, cowboy."

"I wouldn't dream of it."

"Don't bullshit me, boy. Your family is all about games."

Roman tensed, fearing that there was no way to avoid rehashing the past, and at the same time not wanting to get into it. Not with Julia standing right there. But then Marv's cell phone rang, and Roman watched the mental debate as Spinelli tried to decide if he was going to go a round with Roman or tend to business.

Business won out. He spared Roman one hard glance, then moved to the far side of the lobby, his phone pressed to his ear, a slick ducktail bobbing as he nodded in time with the conversation. "What's that? Yeah? Who called? Him, no, I ain't interested in talking to him. Who else? Oh, really?" He turned, his eyes softening as he looked at Julia, then going hard as his gaze landed on Roman. "Yeah, he's a good one, all right. Him, you give my cell number. Tell him to call me. We got stuff to talk about."

He snapped the phone closed and flashed a smile that seemed to scream victory. For absolutely no reason, Roman got a chill. "Good news, sir?" he asked.

"The best, boy." Marv pointed a finger at Julia. "And don't think we're through, Princess. Your sister may have checked your numbers, but you can bet your pretty little ass that I'm going to check your operations. I know the way you think, sweetheart, and I ain't putting up with no frivolous, pansy-ass stuff. Not at my motel."

"Pop, I—"

"Don't start with me, little girl."

"Mr. Spinelli." Roman's tone was like ice, but his blood was fire. He took a step forward, stopping only when Julia's grip tightened on his arm, pulling him back.

"Think you can threaten me, boy? This here's my business, and I'm gonna see it's run the right way."

Marv dug his hand into a bowl of potpourri, let the dried flowers fall. "How much you got invested in this kind of froufrou nonsense, huh, Princess? You don't look at the bottom line, babydoll, you ain't gonna make it." He pointed a finger at Roman. "Romeo there knows it, too."

Julia's eyes were wide and dewy. Roman had the feeling she was working hard not to blink, afraid of releasing tears. He fisted his hand, wanting to pound on the man who'd so cavalierly made her cry.

The frail blonde who'd been parked on the natty sofa rose before he had the chance to lash out. She moved quickly, tottering across the lobby toward Marv on four-inch heels, a tight pink skirt stuck like plastic wrap to her thighs. *Myrna*, he thought. Julia's mother.

"Come on, Marv, honey," she said, her hand on his arm. "It's been a long trip, and I think we both need a drink and a nap."

"I'm not—"

"Of course you're not," she said. "But I am. Now come on with me. Julia and her man aren't going nowhere. Whatever needs to be said can wait."

"Mom . . . ," Julia said, her voice soft beside him.

"Don't worry about us," Myrna said. "We'll get our key from Ford."

"It's Carter, Mom."

Myrna just waved. "I knew it was one of them." She headed out of the room, steering Marv along with her.

"This isn't over," Marv muttered from the threshold.

"No one thinks it is," Myrna said. But she turned then and looked at Roman. Beamed at him, actually. "It's *very* nice to meet you," she said. And Roman knew that, in Myrna at least, he had an ally.

"Well," Julia said brightly the moment they disappeared from view, "that certainly went well."

"Actually, it went better than I'd expected."

She looked up at him, her beautiful face showing both strain and bafflement. "You've got to be kidding. He hates you. He wants to ship me back to New Jersey. And he's going to do everything he can to sabotage our wedding."

Roman pressed a soft kiss to her cheek, wishing he could make it all better for her. "It's not all perfect, I'll admit—"

She snorted, the amusement in her eyes lifting his heart just a little.

"—but I still consider the morning a success. I didn't hit your father," he added, before she could argue some more. "Nor did he hit me. You still have your job. Your parents have left us alone, at least for the moment. And," he added, "your mother is on our side. Or, at least, she's on *your* side."

"Yeah, that was weird. Very *not* like my mom to step in when Pop's in a snit."

"Maybe their relationship is evolving."

That seemed to wipe away the last of her sour mood, and she laughed outright. "Yeah, and maybe Marv is going to pick up the phone and invite your dad over for a beer."

"All right," he conceded, "maybe your parents' relationship hasn't changed. Maybe she's always been able to handle your father."

"Myrna? Get real."

"I am. Relationships are funny business. And they've been together a long time. Your father's a domineering—"

"Jerk."

"I was going to say 'man,' but 'jerk' works, too. At any rate, it's natural that your mom's personality fades a bit into the background. But there must be some give-and-take between them or else they wouldn't have lasted this long. Don't you think?"

She frowned, but he could see her considering the possibility. "I guess it's a little like us, maybe."

He took the hand she offered, squeezed it. "How so?"

She lifted a shoulder. "Nobody seems to understand what's between us. Even Syd and Viv, my sister and my very best friend. They just saw what they wanted to see, what they expected. It took a while for them to believe that we're really in love. And even now, I don't think they understand the full of it. They believe, but they don't really know."

"How could they?" he asked. "We're the only ones who can. For that matter, we're the only ones who need to."

She made a face. "It would help if my father did."

"I'd just as soon keep your father out from between the two of us, if it's all the same to you."

As he'd hoped, she laughed, and the mood lifted a little more. "By the way," he went on, wanting to keep the mood light, "I've never actually seen a pink limo with longhorns before. If nothing else, I can thank your father for expanding my horizons."

"It's still out there?" She looked at him with such distress that he had to laugh. "I thought Pop had sent it back to Austin." She pressed her fingers to her temples and massaged there for a moment. "It was bad enough that he rolled into town in that thing, but if he's going to use it as his regular form of transportation, then I'm going to be a laughing-stock."

"No," Roman said, "your father is."

"Same thing," she muttered, looking absolutely miserable. But she squared her shoulders and headed toward the door.

He followed as she headed into the late afternoon heat, then tapped at the glass.

The driver rolled down his window. "Yes, ma'am?"

"Um, hi. Are you . . . I mean, is my father going out again tonight?"

"Don't know, ma'am. My instructions are to be available."

"Available? So you're not heading back to Austin? To the airport?"

"No, ma'am. I've been retained for a full week."

"Great," she said, her voice chipper, but Roman could see the strain on her face. He stifled a grin, knowing her well enough to be certain that she wouldn't be nearly as frustrated if a traditional black limo were parked in front of her hotel.

"What's your name?" Roman asked.

"Earle, sir."

"Well, Earle, you might as well come inside and get a room."

"But—"

"Don't worry," Julia added. "I'll tell my father. Just be available if he needs you and no one will get yelled at."

"Yes, ma'am. Thank you, ma'am."

They got Earle inside and Roman watched as Julia moved him efficiently through the registration process. As the chauffeur headed off toward his room, Carter reappeared. Julia gave him an update, asked the boy to leave a message for Marv about Earle, then turned back to Roman.

"Not going to tell your dad yourself?"

"I'm avoiding him."

"Good plan."

"Blatant cowardice," she said.

"Good sense," he retorted. Then, before she could say anything else, he went on. "You know, the limo wasn't the only odd thing I saw when I drove up to the motel."

"With a pink limo blocking your view," she muttered, "how could you notice anything else?"

"I realize we're in Texas, sweetheart, but last I recall, there were no hitching posts in the back parking lot."

"What are you talking about?"

"Horses, darling. There are three horses tied up back there."

For a moment, her expression was so baffled that he wondered if she'd been unaware of the equine visitors. Then her expression cleared, and she broke into a broad grin. "They're here? Oh, that's so fabulous! I didn't expect them until tomorrow. This is wonderful!"

"What's wonderful?"

"That, my darling Roman, is my latest surprise." She cocked her head, and when she smiled he saw that all of her earlier worry and frustration had evaporated, leaving only a delighted gleam. "Can you spare an hour or two for your wife-to-be?"

He thought briefly of the stacks of work on his desk and the upcoming meetings he had scheduled in Austin. He'd planned to drive in tonight, knowing that Julia had Syd and her wedding details to keep her occupied. Now, though . . .

"Roman?"

"Sorry. Just thinking."

"You don't have time." There wasn't any judgment in her voice, and when she laid a hand on his wrist, she smiled. "Don't feel guilty. It's okay. You just took a good chunk out of your workday to rescue me from my dad. I totally understand if you need to get back to work."

"I do," he said. Then he lifted her hand to his lips and kissed her fingers. "But it'll wait. I believe you said something about a surprise . . . ?"

"You're sure?"

"I love you."

Her face lit, as if he'd turned a switch on inside

her, and the joy he felt, knowing he could make her look like that, was something he wasn't sure he'd ever get used to.

"In that case," she said with a laugh, "come outside and let me introduce you to Shadow and her friends."

Chapter Four

From: crownjule@aol.com
To: kikid@misstexas95.com
Subject: Vera??

Kiki! My darling new sister-to-be! I'm taking two seconds to e-mail you before your big brother and I escape the madness that is my father, but I just HAD to find time to ask: Do you think Vera could pull together a dress for me after all? I know I said I'd already found the perfect gown, but it turns out that perfection is bankrupt. Which I guess could be some sort of sociological statement if I were so inclined. But I'm not. I just want a dress! Would you? Could you? I'd be ever so grateful. I'd need it to arrive here no later than Thursday, just in case it needs alterations. . . .

Your darling, loving, DESPERATE sister-to-be,

Jules

Shadow *clop-clopped* down Main Street, Roman at the reins, as Julia snuggled comfortably against him. Behind them, the buggy was empty. But if everything went according to plan, in the future it would be filled with flirting couples and laughing families.

A red Mustang convertible pulled to a stop beside

them, waiting, like they did, for the light to change. "Hey, Roman! Nice horse!"

"It's Julia's," Roman said. "For the Inn."

At her name, Julia waved at Dennis Paulson, the high school's band director. With any luck, he'd mention the new endeavor to the students, and her rented carriages would become all the rage with the high school seniors. Come to think of it, she really should advertise in the school's tiny newspaper . . .

Dennis laughed. "Isn't it a little early for a starlight carriage ride? I thought that was an after-dark activity."

"We're giving it a test run," Julia explained.

"Well, good deal, then. I'll have to take my wife for a ride once you get going good." The light changed, and he waved a goodbye, then accelerated, leaving Shadow walking at a leisurely clip behind.

Julia turned to give Roman a smile. "He liked the idea. I think he really liked it."

"Of course. It's a great idea."

"I guess. I wasn't really sure. But it seemed fun, and I was trying to be creative . . ." She trailed off, suddenly feeling over her head. Before Marv had arrived, she'd been feeling clever and in control. Now, though—she shuddered. Weren't parents supposed to make you feel *better*?

Roman put an arm around her and pulled her close. "It's absolutely perfect. How'd you come up with the idea, anyway? For that matter, how'd you pull it off?"

She heard real delight mixed with appreciation in his voice, and the relief that flowed through her left her breathless. Forget about Marv. She was here with Roman, and he appreciated her, and the carriage rides *were* a good idea.

"At first, I thought maybe it was silly," she said. "But I've always loved the horses in Central Park, and so I decided to go with my instincts." She glanced up at him, and from the look on Roman's face, she'd made a good choice.

Excited about sharing her little bit of marketing genius, she leaned forward. "You know how much I've been trying to put the Inn on the map, right?"

"Sure. You've been brilliant." He kissed the tip of her nose, and she sighed, thinking for just an instant that maybe she could talk later, snuggle now. "You started with a simple turndown service and now look where you are," he added, with a small wave toward the horse.

She laughed, then snuggled closer. He was right about the turndown. That was the first thing she'd done for the motel, just a week after she'd arrived.

As she'd settled into town and met Roman and his friends, she'd stopped wanting to make the Inn a success in order to show up her father. Instead, she wanted to make it a success for *her*. She'd grown to love the town and she wanted the Inn to be a part of it—a real part of it.

"Have you started with the community rooms yet?" he asked. "How's that going?"

"So far so good," she said. "We have a local reader's group booked for Wednesday evening, and a Bible study class for the week after."

"Will your father approve?"

"Of the groups?"

"Of converting the only suite into a meeting area."

She shrugged, hoping she looked more casual than she felt. "Not at first, since we're losing money right now. But as word spreads and the room gets more use we'll make even more, since we can charge an hourly rate. Plus, when we arrange for refreshments, we get a cut from the local vendors."

He bent over and kissed the tip of her nose again, a goofy grin on his face.

"What's that for?" she asked, absurdly pleased.

"Because your dad's an idiot. You're doing fabulous with the motel."

"Thanks." She waved her hand to encompass the horse and carriage. "My plan with this is to promote the Inn, but also to give us more of a presence in the community. Twenty-minute rides starting at dusk every Wednesday through Saturday night. Minimal fee. Just enough to cover costs plus a tiny markup."

"You can put the Inn's logo on the side of the carriage."

"Exactly," she agreed. She turned around on the bench and leaned over into the main area of the buggy. She tossed aside the blanket she'd put there earlier and revealed the picnic basket. "Ta-da! The pièce de résistance."

She hauled it up onto the bench, sliding over so she could put it between them. Then she flipped

open the top of the basket, revealing the tiny sand-
wiches, fancy cheeses and, of course, the chilled bottle of Sonntag Reserve Riesling.

"My darling, you have the most discerning taste
in wine."

"Don't I, though? But seriously, I was thinking that
we should make that part of the service. Wine and
cheese in a carriage. Maybe full picnic service to the
park. It could be great, don't you think?"

"I think you're bubbling over with ideas."

"Good ideas?"

"Very good."

She almost exhaled in relief, and the only thing
marring her pleasure at Roman's complete support
of her plan was the absolute knowledge that her father would be entirely less enthusiastic.

"Julia?" His finger brushed under her chin, tilted
her head up to meet his eyes. "What's wrong?"

"I was just thinking about my dad."

He grimaced. "Yes. I can see where that would put
a sour look in your eye."

Out of familial obligation, she whacked him with
the back of her hand. But not hard. Her heart wasn't
in it. "It's just so frustrating. I mean, I worked my
butt off planning this. In fact, I had to cancel a meeting with a potential videographer in order to talk to
the guy who sold me the horses. Do you know how
important it is to have the perfect videographer at
your wedding?"

"I'm sure you'll tell me."

"*Very*," she said. "At any rate, it wasn't as hard

as if I were doing it in Jersey or New York. There it would have taken months of fighting through red tape. Here, I just walked down to the courthouse, explained to Amelia what I wanted to do, and I had a permit in three days." She smiled. "I think I'm turning into a regular small-town girl."

"Good. I want you to."

"So what do you think?" She snugged the bottle of wine between her thighs and went after it with the corkscrew. "Think the owner of the Sonntag Winery will make me a deal on a few cases of wine?"

"I think that can probably be arranged. In fact, your timing couldn't be more perfect."

Something in his tone made her search his face, and she saw the hint of stress and worry behind his cool blue eyes. "Roman? What is it?"

"Nothing you need to worry about, babe." He tugged at the reins, getting Shadow to turn as they began to circle the block. Even as she watched, his mood seemed to lighten, as if he was putting every ounce of effort into it. "Besides," he continued, "you've already made it better by—what? Five cases?"

"At least. Roman. What is it?"

"One of our accounts fell through this morning, that's all."

"A big account?"

"Big enough. Several hundred cases. But I'll fill the gap. I've already got meetings set up in Austin with specialty markets, restaurants. And I have a few other big deals brewing. It'll work out fine."

She had no doubt it would. Roman knew his stuff. "But—"

"But nothing," he said firmly. He lifted his glass, waited until she lifted hers. "To my brilliant fiancée. And to what she's accomplished."

They clinked glasses, and she drank, pleased and a little humbled that he would so easily set aside his problems to celebrate her small victories. And the truth was, she *was* proud. She'd been working her tail off, harder than she'd ever worked before, and watching things come together was a thrill. Almost as thrilling as kissing Roman. But not quite.

"Since you've already got a local winery lined up, you might want to talk to some of the local vendors. Chocolates, salsas, even some of the wursts could go well in a picnic basket."

"I'm way ahead of you," she said. "I've already made arrangements with Rustlin' Rob's for salsas and crackers and stuff. And I have a meeting set with Auslander to talk about hot lunches."

To her surprise, he pressed the palms of both hands to her cheeks, turned her toward him, and kissed her hard. "You amaze me."

"I do?" She felt her cheeks heat from a potent combination of embarrassment and lust. Mostly, though, she felt relief.

And then, to her utter and complete embarrassment, she burst into tears.

He stared at her for a minute, his perplexed expression almost enough to dry her tears, but not quite. She closed her eyes, buried her face in his shoulder and sobbed.

Roman shifted beneath her; she felt the carriage veer off the road and then stop. Roman turned to her then, fully cradling her as she let loose all the frustration that had been pent up since her father had arrived on the scene.

"Can you tell me what this is about?" he asked when her sobs had slowed down somewhat. "Or should I guess?"

"I'll give you one guess," she said.

"Your father."

She nodded against his shoulder, then forced herself to sit up. He'd been dressed in a crisp white shirt, and now she saw the smear of her Clinique Stay Neutral powder on his shoulder, along with a burgundy slash of her MAC Studio lip color. "Sorry."

"About your dad?"

"About your shirt. But him, too." She pulled in a deep breath. She hadn't even realized what she'd been doing—giving him her whole resume, as if he'd missed some of the things she'd been doing since she'd arrived at the Inn. But somehow it was so important for him to see her accomplishments, and not see the daughter of Marv Spinelli. Because now that he'd met her father—seen the kind of family she'd crawled from, all new money and no class— she was desperately afraid that he'd see her like that, too. Like some pretty-faced bimbo with no brain, no ambition, and no class. If he saw her like that, she might just have to curl up and die.

She couldn't tell him that, though. It sounded too insecure, too needy. And that wasn't the woman she wanted to be with him. So instead she just told him another part of the truth. "He makes me crazy. I guess I just let it all get to me."

"Understandable," he said. "Believe me. I met the man. I have every sympathy." He took her hand and squeezed. "I also have an idea."

"Yeah?"

"Come with me to Austin."

"I'd go with you anywhere," she said. "When?"

"How's tonight? I had a meeting scheduled with the head buyer for CenTex Spirits." He glanced at his watch, frowned. "I doubt I'll make it in time now, but you and I can have a late bite, and I'll reschedule with Charles for tomorrow."

"Tonight?" she said. "I can't go tonight." She glanced to her right, saw that he'd stopped the carriage right in front of the Inn. "Mom and Pop just got in, and as much as they drive me nuts, I can't leave. I can just hear what Marv would say if I ducked out and went to Austin. Shirking responsibility, abandoning my post, ignoring my—"

She closed her mouth as realization struck, then turned slowly to face him. "Ignoring my commitments," she said, thoughtfully. "Damn it, Roman, you have an appointment in Austin _tonight_. This is to make up for the contract you lost, isn't it? And you just blew it off? Why the devil did you do that?"

He just stared at her, his eyes warm and filled with love.

She shifted a little, almost melting right there. "Roman . . ." This time her voice was soft. "You shouldn't have. I would've been fine."

"Maybe. But I still wanted to be here for you. I think it's part of the job description."

"What?"

"Husband," he said.

"Oh. Right." She felt the grin spread across her face, couldn't seem to tone it down. "I like the sound of that."

"So do I. Come with me?"

"What about the Inn?"

"You've got Carter. And I bet we could talk Syd into taking your place for the night."

"I don't know. I should stay. Deal with my pop."

"We've got the rest of our lives to deal with your pop."

She frowned. She couldn't argue with that.

She was still thinking about it when the front door to the Inn opened and a figure stepped out, first into a shadow, then moving away from the door and into the late afternoon sun. *Marv.*

"There you are. Damn it, Princess, I been looking all over hell and back for you. We gots to talk. Who gave you the okay to order a different grade of TP, eh? You tell me that? My brand not fancy enough for your pretty little ass?"

"I—" She closed her mouth, looked from her father to Roman, then made her decision. In one quick move, she grabbed the reins from Roman. "Giddup!" she yelled, flicking the reins.

And as she and Roman were tossed about on the bench, Shadow took off at a trot, the *clop, clop* of her hooves almost drowning out Marv's surprised shouts echoing from behind them.

"What da fuck? What da ever-loving fuck does she think she's doing?" Marv paced inside the lobby as he snarled at his oldest daughter.

"Getting the hell out of Dodge," Syd said. "Can you blame her?"

Marv pointed a finger at Sydney, then moved it over to her idiot boyfriend for good measure. "Blame her? Hell yeah, I can blame her. She's supposed to be here keeping an eye on the Inn. It's her responsibility. No—" He held up a finger interrupting himself. "You know what? I don't blame her. I blame me. I musta got shit for brains thinking she'd ever grow up and be responsible enough to run a place like this."

"Stop it, Pop. She's doing a good job here."

"Yeah? Then why'd she just take off with the son of Satan? You want to tell me that?"

"Probably thought she'd OD on sugar if she stayed around you any longer."

He held out a finger, his temper spiking. Beside him, Myrna laid a hand on his arm. He shook it off, not interested in taking any of her crap right now. "Marv," she said—and, despite everything, he felt his temper ratchet down a notch. Damn it, he didn't want to cool off. His little Princess had hooked up with the Prince of Putrid. And that was supposed to make him happy?

"Calm down, Pop," Syd said. "She's hardly shirking her responsibility. She called me, didn't she? If I hadn't agreed to come cover the Inn, she'd still be here."

"Yeah? Well, then I'm pissed at you, too."

"Nice, Pop."

He jammed his hands in his pockets and paced. He'd spent the last twenty-some-odd years working his keister off to build an empire. Make his family secure. Give his girls a good life—the kind of life he'd never had with his own lazy-ass pop. But did anyone give a rat's ass? Shit no. Syd had her back up, and his baby girl had run away. He'd thought they were a handful back when they were spitting formula and dirtying their diapers. Ha! They'd been easy back then.

Now was hard. Now that he was trying to make good for them, protect them. And they were grown and fighting him every step of the way.

Chapter Five

Your wedding will be a feast for the eyes, and your reception a treat for the tongue. Release doves for a visual flair. Accent your wedding cake with dark, exotic flavors. And don't forget about your most overlooked sense: smell. Consider piping in a delicate scent—we recommend eucalyptus—and give your guests the joy of watching you wed even while they engage in a little aromatherapy.

—from Hot Tips for the Cool Bride

The western sky glowed purple with the setting sun, making the Colorado River—ironically dubbed Town Lake by the locals in Austin—shimmer. A crushed-stone path circled the lake, veering off into Zilker Park on the south side, across from where Julia and Roman strolled hand in hand, heading east toward the Congress Avenue Bridge.

They'd left the car with the valet at Mezzaluna, an upscale restaurant where they'd had a marvelous Italian dinner with Charles Travers, the sales rep for CenTex Spirits. Roman had eaten there many times, and he chose the place because he knew about Julia's love of Italian food. Of secondary consideration was the fact that the restaurant was downtown and therefore close to Travers's office.

He'd called Charles from the road, relieved to find that the sales rep had been happy to move their appointment from afternoon cocktails to an early dinner. He hadn't committed to a purchase, but Roman was cautiously optimistic.

"I think it went well," Julia said. They'd made the valet open the car for them so that she could switch out her Jimmy Choos for something a little easier on the feet. Now she was wearing some designer tennis shoes that she swore were comfortable. Roman was dubious, but he knew better than to argue with Julia about fashion footwear. They'd walked the few blocks to the river, then strolled along the path watching the joggers. They'd turned around under the Lamar Boulevard Bridge and now they were heading back the way they came. Since Julia was keeping pace and hadn't once complained, Roman had to concede that he knew next to nothing about women's shoes.

"It's really pretty along here," she said, as they watched some rowers go by, oars rising and falling in unison. "I can't believe I've spent so little time here since I moved to Fredericksburg."

He cocked his head at that. "You come here all the time," he said.

"Well, sure. To Scarborough's," she said, referring to one of Austin's exclusive stores. "And Nordstrom's. And that fabulous little paper store near Central Market." She swung their hands, clearly getting into her topic. "And Central Market, too. I mean, yum." The grocery store was more an anti–grocery store, with fabulous gourmet foods, local delicacies, and the absolute freshest of produce. "And all the stores on South Congress, of course." She held out her wrist, flashing a leather bracelet with JULIA spelled out in individual silver beads. "I got this at Primadora for only a fifth of what I would've paid in New York. And the *most* darling purse."

"That's just a few blocks from here," he pointed out. "You never thought to take a walk?"

She blinked at him with such bafflement that he had to laugh. "Why would I?"

"Hopefully tonight I'll show you."

She grinned at him and squeezed his hand tighter. He squeezed back as they started up the gentle incline toward the Congress Avenue Bridge and, of course, the bats.

"There," he said.

She followed the line of his finger, then stopped. "What on earth . . . ?"

In front of them were dozens of people clustered in little groups, just hanging out on the bridge as traffic whizzed by. A few were sitting on blankets under the bridge, their heads tilted back as they looked toward the sky.

Roman grinned. He hadn't been sure she'd be surprised. Now he knew he'd made the right decision bringing her here. This was going to be good.

"What's going on? Is Sandra Bullock going to bungee jump from the bridge or something?" she asked, referring to one of Austin's more famous inhabitants.

"Not that I know of," he said.

"O-*kay*," she said, tilting her head to the side as she squinted at him. "Then what's going on? UFO sightings? President Bush in a motorcade? Live music on the street?"

"Bats."

Her forehead scrunched up. *"Ew!* What are you talking about?"

"Austin's bats." He pointed to the bridge, wondering if he should be amused or planning an alternative for their evening. Julia had an adventurous personality; it was one of the things he loved about her. But maybe a bat encounter was taking things a little too far. Especially since, at the moment, she wasn't exactly getting into the spirit.

"Austin has bats?"

He chuckled. "Famous for them. Over a million Mexican free-tail bats live under that bridge. They come out around sunset to eat bugs. Well, during the summer, anyway."

Her eyes widened as she pointed to the bridge. "There? There are *a million bats* living under there? And people are here to *watch* them?" She shook her head. "Pop was right. Texans are freaky." But her lips curved up at the corner, and he knew she was intrigued.

"You've really never heard of them?"

"No, and I think I would have remembered." She did a little shimmy, as if maybe a bat had snuck into her clothing and she'd had to get rid of the thing.

"Come here," he said, taking her hand and pulling her close. "Since this is your first bat experience, we really should find a prime viewing spot."

She lifted a brow. "What if I said I didn't want to stay?"

"Trust me. It's worth it."

For a second he thought she'd argue, and he really didn't want to have to fight that battle. Finally, though, she shrugged. "We'd just argue about it until the bats came out anyway, and you'd end up getting your way. We might as well stay." She stared out over the crowd of bat watchers. "Freaky," she said, almost under her breath.

He'd been leading her down the crushed-granite path, and now he found a space on the grass with an excellent view of both the underside of the bridge and the sky above. He sank down, tugging her along with him. She settled back against his chest, and he wrapped his arms around her.

"What now?" she asked.

"Now we wait."

"Oh." She sniffed the air. "Is that bat guano?"

"I doubt you can smell it from here."

"Hmmm."

His chuckle reverberated through her. "Trust me."

"I do," she said. "But I'm beginning to doubt my judgment." They sat in silence for a moment before she twisted around to look at him. "I think dinner went pretty well."

"Me too," he said. "And I'm glad you came." And as a bonus, now he had an entire evening with his fiancée.

It really didn't get much better than this. A clear, sultry evening. A beautiful woman on his arm. And, of course, the bats.

"I, um, really don't mind if you don't want to sit out here with the bugs." She was turned to face him, and her gaze darted around, still just a little wary.

Roman laughed and kissed her forehead. "Darling, if I didn't know better, I'd think you're chicken."

"It's just . . . *bats.* Don't they get in your hair? Suck your blood?"

"You've been watching too many old movies. You said you trusted me."

"I take it back."

"Too late. Sit. And wait. Here," he said, moving his leg and managing to slide up so they were sitting next to each other rather than in a line. "I know a great way to keep you occupied." As her eyes widened, he pressed his lips to hers. Such soft lips. He'd known their touch for only a few short months, but in his heart, he'd known it all his life. Not that he was sappy about the woman or anything.

They fit together so perfectly. He realized once again just how lucky he was. They'd been made for each other, no doubt about it. An instant, primal connection zinged between them, and it had from the very beginning. It had struck them both, almost as if someone had cast a spell. *A love spell*, he thought as he tugged on her lower lip with his teeth. She responded in kind, her enthusiastic kisses doing a number on his body and making him think that maybe the damn bats weren't that big a deal after all.

When her hands slid up his back, her clever fingers having somehow worked their way under the material so that the heat of her palms stroked the smooth of his back, Roman shifted, wanting to stand up and carry her back to their hotel room like a caveman.

But then she stiffened, her head cocking to one side. She pulled away, breaking the kiss and staring not at him, but at something off to the east. Her mouth made a perfect little "O" and her eyes were just as wide.

"Jules?"

"I think I saw one." Her voice was soft, her whisper almost reverential. "There. Do you hear that?"

He did. A hum, unrecognizable except that he'd heard it before and knew what it was—the rhythmic flapping of millions of bat wings as they rose from under the bridge into the sky to hunt for their feast of mosquitoes and other riverside bugs.

"Oh!" Her hand went to her mouth, her eyes even wider as she climbed to her feet, oblivious to the dozens of people around them doing exactly the same thing. "Wow! They're so amazing!"

He tried to see the picture through her eyes—the tiny black bats bursting from under the bridge, their bodies silhouetted against the deep purple sky.

"Was I right?" he asked. "Do you like it?"

She leaned up against him, her hands in his and clutched in front of her. She swayed a little, then sighed. "Yeah," she finally said. "I like it." She smiled at him. "Who would've thought there could be something so . . . I don't know . . . *romantic* about a bazillion bats flooding the sky. But there is. The sound of their wings and the setting sun, and all the

other couples out here to watch them come out." Her
shoulders lifted in a soft shrug. "Thanks for bringing
me. I like. And I never would have come on my
own."

That was the thing about the two of them, he
thought. They seemed to make each other whole. Because although he'd seen the bats before—and
thought they were spectacular—he'd never seen the
romance of it until just now, looking at their stunning
ascent through her eyes.

"The bats are only one of the things Austin is famous for, you know," he said.

"So you say." She turned in his arms. His hands
were clasped in the small of her back, and her breasts
pressed against his chest. "What other delights do
you want to show me?"

He *wanted* to show her nothing except the inside
of their room at the Austin Motel. But she deserved
a better tour than simply what they could discover
between the sheets. They'd come into town, and by
God, he was going to show her the town.

"Music, for starters," he said. "Alex took Syd into
Gruene, but you still haven't seen much of what
Texas has to offer in the way of live music. And
there's no place better for that than Austin."

Julia had never been a huge fan of live music—too
crowded, too much standing around with the potential for serious injury in open-toed shoes, and too
much noise. Tonight, though, she was having too
good a time with Roman to complain. She'd see

where the evening led, and if she ended up calling uncle . . . well, they'd just end up back at their room, and that was hardly a downside.

Since the bat bridge was only five blocks from Sixth Street—one of the town's live music hubs—they started out their magical mystery tour by walking north on Congress Avenue. The Capitol Building glowed in front of them, lit by innumerable well-placed lights, and blushing a sort of brownish pink, the color of the local Texas granite from which the famous building had been constructed. "It's just a little bit taller than the Capitol Building in DC," Roman said with a grin. "We do things bigger in Texas, you know."

"I'm beginning to figure that out," she said. She hooked her arm through his, bumping his hip slightly as they walked. Office buildings lined the streets, new construction mixed with older façades dating back to the nineteenth century. Some successful and not-so-successful dot-com's had started in those buildings, and Austin had earned the rep of being another Silicon Valley.

All in all, the town had a distinctiveness that Julia found charming. Bats, high tech, and music. Definitely an intriguing combination.

Though late on a Monday, the area was hardly dead. To their left was what Roman called the Warehouse District. "Lots of dance clubs and restaurants. Mostly DJ stuff, I think." That wasn't their destination, and they didn't veer off course.

Sixth Street itself lived up to its reputation. The

sidewalks swarmed with people dressed to party—mostly, from the looks of it, students from the University of Texas, located just a few miles to the north. Most of the buildings still had their original façade, squat brownstones with ornate stonework lined up one after the other, the occasional modern building thrown in for good measure. The happening part of the street seemed to extend for several blocks, and as Roman and Julia walked hand in hand, she breathed deep, enjoying the scent of city air mixed with pizza, pretzels and an abundance of alcohol.

The stately Driskill Hotel, which Roman swore was haunted, capped off one end of the street, with the décor—and the decorum—becoming less sophisticated as they walked to the east.

They passed at least half a dozen doormen urging them to come check out the drink specials, but Roman waved them all off. Instead, he pointed out various bars and restaurants, telling her stories about his days at the university, and his nights on Sixth Street.

"I don't know if this is still the center for the hardboiled music crowd," he said. "But it brings back memories."

"I like it here," she said. "It's lively. Fun." She aimed a grin his direction. "A lot more first-datish than our first date, don't you think?"

"That's why I had to bring you here. I had to make up for inadequate courting."

She lifted a brow. "Courting? What are you? Some English lord?"

"Just a country gentleman, ma'am." He tipped an imaginary hat.

"Hmmm." She stopped on the street, forcing the pedestrian traffic to meander around them. She crossed her arms over her chest and looked him up and down. "I suppose I'll buy that. You were pretty gentlemanly on our first date." They'd met when she'd been sunbathing by the Inn's pool, and he'd been working on renovations to Sonntag House next door. He'd been describing her assets to Alex a little too loudly on his cell phone, and in a huff she'd gone over to confront him. Once she saw him, she'd been just as impressed by the view as he'd been of hers. And he was even more impressed that she was gutsy enough to come over and give him a piece of her mind.

He'd apologized profusely—a pure gentleman, just like he claimed—and they'd gone to lunch. Then dinner. Then breakfast. Then started all over again. Not your typical first date, especially since it lasted more than twenty-four hours. But it had been so very special. Especially since only two hours into it, Julia had known that Roman was The One.

Even so, she hadn't slept with him. Not on that first date. "Yeah," she continued. "I guess you were a gentleman on that first date. By our second, though . . ." She trailed off, thinking just how *ungen-tlemanly* that had been. And how positively delicious.

He pressed a hand over his heart, his face contorted in mock offense. "Darling, you wound me.

The way I remember it, it was you who made the first move."

"My point exactly. A gentleman would have rejected me. Brought me to my senses."

"That gentleman would have been an idiot." He pressed a kiss to her lips. "Apparently I've been wrong. I'm not a gentleman after all."

"Guess you'll have to make it up to me," she said breezily.

"I think I can manage that." He took her elbow and they continued walking. "And after the gentlemanly part, I think we can even move on to the decadent part."

"That's what I like. A man who can read my mind."

A few doors down they paused, the sound of an acoustic guitar and a drum meshed with the pure vocals of a bluegrass singer, and Julia caught herself smiling. Roman steered her into the building, entering a narrow bar that opened on the left to a stage area with tables.

It was the bar, though, that caught her attention—a long skinny bar, behind which stood three bartenders in front of shelves filled from floor to ceiling with a variety of beers.

"This was my Friday night haunt during college," Roman said. "Maggie Mae's has pretty much any beer you've ever heard of. What'll you have?" Roman's mouth pressed against her ear, not because the band was so loud, but to be heard over the din of people.

"Um, Coors?"

His mouth quirked. "I think we can do better than that."

He brought her a beer the color of caramel, and she took the first sip cautiously. Beer wasn't her thing, but it was a Texas thing. And if she was going to marry Roman, she'd have to become a Texas girl. And, even if her husband owned a winery, beer was still on the agenda.

To her surprise, she liked it. Smooth and drinkable and, in the stifling Texas heat, deliciously refreshing. When she told Roman, he just laughed. "Why do you think beer's so popular in Texas?"

He led her to a table near the band, and they listened as the singer covered a few country songs, then performed some of his own. They were there for only forty-five minutes, and managed to bump into at least six people Roman knew, including a tall brunette in a tight skirt. She and Roman made polite conversation while she eyed Julia suspiciously. As soon as Roman introduced Julia as his fiancée, the brunette suddenly remembered another engagement. She went through the kiss-kiss-it's-good-to-see-you routine, then sashayed out.

"She looked a little annoyed to realize you're off the market," Julia said, her hand clutched possessively on Roman's wrist.

"She probably is," he said. Then he kissed her—very hard, very deep and very public. He broke the kiss and she gasped, trying to catch her breath and not blush all the way down to her toes. "But I'm not the least bit disappointed about being off the market."

Oh, wow. She just about melted on the spot. The only thing keeping her remotely pulled together was the brunette's tiger eyes staring daggers at her from across the room. Catty, maybe, but Julia couldn't resist flashing a smug little victory smile. She'd won the prize—and she hadn't even known about the competition.

Roman checked his watch, then slid off his stool, holding out his hand to help Julia down. "You ready?"

She frowned. "Are we heading out already?"

He blinked, his face deadpan serious. "You don't want to go back to the room with me?"

"Roman! Of course. It's just we're here, and—"

He cut her off with a kiss. "God, I love you." He pressed his hands to the side of her face and brushed back her hair, then pressed a kiss to her forehead. "Believe me, sweetheart, we are going back to the room sometime tonight, and we'll go before we're both completely tired out. But right now, I want to show you a good time. What would you say about letting a good old Texas boy show you a wild night on the town?"

She pressed a fingertip to her lips, thinking. "Hmmm. Well, if the Texas boy is my very sexy fiancé, then I guess I have to say I'm all for it."

"In that case, let me show you the way."

Since the night was still young, they headed a few blocks to Red River, then turned left and walked a few more blocks until they reached a run-down rock building with a sign announcing STUBB'S BAR-B-Q.

"Dinner?" Julia asked. "It's almost ten. And I thought we were doing music."

"Trust me," he said. "We are."

The band was already into its second set, and music filled the air, getting louder as they paid the cover and moved through a gate into what Roman told her was the Waller Amphitheater. Bars were set up to sell barbecue and beer. Roman snagged them a couple of bottles, then eased her through the crowd until they found a comfortable place to stand and watch the show.

The floor was dirt and uneven, and Julia was once again glad she'd switched shoes. The place was funky and hot and not at all the kind of venue she would have gone to voluntarily. But she had to admit she liked it.

The music seemed to surround them, the beat moving through her as she swayed with Roman. The sky loomed over them, a few stars managing to peek through the glare of city lights.

"You like?" Roman murmured.

"I like," she repeated. She turned in his arms. "How do you do it?"

"Do what?"

"Handle me," she said with a grin.

He lifted his brows. "Believe me, sweetheart, it's a pleasure."

His hands roamed her body, and she swatted them

away, laughing. "Yeah, well, that, too, but that's not what I meant." She took a step back so she could thrust her arms out, indicating the entire amphitheater. "I mean *this*. I never would have come here if you hadn't taken charge. But you did, and you're right. I'm having a fabulous time."

"Good. I like surprising you. I like showing you around, introducing you to new things."

"And you like being in charge," she teased.

"That, too."

They were bantering, but there was a core of truth. She knew that Roman worked best when he felt like he had some control. He'd relaxed visibly after the dinner with the CenTex guy, once it became clear that the company could pick up the slack left by the deal that had fallen through. And she remembered their first week together, when she'd had to get a plumber in to fix a leak in one of the Inn's rooms. Roman had stepped up to the plate, completely taking over as she'd stood back, baffled by the very thought of having to deal with a plumbing crisis.

She'd been grateful, of course. But now that she knew him better, she also realized that he'd needed to step in, to make things right for her. It was part of who he was—riding to the rescue. Putting others before himself: first his dad, now her.

She stood up on her toes and kissed him. "You're a knight in shining armor, you know."

"Just a knight? I was shooting for prince."

She gave him a playful smack before they settled

in to watch the rest of the set. At the end, Julia applauded wildly, just like everyone else in the crowd. "Who are these guys?" she asked. "They're great!"

"The Gourds," he said. "Local band. Really excellent. Tomorrow's Willie Nelson. We could try to come back if you want."

"I'd love it," she said, though she was thinking more about avoiding Marv for one more day than about seeing the famous singer live and in person. Unfortunately, the possibility of staying indefinitely in Austin was slim at best.

For at least a few hours, though, she didn't want to think about her father. Losing herself in the music, with her fiancé's arms tight around her, was a much more palatable way to go. They drank a few more beers, danced to a few songs, and laughed themselves silly.

When Roman finally steered her toward the door, Julia realized she was dragging her feet. Her—the girl who as a rule didn't like live music because of the noise, the crowds, and the cigarette smoke that inevitably clung to her hair.

"Maybe one more set?"

"I knew I'd make a convert out of you." He motioned outside. "Don't worry. We're not calling it a night yet. But I thought we'd continue our tour farther south. An Austin landmark." He brushed his fingers over her hair.

"Sounds like the perfect plan," she said. "So long as the evening involves more than just music and drinks. I want you in bed, mister." Her body already tingled from alcohol and music, and combined now with his soft touch and the heated look in his eyes, Julia wasn't sure she'd survive the night if they didn't fall naked into bed at some point.

His mouth curved into the smile she'd come to know so well. "Don't worry, sweetheart. I think we're thinking along exactly the same lines."

The walk back to the car was long, but they got lucky and snagged one of Austin's rare taxis. They held hands and Julia watched out the window as the driver raced the few blocks back to Mezzaluna. Buildings and people whizzed by, the blur of activity familiar. She thought it should be comforting, too, but the truth was she felt like a tourist—a pampered tourist, but an outsider nonetheless. She told herself it was simply because she didn't know Austin, and she really didn't know the music scene. But that wasn't it. Not really.

Roman squeezed her hand. "Quarter for your thoughts."

She smiled. "Worth a lot to you, are they?"

"Everything about you is worth a lot to me."

"Thanks." She felt her cheeks warm, amazed that he could still raise a blush simply with a kind word or a heated look. "I was thinking about that, actually. You, I mean. Or, I guess, our life."

"Good thoughts?"

"Oh, yeah." The admission came out on a breath, her sigh of such deep pleasure that she almost blushed again. "I was just thinking how this town seems so familiar in so many ways. But it doesn't feel like home."

His brow furrowed. "Well, I've never been to Jersey, but from what I understand they're pretty different. Climate. Architecture. Just general ambiance."

She shook her head. "That's not what I meant. I meant *home*. Fredericksburg. It's small and quiet and if there's a crowd on the streets this late it's because there's some big event the whole town is involved in."

She spread her arms, indicating the whole city. "Don't get me wrong, I'm having a fabulous time. I guess I'm just realizing how much I've gotten used to small-town life."

"Considering I don't plan to let you run off back to Jersey, I'm very glad to hear that."

The taxi dropped them off in front of the restaurant, and Roman gave the ticket to the valet. "So which is it?" he asked as they waited for the car. "You up for more music? Or shall we call it a night?"

"That depends," she said. She ran a finger down his shirt, delighted by the hard feel of his pecs underneath her hand and the heat that flooded his eyes. "If we stay out, you're not going to crash on me at the end of the night, are you? I mean, I want you awake. And," she added, taking a step closer so that her thigh brushed his crotch, "I want you energetic."

"Sweetheart," he said, moving closer so that the length of his erection pressed enticingly against her, "I really don't think that will be a problem."

Chapter Six

*Don't kill yourself trying to pull together your wedding!
Do you want sallow skin? Trembling hands as you cut
the cake? NO SEX BECAUSE-YOU'RE TOO DAMN
TIRED?? An exhausted bride is an unhappy bride. And,
baby, this is your wedding! So do what your mom told
you back when you were a little girl: Eat your veggies,
get some exercise, and by all means GO TO SLEEP
AT A REASONABLE HOUR!*
— from *The Ultimate Wedding Resource Book,*
Fourth Edition

He took her to a country hangout called the Broken
Spoke, a true Texas honky-tonk famous enough that
even Julia had heard of it. When he turned into the
parking lot, though, she was certain that he must be
joking. The place resembled a big red box, sadly lacking in style. "This is really the Spoke? The place everyone talks about?"

"This is it," Roman said, looking altogether
pleased with himself. "I wanted you to see a true
Texas original."

She gnawed a little on her lower lip, wondering if
she shouldn't just beg him to take her to bed. Seduc-
tion would get her out of this, right? Because she
had a feeling the Spoke was a little too general store–
country for her Barneys–New York taste.

But Roman wanted to show her the place, so she
sucked it up, trying to remember whether livestock

was allowed inside buildings in the city limits. Surely there wouldn't be cows or horses inside, would there?

As soon as they stepped through the front door, all of her hesitation vanished. What the Spoke lacked in style, it made up in atmosphere, and Julia Spinelli found herself completely charmed.

They'd entered through the restaurant, and now they bypassed the food, heading straight for the long, low dance floor in the back. So low, in fact, that the singer's black cowboy hat almost brushed against the ceiling.

The claustrophobic ceiling aside, the Spoke was everything she'd imagined in a honky-tonk, complete with good-looking men in white shirts, cowboy boots and blue jeans.

She was still wearing a Dolce & Gabbana halter. And though she'd feared derision by a bunch of big-haired women in dusty boots and cowgirl frill skirts, she was pleasantly surprised. A few stereotypical cowgirls were warming up the dance floor, but the rest of the crowd was a mix of designer jeans and Levi's, cowboy boots and couture footwear. In other words, Julia felt right at home, all the more so when she ran into two squealing girls who looked like they were probably enrolled at the university. One of them grabbed her hands.

"Oh my *god*! Tommy Lee Jones is here. Did you see him? He's right over there, and I swear, that's Quentin Tarantino right beside him."

Julia blinked, not entirely sure of the proper response to such unbridled, lustful enthusiasm. "That's amazing," she finally said. "Uh, good luck."

The girl's eyes widened and she gripped her friend's arm hard. "Oh, wow. Do you think I have a chance? I mean, that would be so . . ."

Julia and Roman drifted away, so she didn't get to find out how "so" it would be.

The band was set up on a platform (raising them even closer to the ceiling than the mere mortals), and the music, though country, was nothing like what Julia had expected. It had a twangy bounce and a bit of a rock undertone.

Roman held out his hand. "Dance with me."

She eyed the people moving across the floor suspiciously, noting in particular the way feet were moving and hips were swaying. "I have no clue what they're doing."

"The two-step," he said. "It's easy."

She frowned. "Easy for you. You grew up in Texas."

"What? Daddy didn't send his little girl to Arthur Murray?"

"As a matter of fact, he did." But ballroom dancing had never been her thing. And besides, the two-step really didn't look like a waltz.

"Come on, Jules. How hard can it be? I mean, like the name says, it only has two steps."

"I don't know . . ."

His eyes went wide with mock horror. "Well, this is a real shocker. The woman who'd never run a motel before but who tackled it head-on, afraid of a little dancing? The woman who made turndown service the new 'it' thing for motels? The woman who single-handedly arranged for the return of the horse and buggy ride to Fredericksburg? The woman who—"

Laughing, she held up a hand. "Okay, hotshot. I get it." She cast a long glance at the dance floor. "What the heck. At least the only one I know here is you."

And with that, she took him by the hand and tugged him onto the floor. He put his arms around her and, as she had from the first time they'd met, she melted into him, their bodies fitting together perfectly, as if they were two halves of a whole.

They were, she knew. And she couldn't wait until the wedding made that official.

As it turned out, Roman was an excellent dance partner, seamlessly leading her across the floor. She should have known that he would be, and without even thinking, she was two-stepping right along with him. Once she even caught herself wishing that she had a pair of red cowboy boots. How fun would that be?

As the band let loose with a big finish, Roman grabbed her around the waist, twirled her, and planted a bone-melting kiss on her. She started to pull away, all too aware of the dozens of pairs of eyes glued to the show they were putting on. But, damn it, she didn't care. She loved this man, loved the feel of his arms around her and his lips hard against hers. She leaned in, opened her mouth, and let the kiss go on and on.

When they finally separated, the couples around them broke into scattered applause. They laughed, then danced a few more dances, until Julia finally had to beg for a break and a beer.

"Not bad," Roman said after they both drained their longnecks. "You'd think you'd been two-stepping all your life."

"Once I got out there, I didn't even think about it," she said. "I just let you lead me." She peered up at him, then rose on tiptoes to plant a kiss on his cheek. "Actually, I do that a lot."

"And that's a damn good plan in general," he said. At the moment, Julia had to agree.

She also had to admit that the dance was fun. She hadn't been kidding when she'd copped to the Arthur Murray classes. She'd had oodles of dance lessons, all at Marv's insistence. A little princess had to know how to waltz. But Marv would have a fit if he realized that the skills she'd learned in the ballroom were being put to good use on a dusty floor in an under-air-conditioned venue.

What was even more shocking—although Julia's shoes were getting scuffed up and dirty, she wasn't even close to freaking out. Shoes could be replaced. Memories like tonight . . . well, she was going to hold on to this one forever.

All in all, it had been a perfect night, and by the time they stepped outside and headed for the car,

Julia realized they'd spent over two hours inside, drinking and dancing and listening to the band. And she had loved every second of it. More, she loved Roman. A given, of course, since she was marrying the man in just a few days, but right then, she *really* loved him. He'd treated her to an absolutely perfect evening, and as he opened the car door for her, she realized with a start that she hadn't thought about her parents, or the botched-up wedding plans, in hours.

"Have I exhausted you?" he asked.

"Invigorated," she corrected. "There's life in me yet."

"Good." He shut the door and moved around the car to his side. "I considered taking you to the Continental Club, too. It's just across the street from the motel. But I'm starting to feel a little too selfish."

She tilted her head back to squint at him, confused.

"I don't want to share you anymore," he clarified. "And besides, right now you look energized. I want to take advantage of that before you crash."

"You think I'm going to keel over on you?"

"You two-stepped for over an hour." He grinned. "Syd will never believe it."

"*I* hardly believe it," Julia said.

The night became even more perfect when Roman took them back toward the center of town. "The Austin Motel," he said, maneuvering into the parking lot. "One of the city's best-kept secrets. I thought about booking us a room at the Four Seasons, but I decided you'd like this better."

She had to admit, the man knew her well. The small motel had been refurbished with love and what had to have been a nice healthy budget. Roman had made the reservation from the road, but since they'd arrived in town, they'd been going strong, and Julia had yet to see the place. Now she couldn't wait.

She told herself that she was just curious about what Roman considered cool, but the truth was she wanted to scope out any tricks of the trade—decorating tips, layout of the reception area, the general décor. Scary to think that already her position at the Inn had seeped into her pores, but apparently, it had.

While Roman went to the front desk, Julia looked around, taking in the furniture—simple lines, but inviting—and the bright artwork. The lighting made the place cheerful, not dark, and there were kitschy things tucked in corners. It reflected the laid-back, artsy personality of the town—a personality that had been somewhat battered by the influx of Silicon Valley money, but never quite defeated.

"I could do something like this," Julia said as Roman led her to their room. "It's very flea market–chic. Some paint, a few slipcovers, and someone who knows how to sew, and I could make the Inn's lobby just as cozy. And I could do it cheap enough that even Pop couldn't complain."

"I thought this place might give you some ideas."

"You brought me here with a plan."

He lifted a shoulder. "Let's just say I thought it would pique your curiosity."

"Well, you were right," she said. She frowned slightly as she looked around some more. "Of course, Fredericksburg has a different personality than Austin. More country. More German. But if I buy from local artisans, talk to the antique dealers . . ." She pressed a finger to her mouth. "You know, I could maybe work a deal with Homestead or someone. Display their pieces in the lobby, but keep them for sale. We'd get nice furniture, and they'd get their belongings set out in a way that featured them to their best advantage."

Roman paused in front of their door, the key in his hand and a goofy grin on his face.

"What?"

"You," he said. "And here I thought that I was the businessman in the family."

She felt the blush creep up her face. "Yeah, well, it might be a stupid idea . . ."

"It's not."

"Tell that to my father."

"I just might do that," he said, then laughed at her look of absolute horror. "Don't worry. I promise to only mortify you a little bit. But the man's going to be my father-in-law soon. He needs to realize that you've got a head on your shoulders, and you know what to do with it."

He looked at her with such fervent sincerity that she was certain her heart was just going to melt on the spot. "I love you, Roman. You know that, right?"

"I figured it out," he said. "I'm perceptive that way."

He pushed open the door and they half tumbled into the room. Julia had a quick flash of the interior, her brain making note of the charming paint job and the perfectly suited furniture. After that, though, her brain moved on to more interesting—and prurient—things. Like Roman's lips on her neck, his hands on her ass, the way the length of him pressed hard against her as he assaulted her senses with kisses and caresses.

Her heart stuttered, and her body started to fizzle under his touch. It had been this way from the first time they'd met—barely able to keep their hands off each other. They *fit*, plain and simple. And the miracle that she'd found such a perfect man never ceased to amaze her.

"I've been wanting to touch you like this all night," he said, his voice as hard as his body. "I can't believe I kept you out in public instead of bringing you straight here."

"Me either," she said, smiling against his mouth. "I figured you were getting tired of me."

Her voice was laced with a tease, but he pulled back anyway, his eyes serious as they looked into hers. With his hands, he framed her face, held her steady.

"Never," he said. "I could never get tired of you."

Her heart skipped a few more beats, and for about the millionth time, she thanked God and fate and good clean living that the Universe had seen fit to bring this man into her life.

His hand slid down to cup her gently between her

thighs, and that was the extent of rational thought. After that, instinct took over, and lust, and the only thought in her head was to touch and be touched. And the only word her addled brain could form was, "Now."

Chapter Seven

For that special wedding night, consider abstinence before the wedding. Hold off for a month, and your wedding night can be just like that first time. It takes a little willpower, but when you get right down to it, who's more motivated than a bride-to-be?
—from *Planning the Perfect Honeymoon*

Now. Just three little letters, one small syllable, but that little word held more power than any he'd ever heard before.

She wanted him. And damned if he didn't want her right back, even more than he'd wanted her yesterday or the day before. Every day with Julia seemed to offer more, and if the desire that flooded his body kept increasing at such an exponential rate, Roman had to fear that he'd be dead before they reached their wedding night.

Not that he intended to linger on that fear. Not with such a warm and willing woman pressed against him.

His woman.

He still couldn't quite get used to that. Lord knew he'd had women before—plenty of women—but none that made him feel the way Julia did. None that burrowed into his heart and made a home there.

"Roman." Her soft voice held a demand.

"I'm right here, baby." His hands stroked her bare back. The woman had a flair for fashion, and Roman thoroughly approved, especially when that meant backless halters held together with nothing more than two strings tied behind her neck and another two tied at her waist.

"How expensive is this top?" he asked, his fingers fumbling with the bottom knot.

"I love you," she said, "but if you rip my Dolce & Gabbana, you'll be hearing about it on our fiftieth wedding anniversary." She reached back herself, pushing his hands away, and her nimble fingers had the tie free in no time.

The halter hung loose from her neck, and as she reached up to take care of the final knot, his hands stroked up, his palms cupping her firm breasts. Her nipples were hard pearls against his palms, and he rubbed slowly, a circular motion designed to drive her wild.

It worked, too, he thought as he heard his name, little more than a moan as it escaped her lips.

A soft brush of fabric over his hands as the halter fell off, and then she stood before him, bare from the waist up. They hadn't switched on a light, but the curtains were open, and the lights of South Congress filtered through, illuminating the interior. The soft orange glow of streetlamps mixed with storefront signs painted her skin with translucent gold, lighting her from the inside.

He reached up and took the clip out of her hair, then watched as the mass of curls tumbled just past her shoulder. The light caught the strands and they seemed to spark in the dim illumination. She was on fire, a wicked angel there just for him.

Roughly, he pulled her toward him, his fingers going automatically for the waistband of her flirty skirt. He tugged it down, delighted by her little shimmy of help.

She eased out of the skirt, kicking it aside to land in a pile a few feet away. A testament to her passion, he thought. Clothes were one thing Julia Spinelli treated with the utmost respect.

Not that he could care less about her clothes at the moment. Not when he was staring at this goddess of a woman, standing in front of him wearing nothing but yellow Sponge Bob panties.

He did a double take, then chuckled. "Not what I expected," he said.

Color lit her cheeks. "I wasn't expecting to see you when I got dressed this morning. They're comfortable."

"I hope so," he said, still fighting back laughter. "I never thought Sponge Bob could look so sexy."

"Roman!" Her voice held both censure and amusement. "Okay, now you *have* to marry me, because you know my dirty little secret. I love cheap underwear from Wal-Mart."

"It's cute." He held up his hands before she could smack him. "I mean it. Got any other dirty little secrets?"

She made a face. "I like peanut butter M&M's. I keep a stash in my purse."

"You're a wild woman."

"That I am." And then, wearing only her cartoon panties, she walked toward him, her hips moving like a runway model's. He tried to swallow, but couldn't quite manage. Julia knew her appeal. She might be unsure about her ability to run a motel or to mix with the folks in his hometown, but she knew her effect on a man. And it awed him that *he* was the man she wanted to bewitch.

"What do you think?" She did a turn, then posed. "Are you going to keep me? Despite my questionable taste in underwear?"

"Sweetheart, you couldn't get away from me if you wanted to."

She moved toward him without an ounce of shyness, in total command of the room. She stopped only inches from him, and the air between them practically crackled with electricity. She reached a finger out and ran it down the front of his shirt, then hooked the tip of her finger over the waistband of his jeans.

"I seem to be at a little bit of a disadvantage," she said.

"I disagree," he said. "I'm pretty sure the advantage is entirely yours."

She laughed, and he pulled her close, kissed her

once again, hard. Her mouth opened to his, and he deepened the kiss even as his hand dipped down, his fingers knotting in the panties. And then, he ripped. Bye-bye Sponge Bob.

Julia's startled gasp, laced as it was with passion and need, told him he'd done exactly the right thing.

"Baby," he said reverentially, "you're so beautiful."

A delightful flush spread over her cheeks, and she shifted a little, one arm moving to cover her breasts.

"No, no," he said. "None of that." He ran his hands over her arms, then pinned them at her sides. He was already rock hard, and he stepped closer, wishing he'd had the foresight to remove his clothes, too. He was so turned on, he was about to burst, and all he wanted was to lose himself inside her.

Except that wasn't really all. No, even more, he wanted to drive her over the edge. To take her as far as possible and then pull her back to him.

He cupped his hands over her breasts, delighted by the way she trembled, as if just that touch would make her come. He stroked and played, then lightly rubbed his palms over her nipples.

In front of him, Julia moaned, her eyes closed. "I can't . . . I can't stand up. My knees . . ."

"Shhh," he said. "I've got you."

He slid one hand down her belly, his fingers finding their way between her thighs as he bent to take one pert breast in his mouth. She gasped and shuddered, and he felt raw male power surge through him.

She was wet, ready for him, and when he slipped a finger inside her, her body clenched around him, her hips bucking as if to draw him in even more.

It was, finally, all he could take.

With his free hand, he fumbled with his belt, managing to loosen it, then his pants.

He couldn't touch her and rip the damn things off at the same time, though, so he spun her around, moving her the few short steps to the wall and wordlessly pressing her hands against it. Her back was to him, her adorable ass right there for him to stroke.

"Roman," she whispered.

"Stay," he ordered, his voice soft, but firm.

He kicked out of his shoes and managed to free himself from the damn pants. His shirt was still on, but he didn't worry about that. He moved to her, erect and full of need, and pressed against her from behind. He slid his hands around her, cupping her breasts as she arched her back.

She lifted herself on her tiptoes, her bottom pressed upward as if silently demanding his touch.

He didn't disappoint her. His cock slid between her thighs, stroking her sex from behind in slow, rhythmic movements designed to take them both over the edge.

She moaned, then spread her legs wider, a little quiver running through her body telling him just how much she needed this.

"Tell me you want me," he whispered, then nipped at her ear with his teeth.

"I want you." Her voice was breathy, full of need. "Tell me to touch you."

"God, yes, please. Touch me."

He pressed his lips to her neck, kissed her. Inhaled the scent of her hair, and concentrated on memorizing the curve of her ear. He had to get his mind off how turned on he was, or he'd come right then. And he wasn't ready for that yet.

"Roman . . ." Her voice was desperate, demanding.

"Hush," he said. "Soon."

Keeping one hand on her breast, he slid the other down between her thighs. His fingers sought out her clit, her startled gasp letting him know when he'd found the perfect place. He stroked slowly, wanting to drive her crazy. And as he did so, he moved his hips forward and back in a slow, undulating motion, so that his cock rubbed gently against the soft skin of her ass and thighs. That way, he was driving them both crazy.

She moved against his hand, and he could feel the need flowing off of her, mixing with his own desperation. She reduced him to passion more than any woman he'd ever been with. Just one look, and she could take him down. But now, like this, he wanted it to be about her. He wanted to be the one to reduce her to neediness, to lust.

He moved his hips, thrusting forward and back in an almost hypnotic motion designed to take them both to the precipice. And then, when he felt himself getting too close, he pulled back. But not for her. His fingers kept touching, kept stroking, until he felt her tense under his touch. She was on the edge, and he was determined to take her over.

"Now," he whispered. "Go over for me."

That was all it took, and he felt her explode in his hand, her body breaking into a million little pieces and him the only thing holding her together.

She twisted as the depth of it passed, turning so that she was facing him, her eyes unseeing, then clearing as she wrapped her arms around his neck. "Roman," she whispered.

"Hmmm?"

She brushed his cheek with a kiss, then pulled back. This time, her eyes were hard and determined . . . and very full of need. "I swear if you aren't inside me in the next thirty seconds, I'm calling off the wedding."

He laughed, then circled her waist with his hands. "Sweetheart, I don't think that will be a problem."

Julia had never thought of herself as the kind of woman to simply let a man take charge. For that matter, she'd always been the one in control in past relationships, leading her boyfriends along on a leash and watching from a pedestal as they did her bidding. It almost made her ashamed to admit it, but it was true.

Not so with Roman.

She was completely lost to his power over her. Totally submissive to him, and loving every touch, every command.

His hands were tight around her waist, and she gasped slightly as he lifted her, pressing her back against the wall, then sliding her down just as he impaled her on him. His hands slid down then, cupping her bottom, as he pressed against her, his mouth crushing against hers before sliding down to nestle in the curve of her neck.

She couldn't move, but it didn't matter. He did all the work, lifting her and slamming her back down against him with each thrust. Their breathing came fast and hard, a rhythm shared as something wild and whirling grew inside them, danced around them, and then determined to push them over the edge.

"I can't—" Roman muttered. "Too fast . . . I'm sorry."

"God, no. Not too fast," she whispered, as his fingers tightened on her and he exploded inside her. They crumpled to the ground as his knees gave out, him on his back, breathing hard, and her sprawled on top of him.

"I think I've died and gone to heaven," he said. His hands were on her back, stroking lazily up and down.

"Yeah?" Her voice was just as languid, but she managed a tease. She rocked her hips just a little, felt him stir inside her. "I don't think you're quite dead yet."

A slow grin started at the corner of his mouth. "What can I say? You've revived me."

She wiggled her bottom a little, feeling him harden and fill her. "Yeah, I guess I have."

It was her turn to be in control now, and she loved that. Loved the give-and-take this relationship with Roman offered. Loved everything about him, for that matter.

She was his, and he was hers.

Even now, that simple fact could make her dizzy.

"What?" he asked, his eyes searching her face.

"I'm going to marry you," she said, and the wash of pleasure she saw pass over his face in reaction to her words nearly undid her again.

"Wife," he said. "I like the sound of that."

"Me too," she whispered. But after that, she quit talking. His fingers had sneaked between their bodies and were now doing a number on her senses. And it was all she could do to keep her head on as she rode him to one more mind-bending orgasm.

Spent, she rolled off him as he murmured a protest. "Not staying on you," she said, managing to force the words out. "Wouldn't survive another round."

"We should move to the bed," he said.

"Can't. No bones."

He started to push himself up, fell back against her. "Me neither." He managed instead to reach forward to grab the end of the bedspread. One tug and he managed to pull it off the bed. He spread it over them, and she started to drift toward sleep in his arms.

A single thought passed through her mind, promising to color her dreams: Today had been perfect. Tomorrow would be perfect. And absolutely nothing was going to spoil that.

*   *   *

Had he known about it, Marv Spinelli would have argued with his daughter's assessment of the next day's perfection. To his mind, the day started off bad when the sun streamed in through the thin curtains at some god-awful early hour, and it got worse when his do-gooder wife dragged his sorry butt out of bed and insisted they walk down Main Street.

Leaving the Inn meant seeing Sonntag House right next door, and that sight sparked his temper all over again. Marv felt his blood pressure spike and he fisted his hands, working to calm himself down. Deep inside, he knew that he should just let it go. He'd won, after all. Putting the Inn up had been the final coup, a middle finger raised and aimed at Robert Sonntag and the whole Sonntag clan.

But Marv had wanted the house and he hadn't gotten it, and that still rankled. He didn't like losing, and resentment had been stewing for years. Maybe he could have burned some of it off if he'd come back to Texas once or twice in the years since the Inn had been erected. But he hadn't. And when Julia had told him who she was marrying, every old injury and pain and resentment had come barreling back down on him and was now churning in his stomach like a monster fighting to get out.

"Marv. Let it go." Myrna's hand was on his forearm, her eyes aimed, like his were, at Sonntag House, a bit dilapidated but still regal.

He snorted and turned away. "I've got it under control."

Myrna pursed her lips, clearly not believing him, but she said nothing, and they walked in silence up Main Street, Marv stewing and Myrna worrying.

When they reached the Old German Bakery, Myrna's hand closed like a vise around his wrist. "Oh, Marv, honey," she said. "Doesn't this just look fabulous?" She'd parked them outside the bakery's window and was inspecting each offering with the intensity of a diamond cutter.

"Looks like food," he said. "You wanna go in, we'll go in. But don't stand out here slobbering like Humphrey."

Myrna's mouth curved into a little moue. "I should have brought him. He's probably missing me something awful."

Marv fought the urge to rub his temples. "He's a slobbering, farting pain in the ass. He's happy if he has some food to eat and someplace to crap it out the other end."

His wife gave him one of her rare sour looks. He held up his hands in surrender. "All right. All right. Sorry. I'm sure the mutt's having a fabulous time. Probably turning cartwheels having the house to himself."

"We should have brought him."

"He's fine with Marcella."

Myrna made a face, and Marv sighed with exasperation. "Damn it, woman, do you have any idea how many girls would give their right arm to have a maid as efficient as her?"

"She steals my underwear."

This was news to Marv, and he slid his sunglasses down his nose so he could get a better look at his wife. "What have you been smoking?"

Myrna's cheeks turned as red as his boxers. "It's just that she—I mean, I—" She waved a hand. "Doesn't matter. I was just saying I miss Humphrey."

"Then ship the mutt down here."

Her eyes lit up, and she threw her arms around him. He returned the hug, holding on to her for a little longer than maybe he should, considering they were out in public, but right then, she felt like the girl he'd married so many long years ago.

"Really?"

He'd made the offer out of frustration, but now that he saw the excitement in her eyes, he nodded. "Yeah. Sure. Why the fuck not?"

"Oh, Marv-baby," she said, throwing her arms around him and kissing him on the cheek. "You're just an old softie." She looked around. "We ought to get some breakfast."

"Breakfast?" he repeated. "What about the dog?"

She shook her head. "He'd be scared to death on a plane. But, honey bear, you offered. And you wouldn't have done that if you didn't love me." She took his hand. "Now, let's eat, okay?"

"Food," he said, staring in the bakery window. "Ain't there a Denny's around here somewhere?"

"Oh, baby. You're not gonna make me eat at a chain, are you? Not when we got so much local color."

He looked her up and down. She wore a big floppy hat to protect her from the already brutal sun, a floral print sundress with spiky shoes that would surely end up costing her a broken ankle. She clutched a small purse with one of the town's tourist maps peeking out. He'd seen the maps stacked on the reception counter at the Inn. Apparently, his wife wanted to do some exploring.

He sighed again. *What the hell.* "All right, already. Let's do this thing." He pulled open the door to the bakery, a little bell announcing their arrival.

"Can I help you?" The question came from a perky teenager with her long hair pulled back into a net.

"You got anything here that isn't made outta a pound of butter?"

"Marv!" Myrna stared at him, looking all shocked, like he wasn't acting the way he always acted.

The girl didn't seem shocked so much as impertinent. She just stared at him, her gaze aimed right at his waist.

He put a protective hand over the paunch that rolled over his belt. "Wha? You think just because I got a few extra pounds on me I can't eat healthy? Babydoll, that's *why* I gotta eat healthy."

"I . . . oh . . . no . . . I mean, I . . ." The startled girl turned away quickly to attend to a beeping coffeemaker, her relief at having an excuse practically radiating off her.

Marv nudged Myrna. "Come on, babycakes. Let's go find us a fruit cup or something."

Myrna crossed her arms across her chest and refused to move. Marv glared, in no mood to play Who's the Boss with his wife.

She stamped a size seven foot. "Don't start with me, Marv. We're down here with half my wardrobe, I don't have my pillow or my dog."

"But I just told you to ship the mutt here."

She ignored that. "The only good thing is that I'm away from Marcella for a few days." She shivered. "That woman gives me the heebie-jeebies."

"Damn it, Myrna." He pointed to the girl behind the counter. "You'd give your eyeteeth to have a maid, wouldn't you?"

"I . . . um . . ."

"Marv, don't terrify the girl."

"Fine. Damn it all. Just give me two of those." He pointed at something round and covered in pastry, like the little mini-wieners he liked to have at parties.

"So what the hell is that, anyway?" he asked, as the girl popped his two into a bag, along with the cheese Danish Myrna had selected. It would go straight to her hips and send her into a ten-day depression, but Marv knew better than to say anything. If he mentioned the Danish, Myrna would take it like he was saying she'd gotten fat. Like he wanted some skinny-ass bimbo with nothing to grab on to.

So he kept his mouth shut and kept the peace.

"They're kolaches," the girl said, then waved toward the front of the store as someone else came in, the little bell tingling once again.

"What the fu—"

"Kolaches," said a firm voice behind him. "A German sausage wrapped in pastry."

Myrna gasped, and Marv turned, his sense of foreboding shifting into hyperdrive. "Judge," he said, when he saw who stood there. "I won't say 'Your Honor,' 'cause you sure the fuck ain't got any."

Judge Herman Strauss stroked his beard, thinking that he should have gone straight to the courthouse and skipped his kolache this morning. His wife kept telling him the damn things would kill him. She probably hadn't meant that his death would come at the hand of Marv Spinelli, a pain-in-the-ass plaintiff who'd lumbered into his courtroom over fifteen years ago.

He'd heard that Spinelli had rolled into town yesterday. The Fredericksburg grapevine was faster than the Internet, and it had been primed for over a month—ever since Julia Spinelli had graced their town's streets.

Poor thing, she'd been the subject of much speculation when she'd first arrived. Not too surprising, Strauss supposed, considering the waves Marv had sent through the town years before. The town's memory was long, and Julia had been watched warily.

The young lady, though, had proved to be nothing like her father, and the judge had been pleased when she'd made friends with the local merchants. He'd been even more pleased when she'd gotten herself engaged to Roman Sonntag. That had caused the tongues to wag some more, of course. Such a fast engagement. But once again, Julia had won the town over.

She was a good kid. Herman liked her, and his own daughter couldn't stop talking about how "fab" her wardrobe was.

The judge looked at Marv, sweat stains from the Texas heat already starting to form under the arms of the Jersey native's polyester shirt. The judge fought the urge to shake his head. The apple might not fall far from the tree in most families, but in Julia Spinelli's case, the apple fell in a whole different field.

"Judge. So, um, nice to see you again." Mrs. Spinelli tottered forward on dangerous-looking shoes. The judge hadn't seen as much of her during the trial, and it took him a second longer to recall her name. Myrna.

"You don't need to be polite to him, babydoll," Marv said. "Judge Strauss's the bastard what screwed us over. Him and Robert Sonntag and his bastard son, that is."

"I only applied the law, Mr. Spinelli."

"Yeah, you just keep telling yourself that if that's what it takes to sleep at night." Marv took a step closer, poked the judge in the chest. "But I know the truth." Poke. "And you do, too. Don't you, 'Your Honor'?"

Poke, poke.

This time, Judge Strauss grabbed Marv's finger. "I really suggest you don't do that again."

"Don't do that? How about do this?" And as Myrna and the salesclerk squealed, Marv pulled his arm back, fisted his fingers and took aim.

The monster exploded out of him, and he heard the resounding *crack* as his fist collided with the judge's nose.

Marv stepped back, nodding with satisfaction. "Damn," he said. "I feel better already."

Chapter Eight

*Not yet in "fighting" shape for your wedding prepa-
rations? Fighting for florists getting you down? Not
quite able to zip up the dress of your dreams?*

No problem.

*Sign up for Bridal Boot Camp! During the two-week
stint, pounds and inches will fall off even while your
stamina increases!*

*Give your husband-to-be the best wedding present
ever: a refreshed, reinvigorated, and raring to go you!*
—from *All About Brides*, Summer 2005 Issue

Julia woke up to the sensation of being petted. A
soft, warm hand drifted up her bare side, following
the curve of her hip, then caressing the side of her
breast. Her nipples peaked; her thighs felt warm and
languid. She stretched, arching her back and silently
inviting an even more intimate caress.

As she'd hoped, Roman was more than happy to
comply. And as the sun streamed in through the
crack in the curtains, they made love in the early
morning light. Soft and sweet, a nice contrast to their
wild coupling the night before.

With Roman, though, just his simple touch was
perfect. Everything beyond that was like a gift.

Spent, they lay spooned together, Roman curled
up behind her, her rear nestled against his crotch.

"Think we can stay this way all day?" she asked.

"I ordered room service for eight," he murmured

back. "We should probably at least toss a blanket over us. I'm not sure the waiter will be able to stand the thrill otherwise."

"Cancel room service," she said. "Who needs food. We can survive on sex. I'm certain of it."

He shifted, leaned up to nibble on her ear. "Yeah," he said. "I'm willing to try that."

She squirmed, laughing, his touch tickling her and making her entire body hypersensitive.

"Assuming we do decide to get out of this bed—"

"Not going to happen," she said.

"—what do you have planned for the day? Anything?"

She rolled over, eyebrows raised. "Does that mean you don't want me with you today? Do you have secret wine meetings?"

"No," he said. "Of course not."

But he answered too quickly and too innocently. "Uh-huh," she said. "You can't play big-shot businessman with your fiancée on your arm." When he started to protest, she held up a hand. "Don't even bother. I know I'm right."

"It's just business."

Julia shook her head as she sat up, her demeanor stern. "It works both ways, Roman. I fell in love with you and let you into all aspects of my life. You know all about my freaky family, you know how completely insecure I am about making the Inn a success, and you even know all about the plumbing and vermin problems at work. More, you've helped me with all of that, and I love you for it." She stroked his cheek, emphasizing her point. "Don't sit there and deny me the right to help you, too. To be there for you."

"I'm not denying you anything," he said. But he didn't meet her eyes, and she knew that she'd totally nailed him. She considered arguing, but what would be the point? Roman was a man of action. In his mind, *he* was the one who got things done. If someone else had to step in and help, then he'd failed. A pretty typical guy thing all in all, and even though it drove her nuts, at least she understood it. Over time, she intended to chip away at it.

"I know you're not telling me something," she said. "But I'll drop it for now. This isn't the end of this conversation, though."

"I love you because you're so smart. You know that, right?"

She laughed. "And I love you because you know precisely how to suck up to me."

"Believe me, babe. I'm happy to suck any part you want."

She laughed again, then rolled over and propped herself up on her elbow so she could watch him. "Does it ever amaze you how quickly we fell in love?"

"Every day."

"Does it ever scare you?"

"Never."

She looked at his face and saw total honesty there. Immediately she felt guilty, because it *did* scare her. She'd never felt like this before.

And to know that she'd fallen under a man's spell was terrifying.

He laughed, then reached over to stroke her cheek. "Don't look so scared."

"Oh, God." She felt her cheeks heat. "Now I'm mortified."

His smile was gentle, not the least bit disturbed that she might be experiencing their engagement as a point of both terror and excitement. She felt the need to explain. "It's just that I've dated my whole life. And it's always been a planned sort of thing. I dated this guy because he could take me to the prom. That guy because he had a discount at Barneys. Another guy because he was an excellent dancer. But there wasn't anything contrived about falling in love with you. And that makes it so scary to me."

"I think love is supposed to be a little scary. Sometimes it hits you in the gut and knocks the wind out of you. Sometimes it's a slow burn. We got hit. No," he corrected, "we got slammed. And now we've got each other to hold on to through the storm."

"I love you," she said. What else could she say after that? He'd taken her fear and turned it into something warm and sweet and special. "I love you more than I'll ever be able to tell you."

"I'm glad." He inched closer, then trailed his fingers along her back and over the curve of her rear. "Of course, even if you can't tell me, that doesn't mean you shouldn't try to show me. Constantly."

Giggling, she squirmed. "You're incorrigible. You

know that?" She reached back and pushed his hands away. "Watch those hands, buddy."

"Shall I cancel my meetings so I can stay here and show you just what I can do with those hands?"

She sat up, trying to affect an expression of aloof indifference even though the offer was so very, very tempting. "That's not necessary. I'll just find something to do to entertain myself."

His mouth quirked. "Uh-huh. And what local fashion establishment is having a sale today?"

"I wouldn't know. I'm only interested in one particular garment."

He frowned, then leaned forward and felt her forehead. "You're not feverish . . ."

She smacked his hand away. "Wedding dresses," she said. "You might recall that I'll be wearing one in a few days."

"I thought you'd already had all your fittings."

She shook her head. She really hadn't planned to tell him, but she wanted the sympathy. More, she wanted to hear him say they'd sue the rotten bastards—even though they really wouldn't, of course. She just wanted to know it meant as much to him as it did to her.

She crossed her fingers and spilled the news.

"*What?*" His question was spewed with such outrage that she felt an unreasonable trill of happiness. He'd be happy if she were dressed in burlap and, like most men, thought that if shown a dozen wedding dresses, then at least one of them had to suit.

He might not understand, but he cared. And since this was her fiasco, it was now his as well.

And what a lovely feeling that was!

"Can we do anything about it?" she asked, hopefully.

He shook his head, which was pretty much the reaction she'd expected. "I can call my lawyer, but even if there's some legal recourse, that kind of thing moves slowly. There's no way it could get resolved before the wedding."

"That's what I expected."

"And that's why you're going shopping today."

"I have to find the perfect dress," she said, as matter-of-factly as if she'd just announced the time. "I won't get married without it."

"You'll be beautiful in whatever you wear."

With a laugh bubbling in her throat, she threw her arms around him and then kissed him. "I knew you were going to say that," she said. "And you're so wrong, I can't even begin to tell you."

"But you love me."

"Bunches," she said.

"Well, then, that's what counts." He hooked his arm around her neck, and her body got that wonderful tingly feeling again as he tugged her closer. His lips brushed over hers, a soft promise of things to come, but they didn't get to the main event. The phone rang instead, startling Roman and making him pull away.

"Leave it," she said, even though she knew it was a futile request.

"Can't. I've got too much on the plate today to miss getting a message."

She watched as his serious business face faded, replaced by the more relaxed expression that she was so familiar with. *Family or a friend,* she thought. And then, when his forehead creased and he shot a quick glance her way, she sat up straighter. Trouble. But what kind?

She wanted to ask, but managed to hold off until he said goodbye and snapped his phone shut. And then she didn't even have to demand. Instead, he told her straight out:

"That was my mom," he said. "I'm afraid you're going to have to postpone hunting for that dress. We need to get back. Your dad's just been arrested."

Julia was a wreck, an absolute wreck, during the entire ride back. She'd said hardly two words to Roman, and she was certain he was worried about her, but she couldn't quite work up the energy to talk—to put up a false and happy face and make it all seem trivial. Like "Oh, gee, look what my pop's gone and done." Because it wasn't light and trivial. It was absolutely horrible.

Not only was she the daughter of that classless putz from Jersey—*now* she was the daughter of that classless *criminal* putz from Jersey.

Roman was being perfectly nice, but Julia knew that deep down he had to be mortified. Would he want to call off the wedding? Postpone it?

"Roman?"

He reached over and took her hand. "Hey, sweet-heart. Almost there."

She nodded. They were passing Wildseed Farms right now. Only a few more minutes to the police station where they had her father locked up.

"You doing okay?" he asked.

"Sure. Yeah. I'm fine." She shot a sideways glance at him. "How are you?" *Mortified to be seen with me?*

"I don't like seeing you upset, but otherwise, I'm fine." He squeezed her hand again. "You need anything—anything at all—you just ask me."

Absently, she nodded. He was saying all the right things, and she hoped he meant them. He loved her. Surely he wouldn't fall out of love with her just be-cause he got a good look at where she came from.

Would he?

She didn't have long to worry about it, because he pulled up right in front of the station. Another plus to small-town life—ample parking.

"Ready?" he asked as he killed the engine.

"As I'll ever be." She pushed the door open and marched up the steps, her chin held high.

She'd never been inside the station before, so Roman led her through the reception area. They were passed into the back by a dark-haired woman who apparently knew Roman, since she didn't even bother to ask for ID.

They moved through a large room filled with a dozen desks, mostly empty, then turned down a cor-ridor. At the end, she saw a cell with bars, just like in the movies. Her stomach twisted. Her dad was a lot of things, but he wasn't a criminal. He shouldn't be locked up like that. They shouldn't have—

She frowned, realizing as they got closer that, apparently, they hadn't.

The cell was empty.

She heard footsteps and turned to see Wesley walking toward them, his uniform crisp and sharp despite the heat. According to Syd, the officer had a weakness for pie and home cooking. Syd had relayed this news with a wide grin, then casually mentioned Julia's driving and suggested she start keeping a tin or two in a cooler in her trunk. Just in case she got pulled over.

As it turned out, the one time Wesley *had* pulled her over, pie wasn't necessary at all. Her innate charm had gotten her off with a mere warning.

"Hey there, Julia. Good to see you again." His eyes widened suddenly, and a red stain started to creep up his neck. "Oh, God. I didn't mean that. I mean, it *is* nice and all. But you know. I wish the circumstances were better. That's all I meant. I didn't mean your Pa—"

"Don't worry, Wesley," Roman said. "Julia knew what you meant." He frowned. "But why are you here?"

Wesley was a state trooper, not a city cop, so the question was a valid one.

The lanky officer shrugged. "My buddy Arvin made the arrest, and when he found out who the perp was, he called me. Seeing as how I know Julia and all. I'm not here officially, but it's a small town, so they don't mind me being around."

"Where is my father?"

"Aw, he was making all kinds of noises about being put in a cage, so they got him in an office." He hooked a thumb over his shoulder. "In there, actually. Last I checked, he was playing solitaire on the computer and cursing to no end."

"He punched out a judge and you just shoved him into an office?" Roman asked.

"Roman! He's my dad."

"That doesn't afford him special treatment."

She stared at him. If that was how he felt, then . . . then . . .

Then she didn't know what. She felt the slow burn of anger start to fill her blood, but before she could lash out at her fiancé, Wesley piped in again.

"Weren't like he was getting special treatment anyhow. Judge already set bail, and Syd and Alex are off at the bank waiting for the wire transfer to come through. So, you know, it's like he's just in limbo. Besides, it ain't like he got arrested in Austin."

"But he's—"

"A pain in the ass, that's for damn sure. No offense intended, Julia. But he's harmless."

Roman put his hand on her shoulder and squeezed. "They've already set bail? That's good news."

She jerked out from under it, flashed him what she hoped was a scathing look. For just a second, she thought she saw hurt cross his oh-so-perfect face, and then it was gone. She stifled the urge to take his arm and say she was sorry, but this wasn't about Roman, and she'd do well to remember that.

"Thank you for that, Wesley," she said instead. "It

means a lot to me not seeing him behind bars. But how'd you get a judge to set bail so fast?"

"Judge Strauss did it."

She blinked. "But wasn't Strauss the one he hit?"

"That's right. Said if he didn't have the right to set bail, no one did."

"But . . . but . . . why would he . . . ?"

Wesley shrugged. "Dunno. But he did." He lifted a hand. "Hey, there's Syd and Alex now." He gestured toward the door that opened into the reception area. "You leave the cash with Irene?" At their nod, he turned back to Roman and Julia.

"It'll take some time for the paperwork to get finished and filed. Half hour or so. You wanna go in and talk to your dad while you wait?"

"Yeah. I'd like that." As she moved toward the door, Roman followed. She stopped, looking at the floor as she shook her head. "I'd, um, rather go in myself. Just me and Syd."

"Oh." She could hear the hurt in his voice, steeled herself against it. Already his perception of her was changing. She could tell just from the way he'd reacted since they got the call. She didn't want to push him all the way over the edge by taking him into the pit with her and seeing just how low Marv could crawl.

That was most of it. A smaller part of her just wanted to be alone with her pop, to tell him she loved him even if he was the world's biggest asshole. But loving her pop might lower her estimation in Roman's eyes. Another reason she didn't want him inside with her.

And last, she'd heard the tone in his voice when he'd thought Marv was getting special treatment. They weren't just like oil and water—they were like nitro and glycerine. Get them close enough, and they'd explode. There'd be plenty of opportunities after the wedding for them to butt heads. No sense getting an early start now.

Mostly, though, she just wanted to go in alone.

Wesley held the door open, and she went in without looking at Roman. Syd lagged behind, telling something to Alex, and for a moment, it was just her and Marv.

He looked up, his eyes sparkling with something that might be amusement, might be love. "Well, hell, Princess. I guess your pop fucked up, huh? Not the first time, kid, and it won't be the last."

And that, she thought as the door clicked shut behind her, pretty much summed up life with Marv Spinelli.

Roman watched, silently cursing himself as Julia slipped into the room with her father. After a few seconds, Syd followed, and still Roman just stood there, feeling a bit numb about the whole thing.

"Roman?" Alex pressed a hand on his shoulder. "What's up, man?"

He shook his head. "I just could've handled this whole thing better." He ran his fingers through his hair. "I don't think I played the supportive fiancé role very well today."

"There's a history there," Alex said. "You did the best you could. You're probably just as shocked as she was. I mean, Spinelli pushed the envelope here. Breaking the judge's nose was hardly what we call typical tourist behavior."

Probably true, but that wasn't an excuse.

A gray government-issue desk was pressed up against the wall, a dangerous-looking desk chair parked beside it. Roman took the chair, balanced so it wouldn't collapse under him, and leaned forward as he rubbed his temples.

Beside him, Alex hitched his leg up onto the desk and sat there as if he owned the place. "The whole town's buzzing," Alex said. "Get used to hearing about this for a long, long time."

"That one I already figured out on my own." He took a deep breath. "The truth is, if it weren't for Julia, the whole thing would be pretty damn funny."

"She's pretty broken up about it?"

"I think she's afraid everyone's going to paint her with the same brush as her father." A fresh burst of anger ripped through him. "Damn the man. How the hell could someone be so stupid? Punching a judge in the nose? What was he thinking?"

"I get the impression from talking with Syd that Marv Spinelli tries to think as little as possible."

"Shit," Roman said, which pretty much described how he felt the last few hours.

"Herman Strauss is a saint, you know that, right?"

"He's doing it for Julia," Roman said. "He may not have said so, but I know the man. He likes her. Wants to make this easier on her. I'm afraid, though, that that's just going to make her feel worse."

"It shouldn't. Everyone in town loves her."

"The sins of the father," Roman said.

"Not here. We know better."

"Maybe we do," Roman said. "I just hope Julia realizes it." He caught the way Alex was frowning at him, and realized he said too much. But he couldn't help it. He was worried. After a fabulous night, today was turning out to be a day filled with nothing but worries and fears. It had been bad enough when he'd had to cancel his appointment with the Barrington Hotel Group's rep. Now he had to add personal worries on top of the business concerns.

He ran his fingers through his hair, hating the way that she'd pulled away from him once they'd reached the police station. The way she'd looked at him when he'd made that stupid, stupid comment about special treatment. Hating even more the impotence he felt, not being able to fix it for her.

He hadn't even been able to post bail, to at least make it a little bit right. Syd had already taken care of that, having contacted the new family accountant to wire funds.

So he couldn't spring Marv, he couldn't change the past, and he couldn't stop the inevitable gossip. Everything his fiancée needed at the moment, and he couldn't manage any of it. Hell, he couldn't even be there for her, since she'd politely but firmly asked him to give her some time alone with her dad.

"Julia loves you, Roman. So much it's embarrassing to the rest of us just to look at the two of you. You're quite a spectacle on the street, you know. The subject of much town gossip."

Roman managed a tiny smile, which was what Alex had been going for.

"And she doesn't love you any less just because she wants a few minutes with her dad," Alex continued. "I mean, it's no secret there's a history between your dad and Marv Spinelli. She drags you in there when Marv has his ire up, and it's not going to be a happy scene."

Roman nodded. "It's like living in a damn Shakespearean tragedy. It's not just our fathers—it's our entire families. You should've seen the way he looked at me yesterday. The man would just as soon not share the planet with any member of the Sonntag clan."

"That bad, huh?" Alex frowned. "You know, I only know the basics. What's the whole story?"

"What do you know?"

"Same thing everyone in town does. Marv wanted to buy Sonntag House. Your dad was going to sell it. Then when he found out that Marv was going to gut it and make it into some monstrosity like all his other motels, your dad backed out of the deal. Marv plunked down the Motor Inn to get back at your dad, and that was that."

"All true," Roman said. "Except Marv looks to be an Olympic-class grudge carrier. And he's pissed off at the entire family."

"Just because your dad backed out of a deal?"

"It's a little more complicated than that."

"Enlighten me."

Roman shot a look at the closed door and shrugged. Why not? They certainly had time. "Marv sued for specific performance, right? Argued that there was a contract to sell land, and that under Texas law, Dad couldn't just back out."

"Right."

"Well, Marv was right. That *is* Texas law. And if Dad had entered into a valid contract, then Sonntag House would be Marv's today."

"I'm not following."

"A few years before Marv rolled into town, Dad set up a small corporation. He pretty much ran things, but technically, everyone else in the family had an ownership interest. Mom. Kiki. Me. It wasn't anything we thought about. We had family meetings once a year and that was that. Dad ran things, the same as always, but the title to the house was transferred into the company name."

"And the contract with Marv was with your dad, not the company."

"Exactly. No big deal if things hadn't gone awry, but once Dad found out that Marv wanted to gut the place, he called in the lawyers. They told him how he'd screwed up."

"So Marv lost out because your dad screwed up?"

"Only partially. If it had just been Dad, the court would have decided in favor of Marv out of fairness. The judge would have considered it a technicality—

the contract was with Dad when it should have been with the company."

"But . . ." Alex prompted.

"But the family had been kept completely out of the loop. We thought it was unfair that this New Jersey businessman was getting screwed, but none of us wanted to give up our heritage if we didn't have to, especially when we realized he wasn't going to keep the house as is. We all voted and it was unanimous. And since we each owned twenty-five percent, no one of us could swing the vote. It really was a family decision."

Alex whistled through his teeth.

"Marv threw a fit, but there wasn't anything he could do. Judge Strauss ruled that the contract was void since it wasn't entered into by the proper party. He ordered Dad to pay Marv damages, and Dad did. But Marv didn't need money then any more than he needs it now. He was pissed at Dad. Mostly, though, he was pissed at the lot of us."

"Family holidays are going to be a load of fun for you and Julia," Alex said.

Roman scowled. "It's been fifteen years. I was hoping the man was over it by now. I mean, he's the one who sullied our view with the Inn. He definitely got the last word, but he's still pissed off. And I hate that Julia has to deal with it."

Alex nodded sympathetically. "She's a big girl, though. And she's been dealing with Marv her whole life."

Roman knew that, of course. But that didn't mean

it rankled any less. Especially since there was nothing he could do to make it better for her. This was in her dad's head. And that was one place Roman couldn't go even if he wanted to.

Alex shifted on the desk, then stretched. "The whole situation sucks, but there's nothing you can do about it. How did the trip to Austin go? Business at least you can get your head around. You told me about the Gristali Market fiasco. Were you able to make any headway filling that gap in Austin?"

"Some," Roman admitted. "But not a lot." He described the dinner with Charles. "Went well, and he's going to put in an order for quite a few cases, but they're a Texas-only operation. Gristali was national. It's still a huge hit." Before his father had called with news of Gristali's breach, Roman had been confident the winery could hang in there by the skin of its teeth. Now, though . . .

Well, now cash flow was even more sluggish, and they had rent and mortgage payments coming due on various properties the winery held. Some creditors could be pushed back. Landlords and mortgagors were not among them. Cash had gone from tight to strangling, and he needed to find a quick solution.

"Sure you don't want me to look into rounding up some investors?"

Roman shook his head. "Not yet. It's a family business and I want to keep it that way. I'm not saying no. But I am saying that's a last resort."

Alex nodded in understanding. "Got anything else in the pipe?"

"Yeah. It's not optimal, but it's a possibility. I had a meeting scheduled this morning, actually, but I had to cancel when we got the call about Marv."

"I'm listening."

Roman stifled a chuckle. By all appearances, Alex was a laid-back country boy—good-looking, with an easy charm and a heart of gold. The man was also a shark where business was concerned, which meant that he was tenacious as hell. Almost as tenacious as Roman himself. If Alex wanted the full rundown on Roman's various business dealings, Roman knew he'd have to either give up the information, or fight a battle to the death if he wanted to hold his cards close to his chest.

Since he didn't have the energy to argue, he caved. "Michael Barrington," he said. "Recognize the name?"

"Hell, yeah," Alex said. "The man's about as well-known as the Hilton family, without the media-trap daughters."

Roman nodded. Barrington kept a much lower profile, but the hotelier had properties all around the globe, with his own fleet of planes to make arriving at the various properties all the easier. If Barrington was on your side, you were golden. For years, Roman had been trying to get an in with the man.

"Let me guess," Alex said. "He's going to set you up as a featured label in his restaurants."

Roman shook his head. "That would be a coup. And, no, these days I'm not that lucky."

"Then what?"

"Barrington's playing hardball. He features Sonn-tag wines at a few locations, but it's not widespread, and I've been pushing for wider penetration. But he's holding back because there's something he wants from me, and he sees it as a bargaining chip."

"What does he want?"

"His own label," Roman said flatly, watching his friend's eyes as the words registered.

"Your wine, his label," Alex said. "And his money backing it up."

"Bingo."

"So what are you going to do?"

"Well, I sure as hell don't want to do that," Roman said.

Alex nodded. "That's not what I asked."

"I know." Roman rubbed his palms over his face, suddenly exhausted. He hadn't managed much actual sleep last night. "I don't want to do it. We're building up to an excellent wine here. The vines are mature, our skill level has increased, I think we're really posi-tioned to break out, and soon."

"And if you're the source for Barrington's label, you're diluting your own."

"Exactly. Not to mention competing against my-self. Best case scenario, we drive each other's prices up. But that's a long shot, and besides, it's only money. I'm more concerned about the vineyard's reputation. I want to produce an award-winning wine, and I want to be recognized for it. I'm not interested in being some winery's ghostwriter. The trouble is, it *is* all about money. We're stretched to the breaking point, and if I want to continue pushing for a stellar vintage, I need the capital to develop the wine. Which means I may have to come full circle and take the deal so that I've got the money to finance all my plans."

"I get you," Alex said, and Roman was certain his friend did understand. A few years ago, they'd both left Fredericksburg to conquer the world, and they'd both done exceptionally well, with money pouring in and hot deals at every turn. They'd both slowed down, though. And for the same reason—family. Roman's father—and the family land—needed him. For Alex, it had been his mother's illness that had drawn him back to Fredericksburg.

And, though nothing formal was in the works yet, Roman knew that the promise of raising a family here with Syd was one of the reasons Alex stayed even though his mom was now well cared for in a facility that knew how to deal with Alzheimer's.

"What does Julia think?" Alex asked.

Roman grimaced. "I haven't told her."

Alex shifted on the desk, everything about his posture telegraphing surprise. "Trouble in paradise?"

"No, it's not like that. It's just . . ." He waved the words away. Shit, this was hard. He drew in a breath, exhaled. "It's just that she knows I came back to make the winery a success. To build it from the small family business into a nationally recognized producer. What she doesn't know is how much money Dad and I have sunk into it. She thinks I need to bring business in to grow the winery and promote the wine. Not to keep the whole thing afloat."

"For God's sake, Roman. Why haven't you told her?"

"Hell, I don't know." He didn't, either. He loved her, he really did. But he hated the thought of coming into the relationship from a position of weakness. "Besides, maybe she already knows. I hear the gossip around town. We bank out of Austin, so no one knows for sure, but this is a small town. Lots of speculation. Especially after the ring situation. Some of it's probably gotten to Julia's ear."

"She would have told you if it had," Alex said, avoiding the mention of the ring. Syd had played a large part in revealing that Julia's engagement ring wasn't really a diamond after all, and Alex was still embarrassed both for Roman and for his girlfriend's role in the whole fiasco.

"Maybe," Roman said. "Or maybe she doesn't believe the rumors. Eventually, though, she'll hear enough and then—"

"What? Then she'll know the truth? Roman, buddy, that's not necessarily a bad thing. I mean, the idea is to be honest with the woman you love."

"I'll tell her when the time is right."

"All I'm saying is that you shouldn't keep secrets from your wife-to-be, my man. That kind of thing will come back to bite you."

"It's no secret that I love her," Roman said. And, really, wasn't that all that mattered?

Chapter Nine

Not even half an hour in a room with her pop, and already Julia had a whopper of a headache. For five minutes, Marv had been blustering on about his civil rights and kangaroo courts and a bunch of other nonsense. God, she needed some Advil.

"It's a plot, that's what it is. A plot to make me spend my attorney's fees. They think they'll break me, but they won't. Damned hicks."

"Pop, you hit a judge. There's going to be red tape. That's just the way it is."

Marv snorted. "Hell, I didn't mean anything by it."

"Didn't mean anything? Then why'd you hit him?"

His hands went out, shoulders rising in a Gallic shrug. "Just one'a those things, baby." He cracked his neck, then inhaled deeply. "Feels good, ya know? Like a load off."

Julia just stared.

Syd moved away to answer a knock at the door, then came back inside, a yellow piece of paper clutched in her hand.

"What you got there, girl?" Marv asked.

"Be nice to me, Pop. This is your get-out-of-jail-not-very-free card."

"So we can leave?" Julia asked. "All the paperwork's taken care of?"

"It's done. Fortunately Judge Strauss is a sweetie. He could have held Pop for a lot longer."

Marv snorted, and Julia waited for the derogatory comment that was sure to follow, but none came. She licked her lips, feeling slightly off balance.

When she couldn't stand it anymore, she stopped him as he was heading for the door. "Hold up a sec, Pop. What's going on in that head of yours? What did you mean 'a load off'? Are you dropping all this feud nonsense?" That couldn't be right. Could it? Could she be that lucky?

"I got screwed," he said. "Make no mistake. But . . ." He trailed off into another shrug, and Julia started to breathe again.

"So you're really okay? You smack the judge in the face and suddenly everything's all right?"

"Eh, you know."

"What I know is that you have to stop hitting as therapy, Pop!"

"Why? And you ain't one to complain, since this whole mess is your fault anyway."

"Mine!"

"You're the reason the wound got opened now, aren't you? I was controlling my temper just fine back in Jersey."

"You've got to be kidding me! I barely even knew Texas was on the map back then. If you'd asked me whether or not to put a motel here, I would have asked why you'd want to rent rooms to cows."

"Well, see there, girl. That's my point. You don't know squat about the motel business."

Julia closed her eyes and fought the urge to clench her fists. "Not then, you're right. But I do now." Marv opened his mouth, probably to argue, and Julia held up a hand to shut him up. "Never mind. That's not important. You're really over this stupid grudge? Really? You're okay with Roman? With the wedding?"

"Hell no."

"Pop! You said—"

"I said I got a load off my chest, and I did. Sonntags stuck together years ago, just like a family ought to, and I won't fault them for that. Not anymore. But that doesn't change a thing between you and that boy."

Julia just stood there, her hands spread and her mouth open, begging the right words to come to her mind. None did.

"I'm not mad at you, Princess. I'm disappointed. Disappointed in you and in my failure as a father. And hers as a mother," he said, waving his hand at Myrna.

"Pop!" Syd and Julia cried in unison.

"It's true. We musta failed you. Ain't that right, babydoll?"

Myrna examined her nails. "I don't know, Marv. I just don't—"

"Don't be such a wuss. You know what? Go check on the limo. Sooner it gets here, sooner we can get the fuck out."

Myrna left, obviously happy to be out of there and not at all concerned about leaving her daughters with the wolf.

"I mean it, Princess," Marv went on, without so much as missing a beat. "Your mother and I musta failed. Why else would you be marrying a man you hardly know? A man you ain't got nothing in common with? And a man who probably only wants you for your money? Huh? You tell me that."

Tears had sprung to Julia's eyes, and she wiped them away violently. "You're wrong, Pop. You are so very, very wrong." She loved Roman. With all her heart and soul, she loved this man.

The door opened once again, and this time, Myrna popped her head back in. "The limo's outside," she said. "And the clerk says there are just a few papers you need to sign, and then we can go."

" 'Bout damn time," Marv said. He stood up and crossed to where Syd and Julia stood huddled together. Without any warning, he pulled them into a bear hug, surprising Julia as much as he squished her. "You two may be screwups, but I love youse," he said. "You're my babies. You remember that."

Julia nodded, her eyes feeling a little misty. Her father might be crass and obnoxious, but she'd never doubted his love. She supposed he was a lot like the devil you knew. But what, she wondered, did that make Roman? The devil she didn't?

No! She *did* know him. And he knew her. They were soul mates. And nothing her father said was going to change that.

She shuddered, scared by the doubt that had invaded her thoughts, and decided to simply chalk it up to a very bad morning. She followed her father out into the hallway, where Wesley and Arvin led them back through the bull pen to the reception area. Roman was there, Alex beside him, both with Styrofoam cups of what had to be really bad police station coffee.

Roman looked at her with such love and concern on his face that all her doubts disappeared in a whoosh. He moved toward her briskly, then took her hand and placed a gentle kiss on her forehead. And right then, all the stupid, horrible, unreasonable doubts that had crept into her head over the last few hours didn't matter one whit. She knew that, no matter what, everything would be okay.

Too bad that assessment was blown to bits when the front door to the station opened . . . and Sarah and Robert Sonntag marched over the threshold.

"Well, well, well," Marv said. "Lookey what the cat dragged in."

Julia inched toward her father. Marv might officially be over his grudge, but apparently bits of dislike still lingered. "Pop, watch yourself."

Marv glared, then gave one quick nod. "Come on, Princess. I think we all should just get outta here."

A fabulous plan. And if she was lucky, she could spend the rest of the day in bed with her covers over her head.

"Now, wait just a minute," Robert Sonntag said. "We need to speak to Julia and Roman for a moment. It's about the wedding."

Marv snorted. "Oh, the *wedding*. We'll just see about that, won't we."

"Daddy!"

"Don't 'Daddy' me. I'm against this wedding, and that ain't no secret. I have no idea what my little girl is doing with that boy," he said, pointing an accusing finger toward Roman. "Lord knows she's had better offers."

"Pop, *please*."

"Please nothing. It's the God's honest truth."

Robert Sonntag's face turned a dozen shades of purple. "Now you just watch what you say, you low-class Jersey shyster. If you think—"

"Robert." Sarah Sonntag spoke the word softly but firmly. "Let's not make this any more heated than it already is."

Robert Sonntag snorted, and as he did, Julia saw the proud man under the sophisticated, old-money façade. The man whose family had worked the land for generations. A man used to doing battle, who wouldn't hesitate to go a few rounds with her pop.

Hell, he'd done it before. He sure as hell wouldn't hesitate to do it again.

"If we could just speak to you and Roman for a few moments," Sarah said to Julia.

Julia cast a glance toward Marv. "Go on and head out," she said. "I'll see you guys later."

"Like hell we will." He crossed his arms over his chest and leaned against the wall, dug in for life or, at least, for a long battle.

Julia sighed. *Whatever*. She moved over to Roman and took his hand, squeezed it. "The Montagues and the Capulets had nothing on us," she said as they moved hand in hand across the room to the corner that Robert and Sarah had staked out.

"No kidding," Roman said. "Why do we have to talk now?" he asked as they approached his dad. "Don't you think it would make more sense to wait until tempers cool?"

"Possibly," Robert said. "But I think Sarah and I owe it to you and Julia to give you as much fair notice as possible."

Julia had no idea what was coming, but her stomach twisted just a bit anyway.

Sarah reached out and took Julia's free hand. "Please understand this is nothing against you. We adore you, darling. You do know that, right?"

Julia nodded, wary. "Um, yeah. But . . ."

"But I'm afraid we can't allow the wedding to be held on the property."

She blinked, as stunned as if Robert Sonntag had lashed out and punched her in the nose.

"But the invitations. The arrangements. Everything's all set. Why now? Why all of a sudden?"

But she knew the answer. Her father. And that answer was confirmed in spades as they turned in unison to look across the room toward Marv.

Panic clutched at her throat. This was a nightmare. The day had officially hit absolute rock bottom.

"But it's just days away! How can I—"

She didn't have a chance to finish the thought, because the front door burst open once again, and this time a man strode in—tall, lean and totally familiar.

With sandy hair, aristocratic cheekbones and an old-money bearing despite his new-money bank account, Bart Winston looked as at home in a small Texas police station as he did at the Lincoln Center.

His eyes skimmed the lot of them, finally landing on Julia.

"Bart," she said, stupidly. "What are you doing here?"

He spread his arms, smiled wide. "What am I doing here?" he repeated. "Julia! Baby! Is that any kind of greeting for the man of your dreams?"

Chapter Ten

Smile! Smile! Smile!

It's your wedding after all, and you're going to be photographed left and right. So remember to show your pearly whites even if the caterer is late or if Uncle Bob gets drunk and dances the polka during the couple's first dance.

No pearly whites, you say? No problem. Before your wedding, have your teeth professionally whitened. Trust us. The investment will be worth it. Those photographs will be on your wall forever, after all!

        —from "Clever Tips and Ideas for Your Wedding," Bridal Bouquet magazine, Spring 2005

Her dreams?

Roman turned the words over in his head, trying to find some other interpretation of "man of your dreams," something that didn't mean that the Abercrombie & Fitch model who'd just walked through the door somehow believed he was attached to Julia. The woman Roman loved.

Nope. Nothing. Not one single thing came to mind.

"Julia?"

She was rubbing her temples, looking almost as upset as he felt. That gave him some hope. The fact that she hadn't immediately called the guy a lunatic, though, gave him pause.

"Julia," he repeated. "Who the hell is that guy?"

"Bart Winston," the model said, his pretty-boy looks marred only a little by the thick Jersey accent.

The interloper held out a hand, one that Roman was tempted to slap away. He fought the temptation. Under the circumstances, he thought that being on his best behavior was the smartest plan. He gave the hand a quick shake, happy to find it limp and slightly clammy. He immediately marked the guy as a pansy-ass. If it came down to it, Roman could take the jerk out. No problem.

Bart grinned, then jerked a thumb toward Julia. "She's my girl."

"Bart!" Julia yelped, her face turning beet red. "I am *not* your girl."

"Julia," Roman said, looking from one to the other, "what the devil is going on?"

She turned to him, the look of frustration on her face directed as much at him as it was at everybody else in the room. "Damn it," she muttered, then took his elbow. She pointed a finger at Bart, her manicured nail looking almost lethal. "You. Stay here."

She turned to her parents next. "Go. The limo's outside. Just go."

"But—"

She held up a hand, turning just slightly so she faced her sister. "You're supposed to be my maid of honor. Doesn't that mean you have to keep me sane?" Her voice was climbing now, easing toward hysteria. Roman reached out, wanting to calm her, then thought better of it. He tugged his hand back and shoved it in his pocket as Julia shrilled, "Do something!" at her sister.

"Pop, Mom. Just get in the limo, okay?"

As Syd and Alex ushered the protesting Marv and Myrna out of the building, Wesley sidled up to Roman. "You know, if there's gonna be a scene—"

"Give it a rest, Wesley. It's under control."

Wesley looked over at Arvin, standing in the doorway, his uniform making him look large and imposing. Arvin nodded, and Wesley continued. "I just mean it's not gonna look good if there's a brawl in the police station. You end up going a round with that boy, you do it outside."

"I'm not going a round with anyone," Roman said. But then he shot another look at Bart. "Okay. If we come to blows, I promise we'll do it outside."

"Thanks."

"Roman . . ." Julia's insistent voice caught his attention, and he immediately looked up. She nodded meaningfully toward his parents.

"Mom, Dad, I think it's time for you to go."

"Roman, we don't—"

He put his hand firmly on his mother's arm. "It's a misunderstanding. We'll get this worked out—*all* of it—later."

"But—"

This time his father was the one who shut his mother off. "Come on, Sarah. Let Roman work this out."

She cast a wary look toward Bart, but she went. And as soon as they disappeared through the door, every proprietary, testosterone-driven instinct welled up in him. Screw that they were in a police station, and screw that two uniformed officers were standing by. It was just him and Bart, and Roman intended to have this out. Right then. Right there.

"Roman."

Julia had moved right in front of his line of sight, afraid that if she didn't, he'd launch himself at Bart, and she'd end up with a father, a fiancé and an ex-boyfriend all being arrested on the same day. That might be the kind of thing Jerry Springer lived for, but it was *so* not her style.

"Calm down," she said, holding on to his wrist and determined to make that fire fade from his eyes. She understood—sort of—what had set him off, but from her perspective, Roman was totally overreacting. Bart was old news. *Very* old news. "Just because we're in a police station doesn't mean you have to take advantage of the facilities," she added, hoping he could hear the tease in her voice.

His eyes stayed hard for a moment, and she wondered if he'd even heard her. Then he seemed to shake himself. "Right. Sorry." He drew in a breath and faced her. "You want to give me that explanation now? Tell me why this guy thinks he's the man of your dreams?"

Not really, since she didn't have much of an explanation to give. She wasn't, however, too keen on the tone of his voice—which meant that what she wanted to give him was a piece of her mind. "There," she said, pointing to the door to the hallway. "I think for what I've got to say, we need a little privacy."

* * *

As soon as they were alone in the hall, she let him have it, and Roman realized that while he knew Julia well, he'd never yet experienced the full fury of her temper.

She might be blond, but she would give a stereotypical Irish redhead a run for her money. That was for sure.

At the moment, his very blond, very angry fiancée stood in front of him, her eyes wild, her finger poking him in the chest.

"Explanation?" she said. "You think I owe you an *explanation*? Are you nuts?"

Apparently he was, because he felt his mouth open and heard his voice saying, "I just want to know who the guy is, Julia. And what the hell he's doing here."

The finger that had been accosting him pulled back. Now one eyebrow lifted in the delicate arch that he so loved to rub with his thumb. Now, though, it was rising with irritation. "Watch your tone, Roman Sonntag. *I'm* not the bad guy here. I didn't invite him. And I have no idea what he's doing here."

"I think he made what he's doing here perfectly clear. He's expecting to give you a ring. Or if not that, he at least wants to get in your pants."

"*Roman!*" she hissed. She took his arm and pulled him farther into the hall.

He took two calming breaths. "I'm sorry," he said, this time managing to keep his voice calm and rational. "But you know what I'm asking. Just tell me."

For the first time since Bart had burst through the

door, Julia seemed to wilt. When he'd first arrived, Roman had watched as she'd shifted from frustration to downright stiffness. The trouble was, he couldn't tell if her ramrod straight posture had stemmed from surprise or guilt. Or if it was something else entirely.

Now the tenseness seemed to ease from her body, and she melted into one of the molded plastic chairs. "Oh, God, Roman. This is a nightmare. A total nightmare. And you! You're not helping matters."

He took a step back, surprised at the vitriol. "Excuse me?"

"I can't believe you're really sitting here wanting me to give you some sort of explanation." She stood up and started pacing the width of the hallway. "As if I had something to do with this? As if I caused this? Because if that's the case, mister, then we have a lot to talk about."

He opened his mouth, but his words stuck in his throat, halted there by the sharp jab of her finger against his chest.

"How *dare* you not trust me! Did I ever once— *ever*—not trust you?" She waggled her engagement ring under his nose. "Everyone was so sure that you sold the diamond. Syd was convinced that you were pulling some scam on me, trying to pass off a fake diamond for a real one. But I never once believed you'd do anything like that, even when I learned the stone was fake. I trusted you, Roman. That's the whole point of love."

"Sweetheart." He took the hand before her fingers

could thump him again. As it was, he probably had a bruise right over his heart. "I do trust you."

Again, the eyebrow cocked up, and he had to grin.

"What?" she demanded.

"It's just that you can express more emotion with one eyebrow than most people do with an entire face."

She crumpled a little at that. "I practiced," she said. "When I was about fourteen. I thought it was sexy to be able to lift just one. So I practiced for hours in front of a mirror. Now I do it without thinking."

He took her hand, kissed her fingertips. "I do think it's sexy."

"I'm glad," she said, tugging her hand back. "But you're changing the subject."

"Yeah," he admitted. "I probably am." The ring was still a sore point to him. When he'd proposed, he'd given her his grandmother's three-carat diamond ring in its original setting. A beautiful stone, it was one that he'd admired all his life. The idea of seeing that ring on Julia's finger had given him a disproportionate amount of pleasure, and he'd been both relieved and thrilled when she'd appeared to love the ring as much as he did.

Unfortunately, slipping the ring on her finger hadn't been the end of the story. When Syd had burst into town, determined to convince Julia to call off the wedding, she'd ended up fixated on the ring. As it turned out, Syd Spinelli had the instincts of a Monte Carlo jewel thief: The diamond, she'd discovered, was nothing more than three carats of glass.

Syd had used that fact to bolster her case against Roman, but Julia hadn't budged, certain there was an explanation. As it turned out, there was. Roman later discovered that his grandmother had secretly sold the stone and replaced it with the fake years before—not an uncommon practice among ladies of means in the past, since it was a way to keep their baubles and also flesh out their purse. No one had known. No one, that is, except Syd.

When he'd learned the truth, Roman had immediately offered to buy Julia a real diamond, just as big as the first. But, stubborn as she was, she said she didn't want one—had said she wanted to keep the ring Roman had given her. Fake or not, it was the one that held the sentimental value. And, she'd pointed out, it ensured that they'd have great stories to tell their grandkids.

Roman, though, still planned to get her a real stone. He hated the fact that he hadn't given her a real diamond, that traditional display of affection and betrothal of a man to his bride.

What bothered him even more, though, was that he couldn't afford it. It had been fabulous that his grandmother's ring had been there to give, even more fabulous that he'd genuinely wanted to share that with Julia. But the sad truth was that if the ring hadn't been in the family, he would have had to scramble to come up with the cash for a decent stone.

All his money was in the vines at the moment. And that left him with little leverage. Not that he needed leverage with Julia, he reminded himself. But he was used to having money, and it bothered him more than he'd anticipated to suddenly find himself in the position of having no disposable income.

"Roman?"

He shook his head, dispelling his thoughts. "Sorry. Got sidetracked."

From her sigh, he could tell that she knew exactly what had veered his concentration. "I love the ring, Roman. I don't want another. Drop it."

He chuckled. "It's dropped," he said. *At least for now.* "But that takes us back to the subject at hand."

"Yes," she said sternly. "I was pointing out that you don't trust me. And then you went wandering around in la-la land. Not very reassuring, you know."

Maybe she had a point. "I *do* trust you," he said. He brushed the back of his hand along her cheek. "Absolutely and fully." He moved closer, then stroked her hair. "I'm sorry if I was harsh earlier. I didn't mean to demand an explanation. That was uncalled for. I just . . ." He trailed off. "I was just a little shaken when your Mr. Winston walked through the door acting like he owned you."

"I was a little shaken, too," she said. "Especially when your parents dropped their bomb!"

He nodded, anger and guilt pressing in. "I know I'm sorry. I'll talk to my mom. They're just—"

She hushed him with a finger to his lips. "I know. And I *really* don't want to think about it right now." She looked at him, then sighed. "Your parents. Bart. My pop. It's crazy."

"I'm focused on your Mr. Winston," he admitted.

She flashed a sharp look at him. "He's not *my* Mr. Winston. We dated a few times about a year ago, but nothing came of it."

"He seems to think otherwise."

"So I noticed," she said grimly. She took a deep breath, then brushed a kiss across his cheek. "All right. We'll deal with this trust thing later. After all, we have years and years to hash out our issues, right?"

A genuine smile sprang to his lips. "Absolutely."

"In that case, wish me luck." She took a step toward the door. "You might as well go on to work. I'll come by later and give you an update." She paused meaningfully. "And get the full story."

"All right," he said, willing to be agreeable.

"Right." She drew in a deep breath, then frowned slightly. "Well, I guess I better go find out why the hell he's here . . . and why he's acting like I should be happy about it."

Chapter Eleven

*Remember that a wedding is about two people uniting,
but you're not turning into one person! Celebrate your
autonomy by having photographs at your reception of
the bride and the groom growing up, graduating high
school, dancing in a fifth grade recital. You know what
I'm talking about. And mix those photos in with pictures of the couple taken during the courtship. Let your
guests know that, as husband and wife, you're still
man and woman. Individuals, united.*
—from *The New Millennium Bride*

Julia paused in front of the door, her hand on the
knob as she thought about what the heck she was
going to say when she went back out into that room.
All in all, she supposed it was a good thing that she
spoke to Roman before confronting Bart. The inter-
lude had calmed her down. The red-hot fury had
settled into a seething anger tinged by curiosity and,
yes, total mortification.

*He'd practically laid claim to her in front of the Sonn-
tags!* Her in-laws-to-be! Would they understand? And
even if they said they did, would they ever really
look at her the same again? She'd worked for weeks
to ensure that they saw her as different—a diamond
forged from the massive pressure of living under
Marv's roof. Not clumsy and classless like her father.
Something new. Something different.

Something *better*.

And then in marches Bart and shoots that all to hell.

She frowned, remembering that things had gone awry even before Bart's entrance. And, just as she'd imagined, it was her father who had altered the Sonntags' perception of her. Why else would they withdraw their offer for the wedding to be held on their estate? Because they thought she was as low class as her pop.

Damn it all.

Not that she had time to worry about her reputation. She had to find a new location for the wedding! *Damn, damn, damn!*

But she couldn't even think about that until she'd dealt with Bart. She cringed, remembering how he'd marched through the door so cocky. God, she'd wanted to lash out and land a good left hook right there on his patrician little nose. The crunch would have been so very satisfying, and so what if she'd ended up arrested for assault? It would have been worth it, even if she'd been stuck for an eternity in a jail cell adjoining Marv's.

That thought spawned another: Marv had gotten arrested for punching someone in the nose. How telling was it that her first instinct as to how to deal with Bart involved the breaking of nasal cartilage?

She sighed, calming down infinitesimally. Maybe the apple didn't fall far from the tree after all.

A little shiver of horror trilled down her spine. *No.* She wasn't like Marv. She knew better than to buy polyester. She had not an ounce of boring brown shag carpeting in her apartment. And she didn't worship at the altar of the almighty dollar.

She wasn't her pop, and she never would be.

With a quick nod to fortify herself, she pushed through the doors. The men—Bart, Wesley and Arvin—turned to look at her. The only female in the room, the young officer behind the reception desk who'd heard the whole thing, flashed a sympathetic smile.

Julia straightened her shoulders, lifted her chin and marched across the room toward Bart.

His mouth opened as she approached, as if he wanted to say something. She didn't give him the chance. "You," she said, pointing to him. "There." The finger moved, indicating the double glass doors leading to the outside.

"I'm picking up on a bad vibe here, honey," Bart said as soon as they were standing on the front steps of the police station. "If I didn't know better, I'd think you weren't happy to see me."

"You're kidding, right?"

He stared back at her, his face impassive, his eyes guileless.

She let out a sigh. The man was either serious or he deserved an Academy Award. She took his elbow and led him down the steps, then steered him to the little picnic table on the green. The intertwining branches of an ancient oak provided some shade, but not enough to make a dent in the late summer heat. Julia kicked off her shoes, clenched her toes in the cool St. Augustine grass, and leaned her back against the table. "Spill it," she said.

"Spill what?"

"What are you doing here?"

"What do you mean, what am I doing here?" He reached out for her hand, and she was so surprised, she didn't snatch it away in time. "I came to see you, of course."

"Obviously. But why?" A few yards away, two women stopped on the sidewalk, then turned to look toward Julia and the stranger. Julia recognized them both—Thelma Lynn with her flaming orange hair and her loyal sidekick Delores. Too late, she yanked her hand away and used it to wave to Thelma. The older woman's lips pursed in disapproval, and she continued down the sidewalk without waving back. *"Why?"* Julia repeated, this time snapping the question as she saw weeks of work toward fitting in go spiraling down the drain.

First the Sonntags, now the whole town. What next? The universe?

"I thought you'd be happy to see me."

Why would I want to see you? She wanted to ask the question, she really did. But he looked so damned earnest, she couldn't manage to get the words out. Instead, she folded her arms over her chest and tried to stay calm. "Not to belabor a point, Bart, but we aren't dating."

"Well, no, not really. Which is why I was a little surprised when—" He broke off suddenly, his face clearing and his eyes narrowing with wary concentration. "You really didn't know that I was coming, did you? And you really don't want me here."

Julia did a double take, ingrained politeness warring with the truth. In the end, she decided on an amalgamation of both. "I'm sorry if I was too abrupt," she said, "but, yeah, that's about the extent of it."

"But . . . why?"

Bart's usually controlled features were fixed in bafflement, the expression almost comical. Julia was pretty sure her face mirrored his, actually, since she had absolutely no idea why he'd be so confused.

"Bart, we quit going out over a year ago."

"But we never officially broke up."

"Well, no. I suppose that's technically true. But I haven't heard from you in nine months. Call me crazy, but I consider that broken up."

"I suppose so," he said, sounding a little morose.

"Maybe I'm being dense, but why on earth would you just bop down to Texas acting like nothing ever happened?"

Even as she said the words, though, she knew the answer. Because when you got right down to it, there was only one reasonable explanation. "My dad."

He nodded, and she mentally gave herself two points. Marv the Meddler strikes again.

"What exactly did he do?"

"Told me to come. Told me you wanted to see me. That you'd been talking about me. That you missed me."

"*Damn it.*" The curse was out of her mouth before she could pull it back.

A wry grin played across Bart's face. "Guess I was misinformed."

Julia melted a little. "Oh, Bart. I'm *so* sorry." She slouched back against the picnic table, feeling sorry for Bart, sorry for herself, and totally pissed off at her father.

The thing was, she genuinely liked Bart. They'd gotten along famously. He was funny and smart and he made her laugh. Their families lived about four blocks away from each other, and Marv and Daniel Winston had a friendly competition going—every time Marv added a new motel to his chain, Daniel rushed to add a new grocery store to his.

Bart and Julia had dated for about eight fun months, and Marv and Myrna had been expecting wedding bells. Julia knew that. But she and Bart had never talked about it, to Julia's immense relief. She might have liked Bart—a lot, even—but something was missing. Some spark. At the time she couldn't define it. Now that she'd met Roman, she knew exactly what it was.

Not that she and Bart had ever talked about the voids in their relationship. Fortunately, they'd been able to completely sidestep that little issue when Bart took a job with a multimedia company. The job took him to Hong Kong, where he'd lived for the last year or so. They'd sent a few e-mails back and forth for a while, but then that had dropped off. Julia hadn't even realized when the notes had stopped coming. By that time, her life had been too filled with other things. Other men. Like Somers, the last man she'd dated before Roman.

She'd put Bart out of her mind and, she'd assumed, he'd put her out of his.

Apparently, she'd been wrong.

She realized that her fingers were once again rubbing circles on her temples. The headache had returned. She pressed her fingertips against her eyes, took a couple of deep breaths, then looked up to face her old boyfriend. "Let's back up," she said. "Tell me exactly what happened. Exactly what my dad said."

"I got back from Hong Kong about a week ago, and I called your apartment in Jersey. Got the message on your machine that you were out of town, and that friends should call your cell phone."

Julia nodded. She'd kept her Manhattan apartment when she'd moved to Texas, but hadn't bothered to forward her calls. Anyone that she wanted to talk to would have her cell phone number. Possibly a little sneaky, but there'd been a few guys in her life at the time that she really wasn't interested in seeing again.

"Go on," she prompted.

"I called, but you must have changed your cell number, because the one I had didn't work. So I called Debbie," he said, referring to the secretary at Marv's office, "and asked if she could give it to me. She said she'd have to get back to me."

"You never called," Julia pointed out.

"Right. Debbie got back to me the next day with the number, but she said before I called you, I should talk to Marv. That was yesterday." Julia made a face, remembering the odd call Marv had received. "Anyway," Bart continued, "I called Marv, and he was blown away to hear from me. I always have liked your dad—he's quite a character."

"That he is," Julia agreed, but Bart spoke with such genuine affection that she couldn't help her grin.

"Well, he told me that you'd come down to Texas to run one of the motels, and that he'd just come down that very day to check on you. And that you were miserable down here. Small Texas town, no taxis. No Barneys or Bergdorf's. No sushi. Just a lot of cow patties and beer."

"He actually *said* that." Julia looked around, as if Marv might materialize out of thin air. She realized after a second that she'd clenched her fist. That Spinelli pound-away-a-problem reaction again, only this time, the urge to hit was directed toward the source of her problem. Her father.

"More, actually. He said that he was so glad to hear from me, and that you'd really missed me over the last year, and that lately you'd been talking about me a lot and wished you knew how to get in touch with me. Let me tell you, I felt like an ass when I heard that. I'd gotten so busy at work that I quit e-mailing you. You're such a social butterfly, I didn't even imagine that you'd be sitting around waiting to hear from me."

I wasn't, Julia thought. But it hardly seemed politic to say it. Instead, she just gestured for him to continue.

"Well, then he said the real kicker—that he couldn't think of anything that would cheer you up more than having me come down here. And, well, I haven't dated anyone seriously since you, and the truth is I've missed you, and since Marv was so emphatic about how much you missed me . . ." He trailed off, looking a little miserable. "I guess that wasn't entirely accurate, huh?"

"Oh, Bart." The words felt like they weighed a million pounds. Julia couldn't remember ever being quite so sad. "I'm so sorry. The man I was with? Roman? He's my fiancé."

Bart just stared at her for a moment, then nodded slowly. "And your father?"

"He doesn't approve." She gave him the Cliff's Notes version of the whole Sonntag House fiasco, the lawsuit and her whirlwind affair.

"Sounds like true love," he finally said.

"It is." She flashed him a wan smile. "Bart, I'm sorry."

He took her hand. "Don't ever be sorry for falling in love, kiddo. I'm happy for you. I'd be lying if I said I wasn't a little jealous, but that doesn't mean I'm not genuinely happy."

"Thank you." She leaned closer and pressed a soft kiss to his cheek. "You're a good guy, Bart Winston."

"Yeah? Well, maybe you can spread the word."

"Maybe I will."

He caught her in a hug, and she squeezed back, her eyes closed tight. When she opened them, she saw that Thelma and Delores were back on the sidewalk again, finishing the circle of their lunchtime walk. Even from this distance, she could make out their shocked expressions. She tensed, her first instinct to push Bart away.

"Julia?"

"Nothing," she said, hugging him tighter. He was her friend, he was a little part of who she was, and she wasn't going to feel guilty about that. Not even if it meant that tongues would be wagging by sundown. Or, more realistically, in the next fifteen minutes.

When she did pull away, she kept her hands on his shoulders, looked deep in his eyes. "You're okay?"

"I'm fine. But I'm not too keen on flying back to New York so soon."

"So stay," she said. "We've still got a few rooms at the Inn. And I'm getting married on Saturday." She squeezed his hand. "I'd love it if you'd sit on the bride's side of the aisle."

"You're sure? Or is this just your social training shining through?"

"My social training was impeccable," she admitted, "but I promise that the sentiment is real. Really. Stay."

"You're sure?"

"Absolutely. I could use the help, anyway."

His brow furrowed. "With what?"

"Finding a new place to have the wedding, for one. Unless I can line up a new location—and fast—I might be saying my vows at the local Dairy Queen."

He pointed across the street. "The park is nicer."

"See? That's why I need your help. I'm too much of a basket case to think clearly on my own." It was a joke, but even so she made a mental note to check with the city and see if the park *was* available to be rented.

He grinned. "You're sure your fiancé won't mind?"

"He won't," she said, fighting a frown. Surely he wouldn't, right? Not once he understood the circumstances.

"All right, then. But your pop won't be happy. I think he wants me standing at the altar, not sitting in the audience."

"You're right about that." She gave his hand a squeeze and stood up. "I guess I know what I'm doing for the rest of the afternoon. I need to go read my father the riot act."

"You're yelling at *me*?" Marv asked, pointing to himself. "You're chewing out your father? You got no right, Princess. No right at all."

"No *right*?" she repeated, pacing at the foot of the king-sized bed in his and Myrna's room. "You invite an old boyfriend down here, fail to mention that I'm engaged, and suggest to him that I'm going to go all mushy when I see him? You better believe I've got a right."

Marv squinted at her, while Myrna sat up near the pillows, wringing her hands. "Your father was only trying to help, baby," her mother finally said, her voice so soft it was almost unintelligible.

"No," Julia said, "he wasn't. He was trying to sabotage. Sabotage is not helping."

"I don't know what's gotten into you, Princess. You used to listen to your father. There used to be some respect. Now you're yipping at me like that damned little dog your mother fawns all over. It ain't right, baby girl. It just ain't right."

"I'm not a baby, Pop. I haven't been for a long time."

"No? You're damn well actin' like one. You wanna know why I invited Bart down here? You really want to know?"

"Yes! I really want to know, because I don't like being pissed at you, Pop. But right now, I'm so livid I can't see straight."

" 'Cause you're acting like a damned fool idiot, that's why. I had to shock some sense into you. You think I don't know why you're doing this?"

She gaped at him. "If by *doing this* you mean getting married, I'm *doing it* because I'm in love."

"Bullshit," Marv said. "You're doing it because of that damn fiasco with Somers."

"You're crazy!"

"Am I? Didn't you swear off boyfriends? Didn't you stand right in front of me and tell me that the next man would stick?"

"Well, yes." She had, too. She'd lost an heirloom necklace, and Somers hadn't been too thrilled. Neither had his family, and neither had Marv when he'd written the check to reimburse them. He'd laid into Julia, but good, calling her a serial dater and all kinds of nasty things, and she'd sworn off men and dating and assured him that the next time would be for real. But she hadn't meant it like *that!*

"Believe me, Pop. You don't intimidate me that much! I'm not getting married just because I made some offhand comment to you! I'm getting married to Roman because I love him."

"You know this Roman boy? You think you know him well enough to love him? You *don't*," Marv said emphatically, before Julia could answer. "You've known the guy for what? A month? How you gonna get to know someone that fast?"

"I know what's important," she said.

"Yeah? Well, I know what's important, too. And I know that family's the most important thing of all. And what do you think this marriage is going to do to this family? Huh? You think about that?"

"Bart's a good boy," Myrna added, her voice almost pleading. "And he knows us. We still go out with Daniel and Charlene. Do you think we'll have family Christmases with the Sonntags?"

Julia stared, incredulous, at her mother and father. "So you're saying I should dump Roman and marry Bart because it'll make the holidays *easier*?"

"You just think about what I'm saying," Marv said, waggling a finger her way.

Julia didn't answer. She couldn't. Because the truth was, she'd already thought about it. And as much as she hated to admit it, Marv was right. Marry Roman, and the holidays weren't going to be a warm, cozy family affair. Marv may have decompressed some, but emotions ran high. And even if the families entered into an all-encompassing truce, that still wouldn't change the basic facts: The Sonntags were class and old money. Crystal goblets and fine china. The Spinellis were classless and newly rich. Shag carpet, tacky architecture and flashy cars.

But she'd made her decision, and she'd chosen love over family. Maybe in her secret heart of hearts, she'd believed that after the wedding, their parents would find a way to get along and their worlds would mesh seamlessly. Now, though, she had to admit that the odds were not in her favor.

She loved her family, warts and all. But she loved Roman, too. She needed to make it clear to her parents that she'd already examined all her options, and she'd made her choice. Somehow, though, she couldn't find the courage to say that, when it came right down to it, her heart had chosen Roman.

So she didn't say anything, even though Marv was squinting at her, clearly expecting her to open her mouth. She kept it firmly shut, afraid that if she spoke, something stupid or hurtful would come out.

After a minute, Marv shifted, his expression altering slightly. She watched him, fascinated at the businessman's mind under the blustery Napoleonic façade. Marv might be full of cock-and-bull, but he hadn't built his empire without understanding how to negotiate, and how to find weaknesses.

Julia's stomach twisted a little as she waited for the jab that she knew was coming.

When he spoke, his voice wasn't the blustery bel-

low she'd expected. Instead, it was calm, rational—
which meant that Marv was playing hardball.

"Your mother and I dated for almost a year before
I proposed," he said. He glanced once in Myrna's
direction, something tender and rarely seen in his
eyes. "We knew everything about each other by the
time I put a rock on her finger. My temper. My background. That your grandparents didn't have two
nickels to rub together. That her pop was in the joint
for stealin' cars. All our skeletons. All our secrets. So
that when we stood up there in front of that minister
and God and all our friends, we both knew that even
though marriage wasn't ever easy, at least we were
going into it with our eyes open."

Julia swallowed. It was the most calm, rational and
reasonable speech she'd ever heard pass through her
father's lips. And that, damn it all, was totally unfair!

"We did it smart, your mother and me. We knew
what we were getting into. Knew each other. Knew
our families. Can you say the same thing, baby girl?"

"Of course," she said, not even aware she was lifting her chin, something she always did whenever
she was on the defensive. "I know him as well as I
know myself," she added. But even as she spoke,
little niggles of doubt preyed on her. What was Roman's favorite color? His favorite movie? Did she
know? *Should* she know?

Marv frowned thoughtfully. "Maybe you do and
maybe you don't," he said. "But how about the other
way around? Does he know you? Does he know *us*?"

And this time, Julia just stayed silent. Because

Roman didn't, of course. The opposite, in fact, since Julia had done everything in her power over the last month to make sure that Roman knew as little as possible about her classless, brusque, tasteless, new-moneyed family.

The Julia Spinelli that Roman saw wasn't real. Somehow, someway, she had to fix his vision. And hope that, once she did, he'd still love her just as much.

Chapter Twelve

*Dear Wedding Guru, I'm suddenly so nervous. I mean,
I'm about to commit the rest of my life to this man, and
do I really know him? I tried to think of his toothpaste
brand last night, and I COULDN'T!!!! I'm in trouble,
aren't I? Signed, Impetuous in Idaho.*

*Dear Impetuous, First of all, you should be congratu-
lated for even having your fears. Every girl has them;
many ignore them. So kudos to you for facing yours.
Now, though, the hard work starts. Are these typical
pre-wedding jitters? Or are there serious issues between you and your groom? Toothpaste isn't the issue,
but there does need to be communication and understanding. Are you in love? Or are you in love with
being in love? Think about it.*

> —from the syndicated column "Dear Wedding
> Guru: Helping You Take a Long Hard Look Be-
> fore You Walk Down That Aisle"

Julia had flipped through every page of *Bride* magazine before realizing that she hadn't focused on even
one of the dresses so beautifully displayed in the
photographs. Obviously, she was distracted.

Not that she'd needed confirmation. At the moment, her entire life was one big distraction. Her
wedding dress. Her wedding location. Her groom.

Her father's not-so-secret desire that she marry another man.

And, most importantly, her sudden overwhelming
fear that somehow she'd managed to keep the heart
of herself completely hidden from Roman these past
months. He was marrying Julia Spinelli. At least that

was printed on the invitations. But did he really know that girl? After all, what was printed on the invitations didn't matter. The lovely script on the thick vellum specifically said that the wedding and reception were at the Sonntag estate. Clearly *that* wasn't going to be happening.

Frustrated, she heaved the magazine across her room, the satisfying *thwack* as the thick magazine hit the drywall not even coming close to allaying her troubles.

She made a face, then got up and moved over toward her laptop. She'd sent Vivien an e-mail two hours earlier, when she'd first gone back to her room. She hadn't really intended to hide away for the rest of the night, but that's how it had turned out, and frankly she was fine with that.

Both Roman and Bart had called, and so had Syd, but she'd ignored them all, turning off her cell phone and instructing Carter not to put anyone through on penalty of losing his job. Considering the way Marv was hounding the boy, she was afraid that might not be a threat, but so far her phone was quiet.

She tapped her fingers on the desk as the computer booted up. In front of her was the laminated to do list she'd inherited from Breckin. She scowled, then grabbed a dry erase marker and wrote across it in big capital letters, "FIND A NEW LOCATION." And then, because she hadn't an idea in the world where to start, she tossed it across the room, too.

God, she was so behind. And the trouble just kept piling up. But the bizarre truth was that she just didn't care. Not really. Not enough. Because right then, the only important thing on her mind was Roman.

In the face of her new fears, her cleverly laminated to-do list didn't seem that important at all. Hard to believe, but at the moment, she really didn't care if she had the wedding of the century. She just wanted some sort of assurance that getting married was the right thing.

Damn Marv for tying her up in knots! And damn herself for letting him!

As soon as the computer screen came up, Julia navigated to her e-mail, and, yes, there was a message from Vivien.

Eagerly Julia opened it, then sagged in disappointment when she read the text:

From: vshelton
To: CrownJule
Subject: Re: Angst

Dammit, Jules, you CANNOT e-mail me with a crisis and then turn off your cell phone. And I couldn't get that little twerp to put me through to your room no matter how much I threatened. You have him totally wrapped around your little finger!

You're probably just taking a nap or something, but I can't call back. My phone died, and I'm waiting until I get to Texas to get a replacement. I'll call the next time I stop for gas or to walk the dogs if there's a pay phone. Don't do anything stupid. Whatever this is, it's just nerves. Roman's great.

And you KNOW I wouldn't say that if I didn't believe it, right?

Love you. I'll be there in time for the bachelorette party! We'll get smashed and you'll have a totally new perspective. See you soon.

Viv

Well, hell.

Julia typed a quick reply, assuring Viv that she was feeling much better. A lie, but she didn't want Viv to worry, especially since Viv was apparently communicationally challenged at the moment. She also didn't want Viv mentioning her onset of angst to J.B., who might mention it to Roman, who might think she was having cold feet.

The love of Viv's life, J.B. Anglin, also happened to be one of Roman's best friends and one of his groomsmen. There was something about the water in Fredericksburg that had all the northeastern girls falling for Texas men.

She shook her head, smiling a little at her own whimsy.

As she was typing, her computer *dinged*, the perky sound signaling yet another e-mail. She clicked to her in-box, then held her breath as she opened the reply from Kiki. *Please, please, please let it be good news.*

From: kikid@misstexas95.com
To: crownjule@aol.com
Subject: Re: Vera??

Julia

You poor thing. What you're suggesting is tantamount to an act of fashion terrorism, and you don't even know it. In this case, ignorance is NOT bliss! Print this out and tape it to your forehead. You don't rethink Vera Wang. Vera Wang rethinks YOU. When you turned down the chance for Vera to design your wedding gown, I thought my brother was marrying Mariah Carey, the GLITTER era. That's how disturbing it was! And luckily, your insane rebuke didn't ruin it for your bridesmaids. We will all be resplendent in Vera Wang, as YOU should be. And what's this nonsense about you once having a dress that you loved? Sweetheart, I don't care if your great-grandmother grimaced through her arthritis hand-sewing the lace train. If Vera Wang is THINKING about MAYBE designing your wedding gown, then even a precious heirloom gets relegated to something you wash the car in.

My advice—kiss and make up with Breckin. He can produce miracles on short notice. Example: Once, back in high school, Sarah Jovies was a wreck before junior prom. Like a fool, she'd gone on the Pill the week before. Her idiot doctor gave her the kind with androgens, which can cause horrible acne. Sarah looked like the very worst of the Proactiv Solution "before" pictures and had to stay home. Well, her mother spoiled her rotten and had driven the girl to Dallas to find THE most fabulous prom dress. Breckin convinced her to let ME wear it. Why should an amazing frock just hang in a closet? A few alterations later, I wowed them at the prom. You know, I've always felt guilty about that night. Not the dress, of course. God meant for me to wear it. But the fact that I made out with Sarah's boyfriend. Anyway, the point is—call Breckin!

PS It's impossible for me to make the bachelorette party or rehearsal dinner. God, I'll be lucky to get there in time for the wedding itself! But I'll make it. Promise, promise. It's just with my book deal, and working out schedules with ABC and Fab's new nightclub, our lives are beyond crazy! But, honey, just point me toward the aisle. If there's any kind of runway and an audience, this girl can wing it.

    Air Kisses,
    Kiki

Julia sighed. *Not* good news. For a second, she considered doing what Kiki had suggested and calling Breckin, but she'd been a little hysterical when she'd fired him. Chances were he was happy to be rid of her.

No, she didn't need her wedding planner. She just needed sympathy. Someone to whom she could bitch about both her dress fiasco and her frustrating fears about her relationship with Roman.

For a moment, she toyed with the idea of calling

Syd. But she dismissed that. Her sister *did* love Roman now, but she hadn't always. And somehow the thought of letting Syd know that there might be even the teensiest bit of trouble in paradise just didn't sit well.

No, this was her problem and her wedding. And she would have to handle it.

Ironic, really. Ever since she'd met Roman, she'd been able to run her problems by him. Most of the time, he'd even stepped up to the plate and helped solve them.

With a sigh, she lay back on the bed, letting her eyes drift over the walls. Blank now, but weeks ago, they'd been covered with pictures of wedding dresses. If a dress had even the slightest detail that she coveted, she'd taped it up so she could study it in the most subliminal of fashions.

Now, she got off the bed and lay down on the floor beside it, reaching far under to find and pull out the box she'd stuck down there—the dress photos. Once again, she taped them to the wall. Because once again, she was on the hunt for a dress.

She *was* getting married. And it *was* going to be an amazing wedding. And so what if she now had to find a different venue? She'd get Syd on the task tomorrow. She could even enlist Bart to help find the videographer.

And that's when it hit her—a true V8 moment. She didn't want to *entirely* spill her guts with Bart, but he was good for talking. And she also recalled that he had some serious shopping stamina. Everything might be going to hell around her, but she could still shop. And number one on her list was finding Roman a groom's gift. And who better to help with that task than a man?

Julia perked up, delighted to have an excuse to get out and hit the stores. If nothing else, she'd consider it therapy.

"You look like you're beginning to calm down," Alex said to Roman. He had a cold beer in his hand, and was leaning back in his chair. The table in front of them was littered with the remains of a traditional Fredericksburg feast: a variety of wursts and piles of sauerkraut. Except for the fact that his best friend was in a funk, Alex would have almost considered the situation perfect.

"It's mostly an illusion," Roman said. He held up a glass mug that still had a bit of foam in it, the remnants of his third beer. "I'm drinking my way to a better disposition."

Alex grinned. Despite the circumstances, he was enjoying himself. He and Roman used to do the beer-and-bullshit thing a lot. Lately, they'd both had too much going on to just kick back and shoot the shit.

Roman noticed the grin and managed one of his own, albeit weaker than his friend's. "You look far too happy."

Alex shrugged. "Why shouldn't I be? Compared to you, I should be the happiest man on earth. I don't have any deep dark secrets that my girlfriend is likely to discover, and by the time I'm in a position for her father to have issues with me, you'll have already paved that road."

Now Roman's smile was genuine. "You're an ass, you know that, right?"

"Been told that over and over. Still not sure I believe it." He stabbed his fork into the last piece of bratwurst as the waitress replaced their empty mugs with full ones. "Anyway, I think coming here was good for you. You needed to kick back. You looked far too worked up about Burt What's-His-Name's arrival."

"Bart," Roman corrected. "And I was."

"But?"

Roman shrugged. "But I'm fine now. Julia didn't invite him. I overreacted. This time tomorrow, he'll be gone, and Julia and I can get back to our lives."

"With the added bonus of having her father in the picture."

"I thought you were trying to *lift* my spirits."

"Sorry," Alex said, not sounding particularly penitent.

Roman waved it away. "It's okay," he said. "Marv doesn't like me or my family, and I guess I understand why. But we're going to work through all of that, I'm going to win her father over, and we're all going to be one big happy family."

"Or else?"

"Or else I'll end up strangling her father and I'm going to have to figure a way to make Julia okay with that."

"Good luck. From what Syd tells me, Marv drives them both nuts. But they still love him."

"Well, they should. He's their father, after all."

"I'm not convinced he has their best interests at heart."

Roman grinned. "I'm absolutely sure that he doesn't. If he did, he wouldn't disapprove of me."

Alex laughed. "Cocky?"

"Just honest."

Feeling a bit better, Roman sat back and took another sip of beer, letting his attention drift over the other patrons. He and Alex were at their favorite table, right next to the sidewalk that ran the length of Main Street. And right then, Thelma Lynn and her husband were walking toward them, all dressed up for dinner.

Roman waved, expecting nothing more than a polite tip of Thelma's head in return. Instead, she stopped cold and held out her arms, as if she wanted to suck him into her embrace despite the five yards and squatty wooden fence that separated them. "Roman," she said. "Oh, you poor, poor dear!"

He had no idea what she was talking about, and considering the way the tables around him started to buzz, he figured that neither did the other diners.

Apparently he was about to find out, though, because Thelma was marching toward the little gate in the fence, leaving her husband on the sidewalk looking slightly baffled.

Despite the short distance, it took almost two minutes for her to make it to his table, because she stopped to make small talk with at least four people along the way.

"Maybe we should make a run for it," Alex said.

"From Thelma Lynn? Trust me. There's no escape. Run, and suddenly everyone in town hears rumors that you have scabies. Or worse."

Alex made a face, then scratched his arms. "Ew. We'll stay. It's your ass she's after, anyway."

"Thanks," Roman said. "Your support is most appreciated."

Alex took the last swig of beer from his mug, then signaled to the waitress for a refill. "Just calling them as I see them."

"Roman!!!!" Thelma grabbed a chair from the next table and parked it next to him, taking his hand as she perched on the hard white plastic. "You poor, poor dear. I feel just terrible for you." Her stage whisper carried across at least a dozen tables, and despite having faced more brutal opponents on the business battlefield, Roman couldn't help but cringe.

She was busily patting his hand, and now he tugged it away. "Thelma, I appreciate the support. But I don't actually know what it's for. You want to give me a clue?"

Her eyes widened, and the hand that had been holding his went to her heart, clutching at the material there. Her face scrunched up, and she looked so flabbergasted that for a moment he feared she was having a stroke.

"Thelma?"

"I just can't imagine . . . *can't imagine* . . . what you must be going through."

"I'll admit to a little indigestion after too much

wurst, but other than that, I'm not going through much at the moment."

"Such a brave, brave boy . . ." She patted him on the cheek, and Roman turned to Alex, hoping his eyes were screaming *Rescue me!* even if the rest of him wasn't.

"Uh, Thelma?" Alex asked. "What's he being brave about?"

"You haven't told him?" she asked, peering deep into Roman's eyes. "I just assumed. He's your best friend, and I . . . well, this *is* awkward."

Considering that every eye at every table within a five-block radius was aimed their direction, Roman had to wonder just how Thelma defined "awkward."

Feeling daring, he took the plunge. Might as well clear up whatever nonsense was on Thelma's mind while half the town was listening. "I don't have any secrets from Alex," he said. "If you're concerned about something you want to discuss with me, you can discuss it in front of Alex, too."

"You were always such a good boy, Roman. It pains me to see you engaged—even briefly—to a woman who would so casually throw you over. She seemed so sweet, too. But I guess blood will tell. Is it because of your financial troubles?" she asked, and he cringed, suddenly regretting not dragging her away to someplace more private.

"My finances are just fine, Thelma."

She patted his hand and made sympathetic noises, while Roman tried to tamp down his temper. Around them, he was certain the gossip was starting to fly. "I remember when that girl's father blustered into town fifteen years ago and started throwing his money around. Well, I thought Julia was different, especially after she didn't make a fuss about that fake ring. Thought she wouldn't care if you were flat broke. But maybe she decided that she just can't marry a man without a fortune."

"Thelma," Alex said, warning in his voice.

"Now, I'm not spilling secrets here. I know your family's been trying to keep a lid on how tight things are, but once word was out about the engagement ring . . . well, we're *family*, Roman. This whole town. We understand when times get tight. But if she's not willing to stand by you, then maybe it's best she found out your troubles and found herself another man."

Roman just sat there in shocked disbelief. Another man? What was the woman blathering on about?

"Alicia Hidalgo," Thelma said, and Roman realized she'd pulled an address book out of her purse and now had it opened on her lap. "She's a lovely girl, and I know she's always had a bit of a thing for you."

"Alicia Hidalgo?" he repeated numbly.

"Right. Now, I wouldn't ask her out right away. That would seem too sudden. You wait a week or two and—"

"*Thelma Lynn!*"

"Oh!" Her eyes went wide and she clamped her mouth shut, her expression that of a woman who'd just met a deranged psychopath in a dark alley. Well, maybe she had.

With superhuman effort, Roman managed to stay

in his seat and not throttle the woman. His hands clenched, though, and Alex must have noticed, because his friend tensed, leaning forward as if to intervene should Roman launch himself at the busybody.

"I'm not sure where you're getting your information, Thelma," Roman said, his voice tight with the effort of controlling his temper. "But I'm hardly on the market. In case you've forgotten, I'm getting married on Saturday. And I assure you that all is well in paradise. Julia and I are doing just fine."

"Oh. I see. Well, that's just . . ." She trailed off, her brow furrowing. "But there was the young man who came into town. He stopped at the bakery. He was looking for Julia. Said he was her boyfriend. And of course Emily told Janet, and she told Betty and then when it got to me—"

"You just assumed it was true."

"Well . . . yes." Now it was Thelma's turn to look a bit flummoxed.

"Just a misunderstanding," Roman said, smiling his most civil smile. "Bart Winston is just an old friend of Julia's who happened to be passing through town on business."

"I'm *so* glad to hear that," she said. She leaned forward, taking his arm once again. "Especially with everything going on, you know."

He knew he shouldn't, but he just couldn't help himself. "Everything?" he asked.

"Well, yes. The way he called himself her boyfriend. And then when I saw them holding hands under the oak tree outside the police station, and then just now. You know, the way they're laughing and carrying on inside that store . . . well, one does jump to conclusions, you know."

"Yes," he said. "I'm sure one does." He kept his voice measured and cool, but he felt beads of sweat break out on his forehead. Not too unusual in the late summer heat, but the heat wasn't the cause. Not this time.

Julia had said she was getting rid of the intrepid Mr. Bart. But if what Thelma said was true . . .

Mentally, he shook his head. He'd never been the jealous type before, and he didn't intend to start now. Surely, Julia had an explanation. After all, there had to be at least a dozen reasons why she'd sit under a tree with her old boyfriend just days before her wedding, holding hands for every wagging tongue in Fredericksburg to see.

Trouble was, at the moment, he couldn't think of one such reason, much less a dozen. And he sure as hell couldn't think of a reason why she'd be shopping with the man, especially since she'd specifically told Roman that she was going to tell Bart Winston to take a hike.

He squirmed a bit, not really wanting to ask. But in the end curiosity and jealousy won out. Careful to avoid Alex's gaze, he met Thelma's eyes dead on. "What store?" he asked. "Tell me where—*exactly*—you saw them."

*   *   *

"Here you go," Bart said, holding up a pair of men's boxers emblazoned with oversized lipstick kisses. "Just the thing for the discriminating groom."

Julia laughed, then forced herself to put on a stern face. "I'm on a deadline here, and you're not helping."

"Really?" His brow furrowed as he held the boxers up high. "You don't think Roman will like these?"

"Bart!" she hissed, then snatched them out of his hand.

"You always were cute when you blushed."

She smacked him with the boxers. "I'm going to fire you if you don't get serious."

"Fire me? A man with my exquisite taste in gifts? I mean, even if you don't think they're right for Roman, surely you wouldn't deny your father. I mean, are these Marv or what?"

"You are so bad!"

"Admit it. Your dad probably wears boxers with cartoon characters. Maybe Jimmy Neutron."

"I think Pop's more of a Daffy Duck sort of guy."

"The episode where Daffy and Bugs found the gold? You're right. That is *so* your father."

She laughed. "Scary, isn't it? I'm not sure what that makes me and Syd . . ."

"Animated," Bart said with a chuckle. "If nothing else, your life is animated."

"You're right about that," Julia said. "Especially this week. And speaking of . . ."

"Hey, I suggested the boxers."

"Bart . . ." She crossed her arms and tapped her foot.

"What? You don't like the kisses? It is kind of Valentine's Day. Well, then how about these?" He picked up another pair of novelty underwear, this time gray with little pink elephants.

Julia clapped a hand over her mouth and tried not to laugh, but she couldn't quite do it. Instead, she managed a very loud, unladylike snort—which, of course, just egged Bart on.

"I mean, it's the perfect wedding night gift, don't you think? Pink elephants. Champagne. I don't know, Julia. I think you're destined to buy these boxers."

"I think you're destined for a mental institution." She pointed a finger across the store. "Now go. Scope me out the perfect present."

But he didn't go. Instead he just stared over her shoulder, his expression entirely unreadable. "What?" Julia asked, but she didn't wait for an answer. Instead, she just whirled around, expecting to see Thelma Lynn. *This* time she'd tell the woman to mind her own business.

Instead, she saw Roman.

"Oh!" She shoved the kiss-covered boxers behind her back. "Sweetheart! What are you doing here?"

"I came looking for you. To prove Thelma Lynn wrong, actually." He aimed a scathing look over the clothes racks to Bart, who'd shoved the elephant boxer shorts back onto a shelf. "However, it's beginning to look as though I owe her an apology."

Chapter Thirteen

OK, girls, it's time to talk money. Yes, I know you're in love, and yes, I know you're going to be married forever, but you need to work these things out. What's the major cause of divorce in this country? I'll give you a hint, and it's not something going on between the sheets. You got it: money.

Even if you don't want a prenup, you at least have to have an open communication system about all that bling bling. You hearing me, girls? Sit your man down and talk to him. Separate checking accounts? Joint? Who pays the bills? Where's the money coming from? You need to work that out now. Before the wedding. Or believe me, baby, you are going to be in for a not-so-sweet surprise.

—from *The Wedding Guru Tells It Like It Is*

"We were just *shopping*," Julia said. They were back at Roman's apartment at the winery, having ridden there in his car in relative silence. "I really don't understand why that's so hard for you to understand."

Roman tensed. The truth was, he didn't know why it was so hard, either. But it was. Apparently, he was discovering a whole new facet of his personality. He didn't particularly like it, but he really couldn't help it.

"But why now? And why with him?"

"Because it's traditional to get the groom a wedding night gift before the actual wedding. If I waited until next week, it would be too late." She crossed her arms over her chest, her posture alone daring him to defy her. "As for him, why not? We're friends. I wanted company. And I figured he'd know what a man would like."

"Novelty boxer shorts? His taste leaves something to be desired."

She glared at him, then dropped onto the couch. "We were joking around, Roman. It wasn't any big deal."

"It was a big deal to me." He was pushing. But he couldn't stop himself. Their laughter had gotten into his bones, into his head. Especially the fact that they'd been laughing about Marv. And with affection, no less. Bart and Julia had a history. Bart and Marv got along. And Julia desperately wanted peace in her family.

To Roman's mind, that left him the odd man out. "I just don't like it."

"You know what *I* don't like? I don't like that you don't trust me."

"Of course I trust you. I—"

"You what? You jump to conclusions about me and Bart. Ridiculous conclusions. Honestly, Roman, I should be a lot more furious than I am. You hardly ever tell me your winery business, and now you're upset about another man. Maybe you *do* trust me, but you're not doing a very good job showing it!"

"The winery business?"

"The meeting? The one you were supposed to have in Austin earlier today?"

"My meeting? I hardly think that has anything to do with—"

Julia held up a hand. "You know what? Never mind." She drew in a long breath as she pushed herself up off the couch. She moved to him and pressed a soft kiss to his cheek as he pulled her close. "He's just a friend, Roman. You're the man I love."

"I know," he said. "I'm sorry." He drew in a breath, trying to shake off the green mood that had settled over him. "At least he'll be gone soon."

"Ah." She took a step backward and studied the floor.

Roman's chest constricted. "Sweetheart?"

"I asked him to stay."

The floor didn't actually fall out from beneath Roman's feet, but it might as well have. "Here? You invited him to stay here?"

"Well, not *here*," Julia said. "At the Inn."

"Oh, right, of course. Because the practical way to handle the arrival of an ex-boyfriend is to invite him to sleep under your roof."

Julia stared him down, the force of her temper spiking again to match the level of his sarcasm. "For God's sake, Roman. I could hardly send him packing after he'd come all this way."

"Why not?"

She clenched her fists, willing herself to calm down. It made sense that he'd be upset. After all, Bart *was* an ex-boyfriend. And considering the story that Thelma Lynn—the snake!—had spewed, she certainly understood why he'd be a little jealous. Mostly, though, she was annoyed.

"I'm sorry," Roman said. "I'm just—"

"Look," she said sharply, "I didn't invite the guy, but he is a friend and he is here, and I'm not going to ignore him. It's not his fault that my father is a manipulator." She was talking too fast, she knew it, but she was irritated. "I have a million things to do before the wedding, and I really don't need this hassle."

"Which hassle? Him showing up, or me being insanely jealous?"

The slight curve of his lips let her know she'd made her point. "Both," she said curtly. "But he's here, and staying. Thelma Lynn can go jump in a big vat of slime for all I care. I'm sure she'd feel right at home."

She huffed a little, calming down only when Roman grinned and pulled her close.

"I do trust you. And I'm so sorry. For all of this."

"Yeah? Well, good. Because I need to be worrying about my dress. Not calming my fiancé down about some old boyfriend who decided to come to town."

He laughed.

"What?"

"I'm just amused at your priorities."

She nailed him with a severe look. "Roman Sonntag! I don't have a wedding dress! That *is* my first priority."

He held up his hands in surrender. "Maybe you should ask Kiki to see if Vera Wang can do your dress, too."

"I already did. Your sister basically called me six kinds of stupid for not jumping on the offer when it was first made." She sighed. "And she's right. It's just that I *loved* my dress." She had, too. It had a fitted waist, a hand-beaded bodice, and a detachable train. She'd put it on, and she'd just known. She'd looked stunning. Like a bride in a movie. It had cost a fortune, but she'd had to have it.

And now she didn't.

She blocked its image from her mind, not wanting to think about that. She'd go to Austin tomorrow and find a replacement. That was all there was to it.

They moved through the apartment to the balcony, then stepped outside and leaned against the railing. They were facing west, and the sun was just dipping below the horizon, the deep ball of orange and the purple haze filtering through the rows of vines to cast a magical glow over the entire vineyard. Julia loved it here. In such a short time, this place had become home. Everything about it felt right and real. Or, at least, everything had until her father had started his interrogation.

She took a sip of wine and eyed Roman over the rim of the glass.

"What?"

"What's your favorite color?"

He laughed. "Are we playing Twenty Questions?"

She scowled. "I just think I should know my fiancé's favorite color."

"I don't really know that I have one." His brow furrowed as he considered the question, then cleared as he pointed toward the sun. "There. That violet haze. That's my favorite."

"Yeah? Why?"

One shoulder lifted. "Because of the way it paints the world, I guess. Because it's a color that comes just before night, just before the world sleeps and renews. It's a lazy color, but it marks deep change."

"Wow."

He chuckled. "Too profound for you?"

"I didn't know you had it in you."

A self-satisfied grin crossed his face. "I'm a man of mystery," he said.

"I guess so." She spoke lightly, but her heart was beating fast. In a lot of ways, he *was* a mystery. And in a lot of ways, she was a mystery to him. Or she had been until her family had rolled into town. As soon as Marv had descended in all his tacky glory, any aura of sophistication and mystery that Julia might have wrapped herself in had been stripped away. Was that good? she wondered. Considering the ridiculous caricature that her parents presented, she didn't see how it could be. Roman had known all along who her father was, of course. But he'd never met Marv up close and personal. Now that he had, did he still want her? He certainly seemed to— why else be jealous?—but she knew that jealousy didn't have to be about her. It could just be the alpha dogs sniffing each other out. Julia'd had a lot of boy-friends throughout her life, and she'd been the object of a jealous rage on more than one occasion.

Just because he was jealous, that didn't mean he still loved and respected her. And after seeing her father in action, *could* he still respect her?

Something of her thoughts must have crossed her face, because Roman took her hand and squeezed. "I love you, you know. It's been a . . . *trying* . . . few days for both of us, but nothing's changed the bottom line. I. Love. You."

"I know. It's just . . ." What could she say? She twirled her hand. "Not exactly the in-laws you'd hoped for, huh?"

"They go with the package," he said. "That's all I need to know." He stood up, his hand held out to help her up, and in silence he led her down the spiral staircase that led to the garden below. There was still enough light to walk by, and they strolled through the garden and into the vines. Julia didn't know a thing about winemaking, but ever so slowly, Roman was teaching her—telling her about the various grapes and the types of wines and all sorts of stuff.

Her favorite part of the winery was the cellar, where stacks upon stacks of old-fashioned barrels were housed. Roman had taken her there on their second date, and they'd made out in the corner, the scent of wine and wood almost as heady as the man himself. He'd told her about how the barrels were specially made by a cooper, and how different types of woods were used for different types of wines. Her mind had gone numb from the description, but had perked up again when he'd told her that each barrel could only be used three or four times. She'd struck her first deal with her husband-to-be then, offering to buy the used barrels from him so that she could use them to plant flowers around the Inn.

All in all, the whole winemaking business was fascinating, but surprisingly scientific. Most of it went over her head. She liked the end result, though. And she liked the passion in Roman's voice when he talked about the process.

Right now, for example, he was talking about the upcoming harvest, then shifting neatly to the vines they were going to plant on the land he'd just acquired, and how they'd have to pinch the buds off for at least two years in order to get a decent grape.

"You're made for this," she said. "Why did you ever leave?"

He shrugged, then swung her hand with his, following the rhythm of their steps as they moved through the vines. "I wanted success. And the trappings of success." He smiled at her. "I'm an ambitious man, Julia. I went off into the world to seek my fortune."

"And you found it."

A shadow passed over his face, but he nodded. "Yeah," he finally said. "I did."

"So why did you give it up?" she asked as they headed back to the house. "Silicon Valley, I mean. You must have been making a fortune. Why come back?"

His smile was gentle. "I thought I'd already told you this story."

"You have." But she wanted to absorb it again. She wanted to absorb everything about him until he was as much a part of her as she was.

"I *was* making a fortune," he said. "But I wasn't

enjoying myself as much as I'd expected. And when my father called to say he was going to have to start selling off the family land, I used family responsibilities as an excuse to come back."

"You would have come even if you loved your work, wouldn't you?"

He thought about that for a second. "I guess so. That's what you do, right? Make sacrifices for family."

"Sure," she said, automatically if not entirely truthfully.

"At any rate, it wasn't a sacrifice. I came here, and we took a good look at the situation and realized that we had some good land and some decent vines. My grandparents had their own label, so it was only a matter of planting new vines, tending the old ones, and expanding the facilities."

" 'Only a matter,' " she repeated.

"Well, that and the money I had to throw at it. Doesn't matter. In the end, it'll pay back tenfold."

"You did a good thing, going to the wire like that for your father."

"It wasn't just for him. It was for me, too. I really do love this life. Love producing something real and tangible. Something with beauty and taste and a life of its own. Because wine does have a life, you know. Even beyond the grapes."

She nodded. He'd explained that to her, as well. How the wine changed day after day, year after year. So a bottle opened on Monday tasted different than if you had opened it on Friday.

She liked that about him, the way he'd sacrificed for his family and ended up winning. He'd gotten something he loved, after all. And all he'd had to do was take a huge risk.

Was he taking a risk marrying her? With her crazy family? Did it matter that he really hadn't known what he was getting into?

She wasn't sure. But even so, she felt better. Roman might not know her, but she certainly knew him. She *had* known the story about why he'd come back. Marv was just plain wrong. She knew Roman. She knew his heart.

Everything else was just facts. And, really, who gave a damn about facts?

Darkness had settled over the vines, and Roman took Julia's elbow, wanting to make sure she didn't trip as they made their way back to the house. The vineyard wasn't lit at night, and the house was secluded. Right then, the only illumination came from a candle on the back porch, and it was to that one beacon of light that he aimed her.

The ground was mostly level, and he kept a light grip on her arm, ostensibly to catch her if she fell. It was a nice metaphor, he supposed, because he did want to catch her. He couldn't quite get a handle on it, but he had the feeling that Julia was falling. Something else was eating at her, and Roman wanted to know what it was. He wanted to help her. To tell her what steps to take to get past it.

But she wasn't asking and he was faced instead

with a void. Something he couldn't control and couldn't fix. He didn't like the feeling.

She'd talk to him in her own time; he knew that. In the meantime, he could lead her home, then into his arms and into his bed.

And he had to hope that, when paired against whatever was troubling her, it would be enough.

Roman moved slowly inside his fiancée, each thrust of his hips matching the rise of hers. Her body clenched around his, and their skin, slick with sweat, glistened in the moonlight shimmering through the window.

She cried his name, urging him to finish, to take her with him, but he didn't want to. He wanted this moment to last. And so he moved slowly, languorously, pushing them both to the point of desperation.

Finally, unable to take it anymore, he thrust one final time, holding tight to this woman he loved as the world seemed to shatter around him. Spent, he collapsed against her, aware through the haze that still filled his brain that satisfaction had been a little one-sided.

"Come here," he said, urging her closer. His hand snaked down over her belly, his fingers finding her slick heat. Her legs parted for him, and he stroked and caressed, her little sighs and soft noises damn near making him hard all over again.

He wanted to take her over the edge, to make her feel as good as she made him feel. And then, when her body tensed and he knew that she was there, he slipped his finger inside, taking her over, and pulling himself along with her.

Her hips arched up, and she cried his name, and as passion whipped through her, he held on tight, wanting her to feel him there with her as she reached for the stars.

"Wow," she said. She went limp beside him, then rolled over, one hand draped over his chest, her fingers twining in the hair on his chest. "Wow," she repeated.

He smiled. "I'll second that."

She snuggled up closer, her mouth pressed against his neck. "Roman?"

"Mmm?"

"Do you think I'm classy?"

He sat up, wanting to see her face. Her eyes were wide, her mouth serious. Apparently, this wasn't a trick question. "You're the classiest woman I know," he said. He pressed a soft kiss to her mouth. "Why?"

She shook her head. "No reason."

He was sure from her expression that there was, in fact, a reason. But he was just as certain that now wasn't the time to pursue it.

"Have you rescheduled your meeting? The one in Austin that you missed?"

Definitely not the time to pursue it. If that wasn't a blatant attempt to change the subject, he didn't know what was.

"Roman?"

"Not yet," he said. That was on his to-do list, of course. But with the wedding so close . . . "I'm going to wait until after our honeymoon."

She propped herself up on her elbow. "I have to go into Austin tomorrow to look for a dress. Why don't we go together and you can meet with him then."

Roman considered the idea and, since he couldn't find a flaw in the plan, he nodded. "All right," he said. He lay back down, watching the way the light of the moon danced across the ceiling. His mind was jumping all over the place, but the one place it kept landing was his earlier conversation with Alex. His friend was right. Especially if he was going to have a meeting with Barrington tomorrow, he needed to come clean with Julia.

"Babe?"

"Hmm?" Her sleepy reply drifted back to him. She sounded so dazed and dreamy that he almost kept his mouth shut. But they needed to talk about this.

"There's something I need to tell you."

She stiffened a little next to him. "Is it bad? Is it about my dad?"

Surprised, he rolled over to see her face. "Your dad? No. Why?"

"Oh." Some emotion reflected on her face. Relief? He wasn't sure. And although he wanted to ask, he was afraid he'd just be stalling. He needed to get this out there. She needed to know that truth.

And so he told her, spilling it all out before he could make himself stop, trying not to look at her face in case he didn't like her reaction. He told her everything, about how he'd had to invest more than he'd planned to get the winery going again. About how his personal finances had been battered by his efforts to keep his parents' land intact and providing capital for the winery. "Alex has arranged for some venture capital financing, but I turned down most of what he brought to the table. I didn't want to be beholden to investors. Not for this."

She nodded, and her apparent understanding urged him on. He gave her the rest of the scoop, sharing with her just how pathetic his finances really were of late, and then ending by explaining why he'd decided to meet with Barrington.

"But if you make the deal with him, no one will know that you're the force behind the label."

Roman nodded. Marv might think Julia wasn't the sharpest blade around, but Roman knew better. She'd just honed in on exactly the point that was gnawing at him. "I know. But the deal is lucrative, and I'm running out of capital."

She nodded, her forehead creasing and her beautiful mouth pulling into a frown. His own stomach twisted. Getting the winery on its feet was taking months longer than his initial projections, and the discrepancy between his plans and his reality had left him feeling unsure and impotent. Needless to say, it wasn't a feeling he liked. And it wasn't an image he liked to project. Even to his fiancée.

Especially to his fiancée.

Julia saw him as a man in control. A man who

got things done. He didn't want her to see him as struggling, even if she believed, as he did, that somehow he'd end up back on top.

He shook his head. He was being foolish and he knew it. That was what couples did, wasn't it? Fought those battles together. Struggled to build something. Hell, that was what his ancestors had done, his great-great et cetera grandparents working side by side to tame this wild land.

"It's not as if I can't put food on the table," he joked, taking her hand. She hadn't said anything yet, and her faraway expression was beginning to worry him. "Jules? A response now would be good."

She shook her head to clear her thoughts. "Sorry. I guess I was just wondering why you didn't tell me any of this before." She didn't care about the money. Hell, Roman could be flat broke, and she'd still love him. But the secrets . . . if he'd kept this a secret, what else had he kept from her?

Beside her, Roman shifted, finally propping himself up on an elbow. "I should have, I know. But I didn't want . . . I didn't want you . . ."

He trailed off, searching for a word, and Julia put her hand on his arm, hushing him. "It's okay. I think I get it." A guy thing. More particular, a Roman thing. He was a man who'd spent his whole life taking care of things: his wild sister when he was little, himself when he was older, his father now. And, of course, her. Not having money meant not being in control; she knew that much from Marv. And Roman wouldn't want to reveal that. Not if he didn't have to.

But she truly *didn't* care about money. She just wanted to be close to him. Wanted to help him. Wanted to truly know the man she was in love with. And how could she if there was layer upon layer of secrets separating them?

"You should have told me," she finally said. "I might have been able to help. I mean, we're a team, right?"

His mouth curved in a gentle smile. "Of course we are. But what could you have done? My problems can only be solved by money. Do you have a secret stash you could have shared with me? Could you have talked Marv into writing a check?"

She made a face. "No on both counts. I mean, Marv set up trust funds for me and Syd, but we can't get at the money. Not for years and years." She sighed. "But that's not the point. We should *talk* about these things."

"You're right. I should have told you. And I'm sorry." He brushed a kiss over her cheek. "Really."

She nodded, then rolled back over, feeling a bit overwhelmed by the weight of his thoughts. She believed he was sorry. But sorry didn't necessarily mean he wouldn't do the same thing all over again. And sorry didn't mean that he trusted her and was going to turn to her to share his troubles. She didn't want to just share the good times. She wanted the whole package. She wanted to be certain she knew

the whole man. More and more, she was fearing that
Marv was right. Pieces were missing. The question
was, were the pieces important?

If only she did have a way to help. Maybe then
he'd realize how silly it was to keep things from her.
But it wasn't as if she could sell her designer shoe
collection (well, she *could* but she wasn't going to),
and every other dime in her name was locked in
trust and couldn't be—

And then she remembered.

With a start, she sat up, then scooted over and
straddled him, almost bouncing with happiness.

Roman grinned, not entirely sure what was running through Julia's head, but enjoying her enthusiasm nonetheless. "Feeling frisky?"

She nodded, the corner of her mouth twitching.
"Mmm-hmm. And you will be, too, after you hear
my suggestion. I just remembered something, and I
have a fabulous idea. You are *so* going to kiss me."

"I'd do that anyway." He stroked his hands over
her hips, the texture of her smooth skin under his
palms sending a rush of lust coursing through him
again. He simply couldn't get enough of her.

She giggled and pushed his hands away. "Stop it!
I can't concentrate, and I need to think this through."

He didn't stop it. In fact, he slid his hand lower,
stroking her intimately. For a moment, he thought
she'd give in, but then she rolled off him and shoved
a pillow between them. "Be good."

"I intended to be very good. But you stopped me."

She made a show of not laughing, then poked him soundly in the chest. "Okay, Mr. Comedian, listen up. How's this for an amazing idea?" She sat up, crossing her legs and shoving the pillow in her lap so that all that was revealed was a tiny bit of cleavage. He shifted as well, intrigued by both her enthusiasm and her nakedness.

"I'm listening."

"Sonntag House."

"What about it?"

"We're living in it, right?"

He frowned, completely clueless as to where this was going. "That's the plan. At least once we finish enough renovations to make it livable."

"And I'm going to keep managing the motel, right?"

He decided it was best to just answer and not elaborate. He had a feeling this might take awhile. "Right."

"And they're right next door to each other."

"Right." He couldn't stand it. "Julia, what are you getting at?"

"Why don't we open a bed-and-breakfast?"

"Well, I don't know. A lot of reasons, I guess. Do we *want* to open a B and B? I mean, we'd talked about opening one here."

"Well, yeah. But this place is so small and remote. They do very well in towns, you know. With Fredericksburg's charm, it's natural that tourists would rather stay in a B and B. And the house is big enough—especially with the guesthouse and if we converted the carriage house—that we would still have plenty of room for ourselves."

"And you'd want to run this?"

"For starters, I could. I mean, we'd have to hire some help, but I've been thinking. There must be dozens and dozens of towns like Fredericksburg across the country. We could do the same thing there."

He must be more tired than he thought. "The same what?"

"Open B and Bs. Make them high class but accessible. And here's the best part." She reached out and took his hand. "We could stock Sonntag wine. You could turn down Barrington's deal."

He blinked, trying to process everything she was saying. Then he sat up, deciding that a prone position wasn't the best for focusing. Not with his near-naked fiancée right next to him.

"Let me get this straight. You want to turn Sonntag House into a B and B, then maybe start a chain of B and Bs across the country?"

"Right."

"And the chain would stock Sonntag wine."

"Exclusively."

"Sounds good," he said. "Except my cash flow problem is now, and this B and B chain doesn't yet exist. And whose chain would it be, anyway? Marv's Motor Inn is hardly the image you're talking about."

She frowned a bit at that. "Yeah, I know. I was thinking that he could be an investor, but that we'd be the face behind the chain. Maybe a subsidiary of the holding company Pop set up. I don't think that name is very public, so it wouldn't mar the image too much."

He gaped at her. He'd known that she was sharper than Marv gave her credit for, and he'd also known that she was getting the hang of the motel business. It made sense, of course. She was smart, and she'd grown up in the business world. She had to have picked tidbits up here and there. But what he hadn't known was just how deeply—and how well—she'd processed all the information.

"That sounds good," he admitted. "But it still doesn't address the winery's immediate cash flow problems."

"No," she said. "It doesn't. I was thinking that you and I should form a partnership—"

"I think we are, babe."

She gave him a quick kiss for that. "A *business* partnership, and the partnership can buy Sonntag House. The purchase money can be invested into the winery. And then, by the time Sonntag House is refurbished, the B and B corporation will be up and running and we can transfer the title into the business."

"I think you forgot one little thing."

Her brow furrowed. "I did?"

"How is our partnership going to get the money to buy Sonntag House? Your dad? Because I don't think I could agree to that. It would be too much like coming full circle."

"Oh, no. I don't need to ask Pop. I can just use my own money."

"Your own money? You just said you didn't have any money." He frowned. "And besides, do you have any idea how much Sonntag House is appraised for? It may be a shambles, but this is prime commercial real estate. And we're talking over an acre of land here."

"I know," she said, tossing out a figure that was remarkably accurate. "I can get that in a snap. I have way more than that in my trust fund."

He couldn't stop staring at her. "Julia, sweetheart, you just told me you couldn't access your trust."

"I can't. Not for just anything. But I totally forgot about the exceptions. I've been allowed to use a percentage of the principal and interest to purchase real estate since I was twenty-five. I just never have, so the possibility never even entered my mind." She bounced a little. "It's a brilliant plan, don't you think?"

"Jesus," he said.

"Roman?" Her brow furrowed and she was looking at him with some concern.

"Sorry. I just didn't realize. I mean, I never imagined you could get your hands on that kind of money."

"But that's a good thing, right? That I can get the money. It can totally solve your problem. *Our* problem."

He rubbed his temples, trying to get rid of the thought that pretty soon she'd be able to buy and sell him several times over. So much for feeling needed.

"Roman? What's wrong?"

He shook his head. "Nothing, babe. Nothing's wrong at all." And it wasn't.

So why did he feel so numb?

"Honey bear? Do you really think this is a good idea?" Myrna's voice was whiny, but at least she kept to a whisper. Marv hadn't wanted to bring her along, but she'd hauled her butt out of bed and blocked the doorway. For a woman who usually resembled a mouse, at times she could be as stubborn as an elephant.

He'd given in because he didn't have any choice. No one knew just how much he gave in to the woman. She was his weakness, damn it all. And, yeah, he loved her.

"Marv? Did you hear me?"

"*Shhhh*. Yeah, babe, I heard ya. Do you want everyone else to hear you, too?"

"Who's gonna hear? Nobody's awake in this town except us."

"Let's keep it that way." It was a quarter past two, and she was right. The place was dead quiet. A streetlamp on Main mixed with the motel's exterior light to give some illumination. But they weren't at the front of the motel. They'd gone out the back and now they were creeping along Orange, moving around the fence until they reached Sonntag House.

He paused at the corner of the property, Myrna so close behind he could feel her breath on his neck. "Damn it all, it shoulda been mine."

"What would you've done with it, anyway?

Ripped it down? Built a bigger one of those?" she asked, waving her hand back toward the Inn. "It's a pretty house. I'm glad it's still standing."

He turned long enough to scowl at her. "Don't you go traitor on me, too. I got enough of that from Julia."

"She's in love, honey bear. And I think he loves her, too."

Marv made a rude noise, then tugged at her hand. "Come on then," he said. "Let's go see what was so all-fired important they had to hang on to this shambles of a house. I asked around, you know. They held on to it, but they didn't have the money to fix it up." From what he'd heard, the litigation and the decline in the oil market had hit the family hard. "It's been sittin' here for the last fifteen years, just falling into ruin." He wanted to feel some glee about that—as if he'd won in the end after all—but somehow he couldn't work up the energy to gloat.

The front and back doors were both locked, but Marv wiggled a window and managed to get it to open.

"Marv, I don't know. What if there's an alarm . . ." His wife's face scrunched up with concern.

"Baby, we're in bumfucksville. No one's got alarms." He hoped.

Figuring he had nothing to lose, he hoisted his leg over the windowsill, then tried to climb through. One of the curses of his life was being short, and he got stuck. He grunted a bit, then felt his wife's hands on his haunches, shoving him through. He landed on his keister with a thud and scowled up at her. She shrugged and offered a tiny smile as she picked her way through the window after him.

"Hmmmph," he said, looking around. The room they were in was open and mostly unfinished, with stripped wallpaper and sanded but unfinished floors under their feet. "Not much to look at considering all the time he's spent here."

Myrna kept quiet, but she started poking around. After a second, he heard her call from the kitchen. "Honey bear, come check in here."

He got there, saw she'd turned the light on, and immediately flipped it off.

"But how can we see if we can't have a light?"

He handed her one of the penlights he'd brought. She didn't look happy, but she clicked it on and aimed it at the cabinets.

"Well, well," Marv said. "Lookey heah."

Myrna nodded. "Pretty nice, huh? And Julia said Roman was doing most of the work himself."

Marv grunted, not ready to like the guy even though he had to admit that the kitchen was pretty damn nice. "Cabinets need another coat of stain."

Myrna just pursed her lips and aimed her penlight into the dining room. An antique chandelier hung there, its facets reflecting the light like a million diamonds. "Oh, honey bear, this is class. Pure class, no question about it."

"Don't mean a thing," Marv said, unwilling to be charmed. "They don't know each other worth spit. Julia's moon-headed over some buff cowboy, and the broke cowboy's just after her money. Probably hoping if he keeps piddling away at fixing this place up, she'll pump some money into it and they can sell at a profit."

"I don't know. I've seen the way he looks at her."

Marv didn't want to think about that, so he headed on upstairs, leaving Myrna in his wake.

The bedrooms were in various stages of progress, with the original furniture shoved to the middle of the rooms to make way for the electrical and aesthetic work going on in the walls. But it was a small sitting room just off the landing that caught Marv's attention.

The walls were painted a muted and familiar shade of pink, and there was a long chaise lounge, just like the kind his princess had had in her bedroom growing up. A vanity was centered against another wall, a drawing table and desk on another. A window box filled with flowers anchored the room.

Marv snorted. "Guess we know which room he set our little girl loose in."

When Myrna didn't answer right away, he turned to see her looking down at a spiral-bound notebook sitting open on the vanity. "What you got there?"

She held it out to him, a little smile tugging at her mouth, and her eyes so bright he could see them sparkle even in the thin light the penlights provided. "I don't think she's seen it yet."

Marv scanned the page, his brain slowly processing the information. The handwriting was cramped and masculine, without any of Julia's girlish flourishes. And the notes were cryptic, as if someone was trying to remember every little thing he'd been told. The notes tracked the room, and with a start, Marv realized what he was looking at—Roman was making a sanctuary for his little girl.

He couldn't know for certain, but something in his gut told him that this room was a secret. That Satan's spawn had gone out of his way to do this nice thing for Marv's little princess.

He shuffled a bit, then tossed the notebook back down on the vanity, not sure how he felt about that.

"Marv?"

"Come on," he said, his voice more gruff than he intended. "We should get the hell out of here before someone sees us."

And with that, he left, and didn't once look back.

Chapter Fourteen

Surprise your guests with thoughtful welcome gifts: maps of the town, local products, hand and body lotions. It's your wedding, but it's also an event. Memories are fabulous, but everyone loves goodies. Make yours the talk of the town!

—from Wedding Tips and Bridal Secrets

Roman stared at his computer screen, willing the numbers on the Excel spreadsheet to expand to fill a vacuum.

No luck.

The winery was running against tough times, and he had to make some decisions.

Fortunately, he had options. Unfortunately, he didn't like any of them.

On the one hand, he could enlist Alex's skill as a venture capitalist, sending his friend out to drum up investment dollars. But that meant selling pieces of the business in some form or other, and the winery had always been family owned and operated.

Strike one.

He got up and moved from the desk to the window, passing the still unmade bed as he went. Julia had gotten up at the crack of dawn, eager to get on the road to Austin and find the perfect dress.

He'd turned down the offer to go with her, and she'd left him with a list of places to call about finding a new location. So far, he'd called the city (the park was already booked), the local VFW Lodge (no answer), and still had four more places on his telephone list.

He'd have to handle that later. Right now, he needed to deal with the business.

He thought again about Julia and the hurdles she was leaping as the wedding approached. He knew she was worried about the little details, along with the larger ones like the location and the dress. More, he knew he should have gone into Austin with her. She certainly wanted him to.

But at the same time, he also knew that she didn't want him to see the dress before the wedding, which meant they would have parted ways—she to go shopping, he to meet with Barrington and possibly strike a deal.

A deal he no longer needed because of Julia's money.

He frowned. He'd told her he was going to stay at home and catch up on work at the winery. The unspoken implication, of course, was that he wasn't going to pursue the Barrington deal. And why would he, after she'd so generously offered her own funds?

He sighed, running his palm over his unshaven jaw as he looked out over the vines and the grapes, ripe and bloated and ready for the harvest.

He should be happy his fiancée had the financial wherewithal to help him weather this storm.

He *should* be thrilled.

So, he wondered, why wasn't he?

Julia had never been a slouch about shopping, but this was ridiculous. She'd hit Austin at ten on the nose, and by two thirty she'd been through every single bridal boutique, department store and even resale shop in the Greater Austin Metropolitan area.

Nothing. Nada. Zip.

Not one dress that tickled her fancy. Nothing that sent her into fantasies of walking down the aisle, twirling with Roman on the dance floor, laughing as they shared a piece of wedding cake. Just . . . nothing.

The way it was going, she'd end up wearing a nice white suit. Maybe Chanel. And she'd tell everyone she did it on purpose. A fashion statement.

Except that wasn't what she wanted. She wanted a Princess Di kind of dress. Tulle and bones and a train and yards and yards of silk.

Apparently, she wasn't going to find the dress today.

Now she was zooming down Highway 290, passing Johnson City as she got close to Fredericksburg. Ramshackle buildings advertising GOOD STUFF dotted the wildflower-lush landscape. Stands of fresh peaches and beef jerky were spaced at appetizing intervals in front of fields housing roaming cows. Things she'd thought so odd when she'd first arrived now seemed perfectly normal. Charming, even.

Very little of the landscape actually filtered through the haze in her brain, though. She was too focused on her dress crisis. She knew what she had to do; she just didn't want to.

Still, it was already Wednesday. Tomorrow was her bachelorette party. Friday the rehearsal. And on Saturday, she was getting married. She was fresh out of time.

And that meant she had no choice.

Reluctantly, she reached into the passenger seat for her phone, then punched in "7," the speed-dial she'd programmed weeks ago.

One ring. Two rings. Three. And then . . . "Hi, you've reached Breckin at With This Ring. Leave a message after the beep, and I'll get back to you with all the ways to make your wedding special."

She considered hanging up, but reminded herself that she was down to the wire. "Breckin? This is Julia Spinelli. Um, about our little disagreement. I was, um, wondering if maybe we could have coffee today and talk about it? I . . . well, maybe I was a little hasty. So, um, anyway. If you're free, could you come by the Inn around six? I'll be in the conference room—we're hosting Ann Marie's book group—but I can get away long enough to chat. Anyway. Thanks."

She closed her phone, her face burning. She *had* been right to fire him, and she hated that she now had to come crawling back. But she wanted the big fancy wedding—had always wanted it. And if she had to eat a little crow to get it . . . well, *bon appétit!*

*   *   *

Julia perched on a stool behind the reception counter, three different bridal magazines open in front of her, and the computer browser aimed at the fashion section of theknot.com. She might be working at the Inn, but she'd be damned if she'd waste time that could be spent on her dress quest.

She heard a clatter in the hallway, then the telltale rumble of her father clearing his throat.

And then they appeared. Julia tried to stifle a gasp, but couldn't quite manage. They just looked so . . . silly.

Marv, with his round little Napoleon body, had crammed his feet into a pair of royal blue cowboy boots. His stubby thighs strained against the dark blue denim of a pair of Wranglers, which were capped off by a belt buckle the size of, well, Texas. It gleamed silver under the lobby's fluorescent light, and she could see that it was in the shape of a star—appropriate for the Lone Star State, of course—inlaid with an etching of one of the state's famous longhorn cattle. He'd topped the outfit with a western-style shirt—already sweat-stained under the sleeves—a string tie and a pristine cowboy hat worn low enough on his head that she couldn't see his eyes.

He looked ridiculous, but not quite as silly as Myrna, who was wearing a similar outfit in even more glaring colors. At least her mother was coordinated, though. Pink cowboy boots matched the pink shirt, pink string tie, and pink cowboy hat. The bloodred lipstick, however, clashed a bit.

What the devil were her parents up to? For a moment, she feared they were making fun, but then her mother smiled and did a little pirouette. "We're getting into the spirit. What do you think?"

She thought they looked like tacky tourists and that they were going to embarrass her mightily. But she couldn't say that. Something in her mom's expression told her they were trying. And so she conjured a smile. "Y'all look great," she said, trying for a Texas accent. "Where are you going?"

"Shopping," her mother said. "When Marv sent you down here, I had no idea how many high-class stores there were."

Julia nodded. She'd managed to do significant damage to her own bank account in the time she lived here. The boutiques rivaled some of the best in metropolitan areas, only with better prices—if a more limited selection.

"Since you're so dead set on staying here," Marv said gruffly, "we thought we ought to get to know the place."

"Oh." Julia blinked, not entirely sure what to read into that comment. Were they coming around to the idea of the wedding? Or just to the idea that she was staying in Texas?

She decided it was better not to ask, and instead just wished them a good evening and waved them out the door. They passed two women coming in, both of whom were rolling their eyes and snickering. They looked up and saw Julia, their faces immediately going red. They mumbled apologies and hurried down the hall.

Julia sighed. She knew both girls—Alice and Mary—and she also knew that they hadn't been giggling about the weather or the scenes in *The Fiery Cross* that they were about to discuss.

She closed her eyes, imagining all her hard work fitting in being flushed down the toilet. Her parents were out wandering the town, about to make fools of themselves. And, by association, making a fool out of her.

The Fredericksburg book club had been meeting every Wednesday afternoon for the last five years, ever since Ann Marie Tolliver had read and loved *Outlander* and foisted it on all her friends. The group wasn't closed to men, but for some reason the male of the species tended not to ask to join. Also, Ann Marie had decided early on to limit the group to twelve. That way, over the course of the year, each participant in the club could pick a book.

This month had been her turn, and the group had read *The Fiery Cross*. It had been out for a while, but the next book in the series was about to be released, and Ann Marie had wanted a refresher. Besides, it was out in paperback, and the club tried to stay away from hardback books, since they were more of an expense for the members, and two of the ladies were retired and living on social security.

Ann Marie herself was only thirty-two and her bank account was doing fine. But she ran her own business and knew the value of the dollar. She also knew the value of networking and goodwill. So when

Julia Spinelli had come to her asking if she'd like to host the club in the Inn's newly refurbished conference room, Ann Marie had put her personal feelings aside and said yes. After all, the bottom line was that there *was* going to be a wedding, and Julia's and Sydney's New York friends were sure to come. If Syd and Jules felt all warm and fuzzy toward Ann Marie, then maybe they'd steer their friends to her shop. After all, didn't New York girls crave funky fashions and handcrafted jewelry?

So here she was this Wednesday evening, their little group totaling fourteen with the addition of Julia, who'd asked Carter to watch the desk, and Syd, who apparently had come just to see what it was all about.

"I still say Jamie is a hottie," Amelia Graham said, referring to the hero of the book. She was pushing eighty, and Ann Marie had to hide her smile at the idea of Amelia thinking anyone was a hottie.

"Not as hot as some of the men in our town," Corinne said. The other women shot her a warning look. Corinne was J.B. Anglin's ex-wife, and she still carried a torch—which would be fine, except that J.B. had fallen head over heels for Julia's best friend, Vivien. Fortunately, Vivien wasn't in the room at the moment.

"You know," Syd said, "I'll second that. I'll take a man with access to indoor plumbing over an ancient Scotsman any day."

The other women laughed, all except Julia. Ann Marie didn't *want* to be concerned. After all, *she'd* been carrying a torch for Roman all these years. But she liked Julia—she couldn't help it. The girl was just so damn bubbly and friendly.

She sucked in a breath, then leaned forward. "Julia, hon, you okay?"

Immediately, Julia's face shifted into a mask of perfection, the worry lines that had been marring her perfect forehead disappearing. "Oh, sure. I'm fine. Everything's great."

Ann Marie knew she should let it go at that. After all, she'd never wanted to like Julia. In fact, she'd fought it all the way. Julia had rolled into town with her designer clothes and personal-trainer-approved body, and Ann Marie had just about gagged. It had gotten worse, of course, when Julia had started dating Roman. Roman had been Ann Marie's property through much of their time at the University of Texas. And even though she wasn't in love with him anymore—didn't even have a crush on him, for that matter—that didn't stop her from feeling completely possessive of him. And protective, too.

So when some little East Coast bitch had honed in, Ann Marie had seen red. But then the red had faded and she'd seen a sweet, charming, smart girl who was trying to make a go of the hideous motel her father had dumped on the town. And a girl who made Roman Sonntag very, very happy.

And on top of that, Julia had spent a small fortune on clothes in her store.

So, yeah, Ann Marie liked her. "Come on, Jules. We're your friends."

To her horror, she saw the girl's eyes fill with tears.

"It's the wedding! All the details are falling apart, and I *so* want it to be perfect and—" She clapped her hand over her mouth, clearly mortified. "Oh, gosh. I'm so sorry. I shouldn't have had those three mimosas before we got started."

"Is something wrong between you and Roman?" Ann Marie asked, and to her surprise, she genuinely hoped there wasn't a problem.

Julia shook her head, almost too vehemently. "No, no. Everything is fine there. It's just . . ." And then she spilled her guts, telling them about her dress horrors, and how the welcome baskets weren't done, and the little packets of birdseed to throw after the wedding, and the flowers, and, ". . . well, just everything." She shot a glance toward Alice and Mary. "And on top of everything, my parents are, well, they're acting kinda silly."

Ann Marie had no idea what that comment was about. She knew Marv Spinelli—from what she could tell, he was a first-rate asshole—but that hardly affected Julia. Alice and Mary seemed to understand, though, because both girls blushed as red as she'd ever seen them.

"Oh, Jules," Alice finally said. "We didn't mean anything. We think it's sweet. Really. They're trying to fit in. They just . . . you know . . . they just kinda look like a New Yorker's view of a Texan. You know?"

"I know," Julia said miserably. Her lips thinned. "You really think it's sweet?"

Alice and Mary exchanged glances and shrugged. "Well, you know. Everyone in town knows about your dad and Robert Sonntag. So, I mean, we were all set not to like him. Or you, for that matter."

"Alice!" Ann Marie sent her a cold look.

"No, that's okay," Julia said. "I want to hear."

"Well, that's just it," Mary continued, speaking for her friend. "We *do* like you. A lot. And, yeah, your father's a little . . . um . . ."

"Brusque and freakish?" Syd supplied.

Mary's face lit up. "Yeah. Exactly. But I don't think he was making fun of us or anything. I mean, I think he's trying to fit in. Really trying. And, well, that's nice, you know. He must really love you."

Julia flashed a watery smile, and Ann Marie lunged for the box of tissues, afraid the girl would start up with the tears again. "You okay?"

Julia nodded. "Yeah. Thanks."

She looked around at the other women, saw the concern on all their faces, and made her decision. "I suggest we table the book discussion this meeting and see what we can do to help Julia out."

"Agreed," said Amelia, and the others chimed in their agreement as well.

Julia blinked as she stared at Ann Marie. "Really? You guys would do that?"

"Of course." She smiled. "You're one of us now, and that means you're family. So tell us. What exactly do you need?"

Roman hung up the phone and leaned back in his chair. A knot had formed in his stomach, reminding him that he wasn't certain he'd done the right thing.

Right or wrong, though, it was the only thing he could do—because his only other option was to accept Julia's offer and use her money to purchase Sonntag House.

He couldn't agree to that, though. It just didn't sit right.

And so he'd made this decision, and he hoped it didn't come back to haunt him.

With a sigh, he looked down at his notes—a page of scribbles that outlined the deal with the Barrington Group. There were still a few points to be hashed out, but it should be final within a week. The winery would be solvent again. And that, at least, would solve some of his problems.

How he felt about Julia's revelation, though . . . well, that was a problem he still had to face. And one that he feared couldn't be as efficiently handled.

"You're sure about this, honey bear?"

Marv nodded as he waited for Earle to step out and open the door to the limo. The back end was filled with packages from their evening of shopping, and beside him, his wife smelled like a flower shop, after having discovered some locally made perfume.

He was glad she'd had a good time, but right now, he had other things on his mind. His little princess. And something he needed to take care of. Right then. Right there.

Earle opened the door, then helped Myrna out. Marv followed, and the two stood there, staring at the limestone and wood house with the simple land-scaping. Boring, he thought. Nothing like his place with the Grecian columns and the grape arbor and the fountain. Still, there was no accounting for taste . . .

He moved to the front door, his wife at his side. He rang the bell, waited, then rang again.

He expected a butler to answer the door and was surprised when Sarah Sonntag herself appeared.

"Oh." Surprise, shock and disapproval registered on her face before she got herself under control. Marv told himself he didn't mind. He'd expected her reaction. "Mr. and Mrs. Spinelli. How can I help you?"

He sucked in a breath, and took off the cowboy hat, felt his hair stuck to his head like plaster from the sweat generated by being under that damn fool thing. "I'd like to talk to your husband." He held out the bottle of wine he'd bought. "If that's okay."

She hesitated for a moment, then stepped back from the door, ushering them in. "Robert's in his study. If you'll follow me." She moved through the entrance hall—very muted and nothing like the palace Marv called home—to a thick wooden door. "Are you both . . ." She trailed off, looking curiously at Myrna.

"I'd love to see your kitchen," Myrna said.

Sarah licked her lips, but nodded. Then she opened the door, told Robert who was visiting, and left Marv on his own.

Marv Spinelli was a man who'd fought countless business battles. Never once, though, had he fought one for his daughter, and he sure as hell had never come to another man with his tail between his legs.

If it would make his little girl happy, though . . .

Damn it all. He was becoming a softie.

Robert stood and came around the desk. "Come to break my nose, too?"

Marv bit back a smart-ass reply. "No, I come with a peace offering." He held out the bottle of wine. Gallo. White Zinfandel. His favorite.

Robert took it, then read the label. His eyes narrowed. "Is this a joke?"

"Like I said, it's a peace offering." Was the man dense?

Robert stared at him a minute, as if he wasn't sure what to believe. Then he shook his head, chuckling slightly.

"What?" Marv demanded.

"You know I own a winery, right?"

Well, shit. Marv hadn't even thought of that. "No point in me bringing your own wine," he said. "You can get that for free."

Robert smiled a little, and Marv had the feeling the other man knew he was spewing a load of bullshit. Marv shoved his hands in his pockets and nodded toward a chair.

"Help yourself," Robert said. "What can I do for you?"

"You can reconsider your crazy-ass decision to fuck over my daughter," Marv said. Then he scowled. "I just mean, she's all messed up, that girl, what with no place to hold the wedding."

"I see." Robert went back behind his desk and started drumming his fingers on the leather blotter. "I was under the impression that you didn't approve of the wedding."

"Yeah, well, maybe I've changed my mind."

"Really?"

"I ain't saying I like what you did back then. Or what your whole family did, either. I'm just saying that maybe it's time to end this thing." He nodded toward the door. "Hell, even *she's* happy I didn't get Sonntag House."

"Your wife?" Robert sounded genuinely surprised.

"Says the place has character. That it'll make a good home for Julia. And I guess she's right." He thought about the place he'd seen last night, could picture his princess walking through the rooms, her modern flair contrasted by the historic lines of the house.

"I see," Robert said, though from the tone of his voice, Marv could tell he didn't really see at all.

He shifted in the chair. This wasn't what he was good at. This relationship stuff. But he was here for his princess, and he kept that firmly in mind. "Look," he said, "I know maybe you don't believe me. Think I'm just playing an angle. But I'm not. I checked the place out last night. Your boy's doing a good job of it. It looks good, ya know? And it's kinda like full circle. I mean, I wanted the place, but now my baby girl's gonna be living there, so maybe it's time for me to just fuhgeddaboudit."

Robert squinted. "Oh. *Forget* about it."

"That's what I said." Marv leaned forward. "Look. You love your boy, right? I love my girl. And I don't want to be stupid about this thing. I don't want her thinking her pop went and fucked up her wedding."

"You probably should have thought of that before you broke Herman's nose."

Another of those snappy comebacks popped to mind. Marv shoved it away. "Yeah. Probably. I gots a temper."

"I've noticed."

"So?"

Robert sighed. "So I'm pleased that you're not going to cause a scene at the wedding. I've been here through their courtship, you know. Roman really does love Julia. And she really does love him."

"Yeah. I'm getting that."

"All right, then." He stood up. "I guess I should say welcome to the family."

Marv kept his seat. "We ain't done here. What about the wedding?"

Robert drew in a long breath, then exhaled. Marv waited, afraid that he really had fucked it up beyond repair for his little girl.

But then Robert nodded, that patriarchal smile once again spreading across his face. "The wedding can take place here," he said, holding out his hand. "We'll be honored to open our home."

Julia was just a little drunk. Well, okay, maybe more than a little. But what did she expect after five—seven?—mimosas during the book club meeting? And then a few more in her room with Syd afterward to celebrate. And, yeah, one by herself after Syd had stumbled home because, well, she was getting married soon and that meant she had to finish off the champagne.

She still couldn't quite believe how everyone had pitched in, and now she had a huge box filled with little net packets containing birdseed, neatly tied with pale pink ribbons. More—Breckin had come by and after Julia had spewed out another apology, he'd pitched in, too. Plus, Syd had made some phone calls during the meeting and lined up a band for the wedding—Two Tons of Steel. It was a real coup, and Julia was thrilled to have the popular Texas band.

What had really astounded her was when Ann Marie had volunteered to help with the welcome gifts. Julia had planned one for every seat at the reception, and Ann Marie had promised they'd be done in time: little tin buckets filled with Emulsion body cream, spicy sauces from Rustlin' Rob's, wildflower seeds, and other goodies that Ann Marie promised from her store "at cost."

Julia had been amazed and humbled at how eagerly the girls had offered to help. She loved this town, she'd thought. Almost as much as she loved Roman.

Of course, the real kicker had been when Alice and Mary had said such nice things about Marv, totally easing her fears that everyone in town thought he was a freak and that she was the spawn of a freak.

She knew she shouldn't care what anyone else thought, but she did. She wasn't sure if that made her stupid or human, but it did make her honest.

And now that she knew they weren't all sniggering at Marv, she felt a trillion percent better.

Still, though . . .

She still wanted him in a *real* tux at her wedding—not the royal blue velvet monstrosity he always wore to formal occasions. It wasn't a question of folks staring and snickering, either. She just wanted her black-tie wedding to be truly black tie.

With a firm nod, she stood up, stumbling only a little as the room tilted to one side. The one errand she had managed to accomplish on this morning's trip to Austin was acquiring a new Armani tux for her father. And she'd spent a lot of time thinking about how she could convince him to wear it.

Finally, she'd decided that she couldn't convince him. If the velvet tux was an option, her dad would be in it—which meant she had to eliminate the option.

And she was just drunk enough to do that.

Actually, though, she might be a little *too* drunk. She should probably get some help.

She reached for her cell phone to call Roman, then stopped. Did she really want to shine a big, bright spotlight on her angst? No, she didn't.

Syd was a natural choice, but she was probably curled up in bed with Alex by now. Julia could just wait until tomorrow . . .

But no. She had the solution. And, she thought, it was perfect.

Chapter Fifteen

Did he get you a winner of a ring or a loser? If you want to determine the stone's quality, you need to know the four C's (and we make no representations as to the groom's quality!).

Cut. Carat. Color. Clarity.

Those, ladies, are your code words for bling.

—from *The Elegant Bride*

"You want me to help you do what?" Bart's expression matched the incredulity in his voice.

"Steal Marv's tux," Julia whispered. She tugged at his arm. "Come on."

"Why?" he asked, but he came. She put a finger over her lips as they eased past Marv and Myrna's room toward the rear exit that opened from the interior hall onto the parking lot.

"Because it's blue," she said, as if that made perfect sense. "And because I bought Armani."

He nodded slowly. "And I'm helping because . . ."

"Because we're friends, right? And I'm just a little tipsy. They might catch me."

"You *are* a little tipsy." He put his hands on her shoulders and looked into her eyes. It was an intimate position, but Julia didn't feel even a tingle. These days, all her tingles were for Roman. She recalled the little tiff they'd had after Roman had found Bart holding the boxers, and she fervently hoped that Roman really did understand that he was the only man for her.

"Why don't you wait until the tipsy wears off?" Bart asked.

She shook her head. "I thought you'd help me, but if you don't want to—"

"Fine. Fine. I'll help."

He didn't look happy, but she didn't care. She stood on her tiptoes and gave him a quick kiss on the cheek.

"So what's the plan?" he asked.

"They're always asleep by nine. So we use the master key to go in, one of us holds the door open so it doesn't click, the other gets the tux, then we get the hell out of Dodge."

"The Armani?"

"Being delivered tomorrow. It'll be so fortui—fortu—*great*, don't you think?"

He didn't look nearly as thrilled as she was, but that was okay. She needed help, he was there, and that was enough.

She took a step forward, stumbled, and decided that maybe that last mimosa had been one too many.

"Jules?"

She waved a hand, steadying herself. "I'm fine. But, um . . ." She reached down and slipped off her Jimmy Choos. This operation called for bare feet.

"Ready?"

"As I'll ever be."

He followed as she crept to Marv and Myrna's door. She used her master key to slip inside, then held the door open about an inch, signaling for him to take it from her. Across the room, Marv and Myrna snoozed in bed, back to back, Marv's snoring so loud that Julia wondered how her mom had managed not to go deaf.

With a quick nod to Bart, she headed across the room to the closet. She rummaged around, found the tux, and pulled it free. She kept it on the hanger and draped it over her arm, treating it better than a blue velvet tux had a right to be treated.

She backed out of the closet and was just about to tiptoe back toward Bart when Marv sputtered and snorted and sat bolt upright.

Shit!

She glanced around, realized the only hiding place was the closet, and closed the door.

Through the slits in the louvered door, she saw Marv scratch himself, then yawn, then stand up. And then—because, really, it couldn't get any worse—he headed for the bathroom, which, of course, was located right by the door. She held her breath, waiting for his scream of outrage when he saw Bart standing there. But no scream came, and she exhaled. Bart must have slipped out before Marv saw him.

All she had to do was wait her father out.

"Myrna!!" His voice echoed through the small room. Her mother made a small noise in response, and Julia stiffened in fear. "Damn it, Myrna, that rash is back. It's these fuckin' pajamas in this fuckin' heat.

Bring me my red ones, will you? They're in my suitcase in the closet. I gotta change before I spend the whole night scratching my ass."

Julia froze. *The closet*? He wanted Myrna to open the closet? She was doomed.

Myrna, however, hadn't stirred. And if Julia knew her mom, it would take a nuclear explosion—or at least three more tries from Marv—before she did.

She just might have time to sneak out . . .

Slowly, she opened the closet door, then stepped out, still clutching the tux. The front door was all the way across the room, but the window to her right was open. Why it was open in this humidity, she didn't know, but she wasn't going to ask. It was an exit and it was close.

And when Marv's second bellow caused Myrna to stir, Julia knew she had no choice. She tiptoed to the window, shoved up the sash, then dove through the opening. She landed in a freshly watered bed of flowers, and too late remembered that she'd made the decision to use real manure for fertilizer. Cheaper, she'd thought, and also better for the environment.

What she hadn't factored in was the smell.

She bit back a curse, afraid her voice would filter up through the window. She put a hand down, trying to push herself up out of the garden, and only managed to slip again.

So much for her tentative hold on sobriety.

"Julia?" Bart's whisper drifted over the bushes and flowers toward her.

"Over here," she whispered back.

He came over, took one look at her, and burst out laughing.

"Shhh!" She pointed to the open window.

He nodded, stepped over her and tugged it shut. "Now why don't I help you up?" he said, extending a hand.

She took it gratefully, but misjudged the slickness of the ground. As soon as he'd pulled her almost all the way up, she lost her footing and tumbled backward, bringing Bart with her. He fell forward, straddling her in the mud, Marv's blue tuxedo all that separated them.

"I hope I'm not interrupting anything . . ." Roman's voice cut through the night, his amusement sharp-edged.

Julia squealed and rolled to the side, mucking herself up even more. Bart just sat there in his jeans, a stupid grin on his face.

"Roman! You scared me!"

"I told you this was a bad idea," Bart said.

"No you didn't. You—"

"What idea was that exactly?" Roman asked.

Julia and Bart exchanged a guilty look.

"All right," Roman said, his face hardening. "Let's try this again. What are you doing lying down in a garden with *him*?"

"Watch it, buddy," Bart said, pushing himself to his feet. "Julia asked me to help her because she couldn't ask you. I'm not sure what that means, but I think you should think about it."

"Bart!" Julia looked from one to the other, absolutely certain that she should have gone with her first instinct and not involved her ex. "Look," she said to Roman. "It's not what it looks like." She frowned, her brow furrowed. She was crawling through the bushes, her ex-boyfriend behind her, with a tacky blue tux rolled up and tucked under her arm. "What *does* it look like?" Surely not some sort of weird sexual liaison.

"Honestly," Roman said wearily, "I have no idea." He scowled, then reached down to help her up. When she was on her feet, he offered a hand to Bart, too. Bart hesitated, Roman shoved his hand farther into the bushes, and Bart finally latched on.

"Thanks," he said, brushing at the knees of his pants. For a moment, the two men just eyed each other; then Julia saw something soften in Bart's eyes. "Look, man," he said. "I promise you there's nothing weird going on here." He made a face. "No, I take that back. I'm helping your fiancée steal her father's tux. That qualifies as weird. But there's nothing weird going on between me and Julia."

"I believe you," Roman said.

"You do?" Bart asked.

"You do?" Julia asked at the same time.

"Yeah," he said. And the fact was, he really did believe them. Despite finding an ex-boyfriend on top of his apparently drunk bride-to-be, he really did believe them. Hell, how could he not? "I love you, Julia. I love you and I trust you."

It was, he realized, exactly the right thing to say. The suspicious protective-wolf look in Bart's eyes had faded. And Julia's own expression was one he'd seen on repeated occasions in his own mirror: love.

She moved into his arms, and he pulled her into a hug, marred only by the rolled-up ball of clothes between them.

"Now tell me why, exactly, were you stealing your father's tux?"

"I think that's my cue to leave," Bart said. "Julia, it's been fun. We'll have to do this again sometime." And with that, he turned and moved along the building toward the Orange Street entrance.

"Julia?"

"Let's go inside," she said. "I'd rather not be out here when Pop and Myrna decide to open that window back up. If they catch us, I'll be stuck."

"Stuck?"

"With Pop wearing that god-awful thing at our wedding."

"Ah." Roman thought he understood. "Only high fashion at the Sonntag-Spinelli wedding festivities?"

"Um, right."

"You know that I don't care that he rides around in a pink limo, don't you? And I don't care about the blue velvet tux, either."

"Really?"

"Promise."

She sighed. "You know, I believe you." She gave him the rundown of what had happened at the book club.

"But that's great," he said. "The town isn't going to care if your father's not exactly *GQ*."

"*I* care," she said. "And I shouldn't."

"Why not?" He hooked a finger under her chin and tenderly lifted her face. "It's your wedding. Shouldn't it be exactly as you want it?"

She scowled a bit. "It's *our* wedding, and it already has so many problems that I shouldn't worry about one more."

"Well, I came here to tell you about one less."

"Really?" She couldn't imagine what, but his grin was broad enough that she knew it was big. "What?"

"Dad's agreed to have the ceremony and reception on the property. We don't have to find a new place, and we don't have to figure out a way to steer all the guests toward a new place."

"But . . . but . . . that's wonderful! Why? How?"

"I guess he talked to your dad."

That she wasn't expecting. "He what? They spoke? In person? Without blood?"

"Apparently. According to my father, your pop was pretty eloquent. Wanting to step up to the plate for his little girl. That kind of thing."

"Oh, wow." Tears welled in her eyes and she looked guiltily at the tux balled up in her hand. "Roman . . ." She didn't know what to say, and so she decided to just lose herself in his touch.

He held tight for a minute, and she breathed in the scent of him, which was a lot better than the scent of *her*, what with the mulch and all. Roman didn't seem to mind the smell, though. He tugged her closer, his hands moving to cup her breasts. Her nipples peaked, and she felt a dampness in her crotch. She wiggled a bit, rubbing against him, wanting to lose herself to this man.

But she couldn't. Not yet. There was something she had to do first.

Reluctantly, she pulled away. "Hold that thought."

"What's wrong?"

"I need to take the tux back."

"But you just went to so much trouble to steal it."

She nodded, exhaling as she searched her soul for courage. "I know. But I was thinking about something you said. Remember? That night we walked through the vines? I asked you why you came back to Texas. And you talked about how sometimes you have to make sacrifices for family."

She unrolled the tux and smoothed it out. The velvet was a little crushed and it smelled a bit like fertilizer, but surely that would fade by the wedding. "He's so damn proud of this thing, and all I could think about was how much it would embarrass me. But he's my dad and I love him and I shouldn't be embarrassed."

She drew in another breath. "So, my darling. That's *my* sacrifice. Not forcing my taste in clothes on my family. Even if I am the only one in the whole gene pool with any concept of style."

"I'm proud of you," he said. "And your father will be proud as a peacock in that tux."

"You mean he'll *look* like a peacock."

"Exactly."

She scowled. "Don't laugh, Roman. I need to sneak

this back into his room. Now. Before he wakes up. And you, oh husband-to-be, get to help me."

The night with Roman was positively glorious. And the next morning, Julia was certain she had a glow on her skin equal to that of any of the diamonds in the Jeep Collins jewelry store window. She paused a bit, actually, just to scope them out before she and Roman went inside to get their rings.

"Roman! Julia!" Tony, one of the men who worked in the store, came over as they entered, his hand outstretched. He shook Roman's hand, then led them both to a small desk. "Everything is ready. Just wait right here." They took a seat as he hurried off, returning quickly with two ring boxes that he set on the table in front of them. "Titanium, just as you'd asked, engraved with each other's names and the word 'forever.'"

Julia nodded, held her breath and opened the box. They'd decided on titanium for what it symbolized— strength and endurance. Absolutely one of the hardest metals out there. Nothing was going to happen to that ring, just as nothing was going to happen to their relationship. From a practical point of view, the metal was a color similar to silver or platinum. The ring would look fabulous on her finger next to Grandmother Olga's heirloom ring.

"Oh, Roman. It's beautiful." And, indeed, it was. The ring gleamed in the store's lighting, its polished surface looking even more fabulous than she'd imagined.

"As beautiful as you are," he said.

She laughed and leaned over to nudge him with her elbow. "Flatterer."

"I speak only the truth." He slipped her ring out of the box and held it out for her. "Try it on."

She nodded, but took the ring from him. "You get to put it on me at the altar. Until then . . ." She slipped the ring on her own finger as he did the same with his. They both extended their hands to Tony, who nodded, clearly pleased.

"Perfect fit," he said.

Roman and Julia grinned at each other, then slipped the rings off and handed them back to the jeweler. She pushed her chair back. "Wow. I can't believe it's so late. I hate to try on and run, but I have to meet Breckin."

Roman took her hand as she stood. "Just a little longer. I've got a surprise for you."

"Yeah?" Her mind ticked off the possibilities. A bracelet, maybe. Something she could wear all the time. Or maybe a diamond drop necklace. How classy would *that* be? "Well, in that case I think I can keep Breckin waiting."

She settled back and waited for Tony to retrieve another jewelry box from the back. She was expecting long and thin, so when he set what was clearly a ring box in front of her, she looked at him in surprise, then turned to Roman, still just as confused.

"What's this?"

"Open it and find out."

Her stomach did a little flip, and she rubbed

Grandmother Olga's platinum and glass engagement ring protectively. Surely he wouldn't . . . Not after she told him a hundred million times how much *this* ring meant to her. Not when she knew how tight his cash was . . .

"Go on," he urged.

She nodded, decided that she had no choice, and opened the box, revealing one of the most stunning engagement rings she had ever seen. A perfectly cut stone flashed brilliantly in the store's lighting, centered perfectly over the platinum setting. Around it, a dozen smaller diamonds winked, calling attention to the center stone without overpowering it.

Julia realized her hand was at her mouth. The ring was exquisite and, based on what she knew about jewelry—which was a lot—she knew that this ring had cost a pretty penny.

She didn't want it. She didn't want it at all.

"Roman, this is . . . I don't know what to say."

He took her hand, slipped off the heirloom ring. "I wanted to get this for you. A real diamond. As beautiful as you are."

She tugged her hand back. "But I love that ring!"

"Sweetheart, it's glass. I didn't know. I would never have given it to you if I'd known."

"But . . . but . . ."

"Julia." She met his serious eyes. "This is important to me. To be able to give you this. It means something to me. Please. Let me do this."

She wanted to protest, wanted to reach out and snatch the heirloom back and hold it to her chest.

But she knew Roman, and she knew what that dark, haunted look in his eyes meant. He wanted to buy this for her, and she couldn't take that away from him, even if the thought of losing the heirloom made her want to cry.

She couldn't speak, so she just nodded. And he slipped the new ring on her finger.

"I love you," he said.

The smile that touched her lips was genuine. "I love you, too."

Across the desk, Tony oohed and aahed, going on and on about how exquisite the ring looked. Julia just blushed and fought the urge to bolt.

It wasn't until they were outside that she finally relaxed. They were walking again, heading toward the Inn so she could go meet Breckin. "Roman, I . . ."

"Don't say anything, babe. Don't say anything except that you love the ring."

"I do. It's stunning. But you can't afford it. And you don't *have* to afford it. I loved Olga's ring, too. You proposed with that ring. It belongs on my finger."

"The best belongs on your finger. And I want to give you the best."

She gnawed on her lower lip, not sure what to say next. She'd told him a zillion times that she loved Olga's ring, that she didn't care that the stone was fake, and that she wanted to keep the ring. He hadn't heard her, obviously. And now she was certain she knew why—money. She hugged herself, suddenly chilled despite the already oppressive Texas heat.

"Roman, if this is about the money . . . If it's about

my money . . . well, I mean . . ." She drew in a breath, let it out again. "I just mean that if it makes you uncomfortable that I have some money, then you can just forget what I suggested about the B and B and the wine. It was just an idea. We don't have to use my money for—"

"I've already talked with Barrington."

She stopped. "What?"

He met her eyes, his own unreadable. "I called him last night. I think I can work it out with him. Come up with a business plan that gives him a label for his hotels and pumps enough money into the winery to make it worth my while."

"But . . . but I thought you didn't want to be the invisible source behind a label."

"I did a cost benefit analysis," he said. "This is the best solution." He reached out and squeezed her hand. "It was sweet of you to offer, but this is how I want to handle it."

"Oh." She tugged her hand back, shoved it into the pocket of her Seven jeans. "Okay." She didn't know what else to say. A thousand words—a thousand recriminations—raced through her head. She wanted to cry, to shout out, to scream in frustration and pound her fists against him.

In the end, though, she didn't say anything at all, just let him walk her to the Inn and open the car door for her. And then, as he got into his own car and drove off toward the winery, she let herself go. And cried.

*   *   *

The Texas sun was already frying the pavement by the time Julia and Breckin reached the Sonntags' home. "Thanks again," Julia said as they walked up the flagstone path to the front door. "You're really saving my ass."

"Well, it's a cute ass," Breckin said. "I don't mind saving it." He flashed her a haughty look. "At least not since you've now apologized properly."

"Right." She had, too. When he'd returned the call, she'd all but groveled. What the hell? She probably had been out of line. And she had to admit it was nice having him back in her corner. Breckin was tall and blond and lean, and somehow managed to look like a man who'd be equally at home starring in *Queer Eye for the Straight Guy* as he would fighting with a supplier about *exactly* the right napkins to ensure the perfect look for a table.

And she had to admit that her groveling had paid off. Already, Breckin had confirmed the photographer, the videographer, the caterer, and the makeup artist. He'd also convinced Julia that she and Syd and Vivien should not be having Julia's bachelorette party at Cuvée, a local bistro. "*Quelle* dull, darling," he'd said. And then he'd promptly booked them an evening package at the Hill Country Spa.

It had, Julia thought, made up for every nutty thing he'd done over the last few weeks.

Now they were at the Sonntags' in order to meet the delivery truck bringing the tables, chairs and linens. The linens wouldn't go on until Saturday morning, but Breckin wanted to set up the tables now so that he could, as he put it, "see the full tableau."

At this point, Julia was happy to just tag along. From her perspective, Breckin was fast filling the role of superhero. She was even convinced that he'd do something about her flower crisis. When she'd told him that Syd was handling that aspect, he'd looked at her with shock. "Julia, darling, you put *Syd* in charge of the flowers?" He'd taken her hand and squeezed. "Honey, you *are* desperate."

He'd immediately called Syd and co-opted the project.

"But what are you going to do?" Julia asked.

"Honey, do you trust me?"

She'd thought about it and decided that she did.

He'd kissed her on the cheek and that was that. The flowers, she supposed, she was leaving to fate. Or, more specifically, to a gay man with exquisite taste.

Well, she thought, *it could be worse.*

Sarah Sonntag answered the door, her smile welcoming. "Julia! Breckin! Darlings, come in. Come in."

Breckin and Sarah did the air kiss routine, and then Sarah took them through the house and out the back door to the expansive yard where the supply company was just beginning to bring in the tables and chairs. Breckin put his hands on his hips, nodded at the women, then made a shooshing motion. "Go," he ordered. "I have my work cut out for me here."

As Sarah and Julia stared at each other, Breckin

held up a hand and hollered to one of the workers. "You there! What are you thinking? That table is blocking the view of the creek! One foot to the left, man!" And as they watched, he stormed off over the grass, a general charging into battle.

"My," Sarah said.

Julia nodded. That about summed it up. And she was *so* glad she'd pulled him back in to help her. Kiki might be a case, but she definitely knew who to contact to get the job done.

Sarah took her arm and steered her inside. "While Breckin terrifies the hired help, I have something I want to show you."

Julia dutifully followed the older woman up the stairs to the master bedroom. A garment bag was laid across the bed, and Sarah pointed at it, a cat-ate-the-canary expression on her face. "Roman mentioned the trouble you'd had with your dress. I think this will fit you."

"Oh." Julia took a step forward, not knowing what to expect. She'd already had a ring foisted on her. Was she about to endure a wedding dress, too?

Sarah was busy unzipping the thing, and as soon as she pulled it out, Julia knew that there was no way—no way—that she was wearing that dress. She took a step backward. "Um, that's really sweet of you, Mrs. Sonntag, but Breckin already has a dress coming in for me. You know. With a train, and beading. The whole nine yards."

"Of course. Yes. I shouldn't have assumed . . ."

The older woman looked so disappointed that Julia felt her will begin to melt. *No.* She was *not* settling on the dress issue. The dress *made* the wedding. She was going to be a princess, damn it. And that was all there was to it.

"I had hoped that Kiki would wear this, you know. But she told me when she was sixteen that I should just forget that." Sarah smiled softly. "I hung on to it hoping she would change her mind. I know it's not the most amazing dress ever, but I don't think it's that bad. Do you?"

Julia shook her head. "No, it's actually quite beautiful." It wasn't. In fact, it was rather ugly, made out of some coarse material that had slightly yellowed with age and improper storage. It had a high neckline that wouldn't show any cleavage at all, and horizontal piping that cut right across the breast line. It was a sheath, and had no waistline, and in the back, a big bow was positioned right over the bridal butt.

"Was it yours?" Surely no sane woman would have worn this dress.

"Yes. My mother made it for her own wedding, and then I wore it. I thought, since you didn't have a dress, that you could wear it. You're going to be part of the family, after all."

"I . . . well, I'd be honored. But, you know, I've already paid for the dress, and my mother helped Breckin and me pick it out, and it's a design that she's dreamed of seeing me in. You know. With a train and all." Lie, lie, lie. Oh, surely she was going to hell for that one. But she couldn't wear that dress. Not Julia Spinelli, the girl who'd never in her life made a fashion faux pas.

"Of course." Sarah licked her lips. "How about you just try it on. Your mother can see you in her dress on your wedding day, and I can see you now. Just for a moment. The dress won't last another generation. You're the last to have the chance to wear it."

She didn't want to, but she figured it was the least she could do. And so she sucked in a breath, tried to keep the grimace off her face, and started to strip down.

The dress wasn't any better on. If anything, it was worse, especially considering the way that ridiculous bow bounced when she walked.

Sarah, however, apparently didn't realize the extent of the atrocity. She clasped her hands over her chest and sighed. "Julia, sweetheart, you look beautiful." Tears filled her eyes. "Thank you, darling. Thank you for trying it on."

"I . . . sure." A little demon inside her *almost* offered to wear the thing at the wedding. Thank God she caught herself in time. "I should probably change and get outside. I'm sure Breckin could use some help."

"Of course."

She started to pull off the dress, but her new ring snagged on the material. Sarah helped her maneuver her way out of the thing, and as Julia stood there in her underwear, Sarah took her hand. "Oh, Julia, darling, is this the ring Roman bought for you?"

Julia nodded and then, unable to help herself, she started to cry. "Damn it! I'm sorry! I don't mean to . . ." She trailed off, wiping at the tears that dribbled down her cheek.

"Honey, what is it?"

"It's just . . . well, I loved the old ring."

"The fake? Well, yes, it was beautiful." Sarah Sonntag cupped Julia's face in her palms. "Brides are supposed to be emotional, you know. And I guess grooms are, too. Roman wanted to get you something worthy of you. He loves you dearly. And he wanted you to have something you could truly cherish."

Julia nodded, trying desperately not to cry again. She understood what Sarah was saying. The only problem was that she'd *had* a ring she truly cherished—Olga's fake one. And if Roman couldn't even see into her heart when she flat-out told him what she wanted, then how could she believe that her fiancé really knew her at all?

"So?" Alex asked, his voice tinny through the weak cell connection. "How did she like it?"

"Like what?"

Alex laughed. "Come on, buddy. It's all over town that you bought Julia the biggest, baddest engagement ring this town's ever seen. How did she like it?"

"She loved it," Roman said, but he frowned as he spoke. She *hadn't* loved it. And her reaction had baffled him.

"Curb your enthusiasm, man. You're burning up the phone lines here."

"Sorry." Roman got up and went to the window. He knew he shouldn't feel this way, but he couldn't help it. He wanted to take care of her. Provide for her. It was a caveman attitude, but damned if it wasn't his attitude. And the fact that Julia had different ideas about how she wanted to be taken care of was messing with his sense of order in the universe.

"Spill," Alex ordered.

"She liked the fake ring," Roman admitted. "I bought her the most amazing ring I could afford— no, I *can't* afford it—and she still would rather have the fake one."

"So give her the fake one. What's the problem?"

If only it were that simple. Roman sighed. "She offered to buy Sonntag House so that we could use the proceeds to fund the winery."

"Marv? He must love that. He wins after all."

"Not Marv. Julia. Apparently she has a trust fund. She doesn't have access yet, but she is allowed to use the funds for real estate purchases."

"Ah," Alex said. "Suddenly it all becomes so clear."

"What?"

"Your attitude."

"Alex," Roman said, a hint of warning in his voice.

"Get mad at me if you want, buddy, but I'm laying it out for you. This woman is the best thing that's ever happened to you. If she has more money than you do, then that's just too damn bad."

"It's not that simple," Roman said. He wanted to

take care of her. Wanted to wrap her up in his love and keep her safe. Wanted to be able to step in and fix her problems. And it rankled that he couldn't even fix his own. "It's not that simple," he repeated firmly. "I love her, but it's just not."

"Yeah? Well, maybe it should be."

"Julia Spinelli! You cannot just sit there with mud on your face and not tell us what's wrong. This is your bachelorette party! The operative word being *party*!" Vivien crossed her arms over her chest, the stern expression marred only a little bit by the fluffy white spa robe she wore.

"I'm sorry, I'm sorry," Julia said. This was supposed to be her bachelorette outing with her bridesmaids. Sans Kiki, of course, who was hopefully going to arrive in time for the wedding. Unfortunately, the incident with Roman at the jewelry store, and then the talk later with Sarah, had soured Julia's mood. More—they had confused her. "I'm just a little distracted."

Viv and Syd exchanged a look.

"What?" Julia demanded.

"Cold feet?" Syd asked.

"No." Julia shook her head. She tried to frown, but the caked mud had pretty much set her features into one singular expression. "I don't know," she reluctantly admitted.

"It's about that ring, isn't it?" Syd asked. "I knew that stupid fake ring would get you in trouble."

"I *love* that ring," Julia said. "Would you please get over the fact that the stone is fake?"

"I will if you'll tell me what the problem is."

Julia shrugged. "I don't know. I guess . . ." She trailed off, because she *did* know. She just didn't want to say it out loud. "It's just that I don't think Roman's comfortable with me having money." There. She'd put it out there.

Viv gaped at her. "Your father is Marv Spinelli. I tried to foist a prenup on the guy. Are you saying he just now realized you've got funds?"

"Well, he knew about my family, of course. But I don't think it's even the money so much. It's just that . . . I don't know."

"Oh, sweetie," Syd said sympathetically.

"And when I suggested a business partnership, he practically ran screaming in the other direction. I don't know if the money makes him nervous or if he thinks I've got no head for business, but either way it . . . well, it bothered me. And then top that with this business about the ring, and I guess it just made me realize how little we know about each other. I mean, *really* know." She licked her lips. "Does that make sense?"

Another look passed between her sister and her friend. "Honey, that was our perspective weeks ago. And you read us the riot act and completely turned us around. Remember? You swore up and down that you and Roman were perfect and would be perfect together."

"And you guys believed me?"

Syd shrugged. "The man's crazy in love with you. I'd have to be blind not to see that."

"It's true. He's a goner," Viv agreed.

Julia managed a smile, the mud cracking on her face as she did so. "You know, you guys are right. I'm just feeling nervy. The wedding, and Marv being such a pain. But Roman does love me and I love him. And that's the bottom line, right?" She didn't wait for an answer. "Right. I've got a beautiful wedding in less than two days, Breckin actually managed to find me a gown that he's driving to San Antonio tonight to pick up, and there's no way I'm going to spoil it by worrying about stupid little things."

She looked around the room, squinting in the dim light. "So where is it? This is a party, right?"

"Where's what?" Syd asked.

"The champagne, silly. Aren't we three supposed to get totally tipsy? This is girls' night out, right? And girls, I'm *dying* to get totally wasted."

Chapter Sixteen

Your Bridal Checklist
  What you should be doing two days before the wedding: NOTHING. This is your time to enjoy. By now, everything should have been delegated. Relax, refresh, and restore. Trust us, honey. You want to save your energy for the honeymoon.
                              —from *The Organized Bride*

The next morning, Julia had to admit that maybe spa night with the girls had been just a little *too* fun. Or at least they'd drunk a little too much champagne. Because as she stood up there with Roman under the arbor while the minister walked them through the service, all she could think about was how she really, really, *really* needed to sit down.

Fortunately, as the bride, there wasn't much to do other than walk down the aisle, say her lines on cue, and kiss the groom.

Also fortunately, this hangover would be gone by the wedding tomorrow. And, if she was lucky, and if the aspirin did the trick, it would also be gone by the rehearsal dinner.

"Are you okay?" Roman asked her, pulling her aside as the rest of the wedding party mingled.

"I'm fine. Just a little too much fun last night."

He examined her face, his own expression worried. Then he picked up her left hand, the one with the new ring on it. He looked at it, and his eyes darkened. Julia held her breath, surprised by how much she hoped he would tug it off her finger and ask if they could have a do-over of the previous day.

But that didn't happen. Instead, he simply turned her hand over and kissed her palm.

"I love you," he said.

For some reason, the words made her want to cry. Her answer, however, was the complete truth: "I love you, too."

She wanted to talk more, though she wasn't entirely sure what she wanted to say. But she didn't have time. The photographer was there, wanting to take the "before" candids that Breckin insisted they have made for fabulous scrapbooks.

Breckin himself was bustling about, trying to hurry things up so that he could sweep Julia off to the local dry cleaners/alterations place, where he'd bribed the seventy-three-year-old seamstress into closing shop for the day so that she could concentrate on nothing except the alterations to Julia's new—and totally fabulous—princess wedding dress.

"Julia?" Syd sidled up. "You look lost."

"Just a little overwhelmed. And a little hungover."

"Well, everything's coming together."

Julia nodded. She had to agree. Considering that just a few days ago the wedding had more loose ends than a cheap pashmina, she was amazed at how smoothly everything was running.

"Julia!" Breckin called, moving toward her in long, determined strides. "You can stand around mooning *after* you're a married woman. Right now, you need to be photographed." He made a shooing motion toward Syd. "Don't you have a list of things to be working on? Go on. Shoo!"

Syd saluted, then made a face, making Julia laugh.

"You laugh now, but you'll thank me when we pull off the wedding of the century."

"I'm already thanking you," she said. She pulled herself up on her toes and kissed his cheek. "Thanks, Breckin. I really couldn't have done it without you."

"I told you *that* when you fired me."

Since he had a point, she didn't bother responding. She and Roman followed him around the house, then went through the motions for the photographer, taking a lot of staged shots that were designed to look candid. Julia fought the urge to protest. She'd decided to trust Breckin, and trust him she would.

"Good. Great." Breckin came up and took her by the arm, just as Roman took the other one. "No, no, no," he said. "She's yours forever after tomorrow. Right now, she's mine." He aimed a stern glare at her. "Alterations, darling. Unless you want your gown to sag."

"Priorities," Roman said with a smile.

"Absolutely." She blew him a kiss and hurried after Breckin, who was apparently in training for an Olympic racewalking team. They were almost to Breckin's car when Marv caught up with them. "Princess, hold up there. I gots to talk to you."

Breckin sighed. "Damn it, Julia. We'll never get everything done if you keep stopping to chitchat." He aimed a reproachful glance at Marv. "You couldn't have had this tender moment last night? You can't save it for tomorrow? You're her father. How many years have you been wasting? Mister, we are on a schedule here."

Julia expected Breckin to experience the Wrath of Marv, so she was surprised when Marv just nodded and said, "Yeah, yeah. I shoulda told her a long time ago. Just give me a couple of minutes."

Breckin crossed his arms over his chest and started to tap his foot.

"Alone, Breckin," Julia said. "Please."

Breckin huffed a bit, then nodded. "Fine. I'll go call about the flowers." He pointed a finger at Marv. "Five minutes. And then she's out of here. She's not your daughter today. She's my bride."

He sprinted away, leaving Marv and Julia looking awkwardly at each other. Finally Marv opened his arms wide, and Julia slipped inside, for the first time that day feeling truly warm and safe. "Oh, Daddy," she mumbled, then sniffled. She wasn't going to cry—she wasn't—but damned if she didn't come close.

"Hey, there, Princess. Don't you go cryin' on me. This is a big day. My little girl getting hitched and all."

She leaned back to look him in the face, expecting to see disapproval reflected there. She didn't. All she saw was love—which, of course, made the tears flow in earnest. "I love you, Pop," she said, throwing her arms back around him and sniffling. And why not? Weren't brides supposed to be teary and emotional?

He stroked her hair and made soothing noises. "Hey there, baby girl. Hey, hey. You know, you shouldn't oughta be cryin'. I figure big-shot business women don't cry, you know?"

She sniffed and pulled back again, her curiosity getting the better of her. "Huh?"

"You. You're doing good, you know? I, well, I just thought I ought to tell you."

"Really?" She wiped the tears away with the back of her hand. "You're not just saying that?"

He snorted. "You ever know me to say something I didn't mean?"

He had a point.

"No, Princess, it's true. You done good here. The Inn. The crazy idea you got for a B and B. Even your numbskull fiancé ain't so bad."

"The B and B?" She was so intent on his comment that she barely registered the praise. "How do you know about that?"

"Your sister's boyfriend. He told me about it. Sounds like a good idea."

"Really? You think I could pull something like that off?"

He adjusted his stance, his pudgy arms crossing over his chest as he nodded. "Yeah, Princess, I do. I been lookin' at your books, you know. You got a good head."

"Pop . . ." She felt her lip quiver.

"Don't go getting all emotional on me. That's the problem with women and business. They just can't take a damn compliment."

"I can take it," she said. "And thank you." She just wished . . .

He squinted at her. "What?"

"Nothing." She looked away, focusing on her toes.

"Don't nothing me, baby girl. What's going on?"

She sighed, not wanting to tell Marv for fear he'd gloat, and at the same time wanting to dump all her fears and frustrations on her father and let him sort them out for her.

"Princess? This is your pop. Am I gonna have to smack you across the backside or are you gonna tell me?"

She grinned. That was the Marv she knew how to answer to. "It's just . . . well, it's Roman. When I told him about my money and suggested we form a partnership to buy Sonntag House, he kind of freaked."

She frowned, realizing that wasn't true. "No, actually, he didn't freak. But he didn't do it either. He lined up some other business deal. A deal he didn't even want, and I know he did it only so he wouldn't have to partner with me."

"Aw, Princess. You really think so?"

She licked her lips, her eyes brimming. "I don't know what to think. I mean, if he thinks it would strain the marriage for us to have a business together, he ought to just tell me that, right? But what if he thinks I've got no business sense? What if all his compliments have just been, I don't know, pats on the head? Or what if he's uncomfortable with the fact that I have money? It's not like I can change that. I mean, I'm not going to just give it all back to you!"

Marv laughed. "I wouldn't take it even if you tried. Why you think I been working my keister off for all these years? For my health? I been wanting to give you girls something solid. Don't you ever be ashamed you got money. Your pop worked his tail off for it. And it's yours because I love you."

"Pop . . ." She got all misty-eyed again—apparently that was par for the course this close to her wedding day. "I don't think you've ever said anything like that to me."

"Yeah, well, just because I don't say it doesn't mean I don't mean it." He shifted a bit, trying to find a position where he could look her in the eyes. "About that boy of yours—"

"I know you don't approve of Roman, but I love him, Pop. It's probably just wedding nerves, but this whole money thing has got me all worked up, and I just—"

"I like him just fine."

She blinked. "What?"

"You heard me. I ain't gonna say it again. Let's just say I been watching the boy. Seen some things he's done for you. And I've been doin' a little thinking on my own. I don't like what happened all those years ago, but that's the past. And right now, that boy's in love with you. That much I'm sure of."

"Then why is he walking on eggshells about this

whole money thing? And the ring. He made a huge deal out of going into debt to buy me a ring I don't even want."

Marv nodded, looking like a man who was truly considering the problem. "He wants to take care of you, Princess. It rankles him because he thinks that he can't. That you don't need him that way."

She nodded slowly, considering the possibility. It did make some sense. "You really think so?"

"Princess, I been there. Trust me. Just give the boy some time to come around."

"Time," she repeated. Except she didn't have any time. Tomorrow she was going to be at the center of the grandest wedding the town had seen in decades. It was what she'd always dreamed of, and she wasn't about to sacrifice that or postpone it or do anything at all to risk her dream. "Time," she said again. And she really, really wished she had some.

"Dance with me?" Roman held his hands out to her, and Julia slid into his arms, wanting to stay there forever. After tomorrow, she thought, she wouldn't have any reason to leave. They'd be married. Bound to each other. For better, as the saying went, or for worse.

Damn.

These doubts and fears kept running through her head and she didn't know if they were legitimate or just nerves. Now, of course, wasn't the time to be thinking about it. They were at their rehearsal dinner, dancing among the tables filled with good food and good friends. Their families were actually at peace with each other (more or less), the final wedding arrangements had been made (Breckin swore the flowers were taken care of, though he wouldn't tell Julia how), and all that was left was to eat, drink and be merry before the big day.

So why, why, why did she have this niggling feeling of doom?

"Julia?"

She sucked in a breath, planned to tell him everything was all right, and heard herself saying, "We need to talk."

"Yeah," he said. "I know."

They moved through the restaurant, stopping at tables to chat with Syd and Alex, Vivien and J.B., their parents. Then they made some ridiculous excuse and stepped outside, walking hand in hand down Main Street in the fading light.

She didn't say anything at first because her nerves were too raw, but finally she decided that she had to speak up or they'd be all the way to Austin before her courage kicked in. "I need to know if you're okay with the money," she said, then held her breath.

He didn't even pretend to misunderstand. He just stopped, and took both her hands in his. They stood that way, drawing the odd glance from the few passersby, as he fought to find the words. "I am," he finally said, and Julia felt her heart lift with relief. "I wasn't at first, and I'm sorry. Babe, I'm so, so sorry. I wanted . . . I guess I wanted to give you everything. Old-fashioned and ridiculous, but I just wanted to be the man you relied on. But when I learned that you had access to money that could get me out of a bind . . . I don't know. Maybe I was a little bit jealous. Maybe I felt emasculated. Maybe I was just being an ass."

"Then it didn't have anything to do with my business skills?"

His forehead furrowed. "What do you mean?"

She looked down, studying her shoes. "Just that I suggested we form a partnership to buy Sonntag House, and you practically ran screaming in the other direction."

"Oh, babe." He shook his head, holding tight to her hands.

"And that time in Austin when you didn't want me in the loop for your meeting. I mean, we're about to enter a pretty intimate partnership, and yet you don't seem to want me anywhere near your business. Don't you trust me?"

He closed his eyes, a flash of pain coloring his face. "Sweetheart, I promise, it's nothing like that. You're brilliant at business. You have an amazing knack. You've blown everyone away, including yourself."

"Everyone but you, you mean."

"Me too. I promise. It's not you, really. It's me."

She choked back a sob. "Funny. I think that's the line I used most often every time I broke up with a boy."

"Well, you're not breaking up with me." He brought her hand up and kissed her fingertips. "Julia, all I know is that I love you and I want you and I want to take care of you. I want to make you happy."

"You do make me happy, Roman. And the things I want from you—the things I want for us—don't have anything to do with money."

"I know that, babe."

He was holding her left hand, his finger brushing the edge of the new engagement ring. She held her breath, expecting him to take the ring back, to promise to return his great-grandmother's ring to her finger. He didn't, though. And all of a sudden, Julia's heart got a little bit heavier.

The ring really was a symbol; she realized that now. And not a symbol of their engagement, either. Or at least not exclusively. No, it was a symbol from Roman to the town. A symbol that he was still successful, a man with money enough to buy his wife a fabulous diamond—even if his wife didn't really want one.

"You know I love you, don't you?" she asked.

"Of course."

She licked her lips. "Remember what you told me when you found me and Bart in the flower bed? You said that you loved me. And that it didn't matter about my dad or his blue tux or any of that. You just loved me."

"I remember."

She nodded. "Do you really know the woman you love?"

He cocked his head, wary. "Of course I know you. Sweetheart, I—"

"What's my favorite color?"

He closed his mouth. Frowned. "Yellow?"

"Good guess. But wrong."

He shook his head, concern and confusion marring his features. "Julia, I—"

She pressed a finger to his lips. "Don't worry," she said. "It doesn't matter. It's red. And in time you'll learn that. And all sorts of other little things about me." She nodded down the street toward the restaurant. "We ought to get back," she said.

They walked silently back, not speaking. But the silence between them seemed heavy and awkward. She knew without a doubt that Roman was the perfect man for her. But she was no longer certain that she was his perfect girl.

Nerves, Roman thought. That explained why even after their talk, Julia still seemed distracted during the rehearsal dinner. Nerves and maybe something else. Like that she was still irritated with him because of his reaction to her money. Not that he could blame her for that. He had reacted badly. Stupidly. But he couldn't go back in time and fix that. They'd just have to keep moving forward. And the fact was, with less than twenty-four hours to go until the wedding, it was understandable that emotions were running high. Wasn't that the very definition of a bride?

Not that he had the luxury of analyzing the situation. He was too busy shaking hands and listening to toasts and stories from his family about all the girls he'd left with broken hearts in high school.

He wasn't even paying attention, in fact, when Julia stood up, her spoon tapping against the side of her water glass. But the ambient noise in the room died down, and he turned to find his bride-to-be facing the crowd, looking strong and beautiful and a little too serious for the night before her wedding.

"Hi," she said, her voice more timid than he'd ever heard before. "Um, I . . . I mean, *we* . . . have a little announcement to make." She smiled at Roman, her expression ever so tender. He swallowed. This was going to be bad.

"So, here's the thing." She stood up a little straighter, and he knew she was gathering her nerves. "Roman and I just had a long talk, and we've decided that we need a little more time to get to know each other." She held up a hand, ostensibly to cut off the chatter that had started in the room. "We're not cancelling the wedding. We're just postponing it. And there's still going to be a party tomorrow at the Sonntags' house. The wedding reception will just be an engagement party instead. And when Roman and I are ready, we'll go visit a justice of the peace. Or maybe Judge Strauss will do the honors," she added, and everyone laughed, albeit a bit nervously.

Roman stood up. He had to. She'd included him in this speech so as not to embarrass him; he knew that. But he also knew how much a big wedding meant to her. And there was no way they could pull this off more than once. "Julia, sweetheart. This wedding—"

"No." She shook her head, her eyes sad despite

her smile. "No. I thought I needed the big wedding. You know, the wedding I'd always dreamed about. A fairy-tale dress and a fairy-tale wedding. But the thing I've learned is that it's not about the wedding being perfect. It's about the marriage being perfect." She paused a bit, then aimed her smile at all the guests, who were sitting there looking just as shell-shocked as Roman felt. "Give us time, and we'll get there. Tomorrow, though, we just want to celebrate the engagement with our friends and family."

She dragged her teeth across her lower lip, a sure sign that she was fighting back tears. Then she squeezed her father's hand and sat back down.

Roman realized he was still standing, all eyes on him. They all knew he was as shocked as they were; surely they could see it in his eyes.

He exhaled, doing nothing more than watching his bride. He'd known from the day that Julia had walked into his life—a vibrant woman in a tiny bikini determined to read him the riot act—that she would never stop surprising him.

This, however, really wasn't what he'd had in mind.

"I can't let her do this," Roman said.

Alex took his empty beer bottle and replaced it with a full one. Then he tossed J.B. a bottle as well. The men were in Roman's apartment, their bachelor party plans cancelled. Instead, they were commiserating with their friend.

"You have to let her do this," J.B. said. "Roman, man, if what you're saying is right, one of the reasons she's backing off is your little issue about control."

"She wants the big wedding. And, yes, maybe I do like to be in charge, but that's never been a problem. I mean, we laugh about it." They did, too. His personality was one of her favorite things to tease him about. He shook his head, slightly baffled. "I've never steamrollered her decisions. Hell, she's the one who's built up the Inn. I barely even helped her."

"You never steamrollered her until she tried to step in and do some control maneuvers on your turf," Alex pointed out. "Until she wanted equal billing in a business deal."

"Put together with her money," J.B. added.

And, because they were absolutely right, Roman didn't say anything.

He'd been an idiot, a fool, and a hundred other derogatory names. He'd been trying so hard to be the perfect husband, able to give his new wife the perfect life, that he hadn't been able to see the big picture.

And now the picture was nothing but a mess.

The truth was he *did* trust Julia—on all counts. He trusted her business sense and he trusted her with his heart. But he'd been such a damn fool about keeping his pride that he'd wounded the one person who mattered more to him than himself.

He had only one chance to make it better. It was a risk, but it was a risk he had to take. He only hoped it would work.

Determined, he took a long swallow of beer and then stood up. "I need your help, guys. I know what I need to do. But there's something I need if I'm going to pull it off."

"Sure," J.B. said.

"What do you need?" Alex asked.

"Breckin," Roman said. "I need you guys to track down Breckin."

"It's really beautiful," Claudia said.

"Oh, yes," said Daisy. "Truly."

Julia nodded. Her friends from school had flown in that morning. They were a little—no, *a lot*—surprised that the wedding had morphed into a party, but they were doing a good job of masking their concern. And their curiosity.

As for it being beautiful, about that, they were right. Breckin really had come through. The tables and chairs were covered with crisp white linens and spaced the perfect distance apart. Welcome gifts were at each place setting. And the flowers—well, the flowers were perfect, Texas wildflowers strewn delicately around. He'd even found a private source for bluebonnets, the state flower that couldn't be picked from the wild.

She felt a little twinge in her stomach, a knot of regret that this was just a party and not her wedding reception. She hadn't even gotten to wear her dress. Instead, she was decked out in a white Chanel suit. Sophisticated, glamorous, regal. But not the attire of a bride.

She told herself she'd done the right thing.

She hoped she was telling herself the truth.

"Chin up, sweetie," Viv said, moving up to press a champagne flute into her hand. "You did the right thing."

"Are you sure?"

"Did it feel like the right thing when you did it?" Julia nodded.

"Well, there you go." She gave Julia a tender smile, then waved at J.B., who came over and slid his arm around Viv's waist before planting a quick kiss on her shoulder.

"How you doing, kid?" he asked Julia.

She shrugged. She'd been getting that question a lot. "I'm trying to remind myself that it's one hell of a party."

"That it is."

Syd and Alex ambled up. "Anyone else think it's ironic that I got the last word?" Syd asked. "And believe me. When arguing with Julia, I *never* get the last word."

Julia squinted at her sister. "What on earth are you talking about?"

Syd smiled angelically. "I came to Texas to postpone the wedding, remember?"

Julia rolled her eyes. "Doesn't count. You do *not* get the last word."

"Of course I do. I—"

But she was cut off by the flurry of flashbulbs and trampling feet. Julia turned sharply, her eyes widening at the sight of Kiki leading Roman by the arm, photographers following in their wake.

"Julia! Julia, honey, this just won't do. You can postpone the wedding if you need to. I mean, do what you have to do. But you simply can*not* postpone Vera Wang." She pointed a stern finger at Syd and Viv. "Photo session now. On the veranda. Zachary is just the best," she added, waving a hand at a short man laden down with cameras. "You'll have a portrait and, if you're lucky, you might even end up in *Vogue.*"

As Syd and Viv shrugged at each other, communicating only with their eyes, Julia moved to Roman's side. He took her hand, their fingers twining automatically as Kiki swept out as quickly as she'd swept in, this time with Syd and Vivien in her wake.

"Your sister is a force of nature," Julia said.

"Scary, but true." A slow smile slid across his face. "Can I have this dance?"

"Will it make the news?" She nodded toward the crew from *Entertainment Tonight* or *E!* or one of those celebrity shows that had been left milling about the lawn while Kiki ran off to change.

"You just never know," Roman said.

"In that case . . ." She slipped into his arms, and was caught up once again by the sense of perfection. This was where she belonged. With him. But doubt taunted her. Had she made a fatal error? Roman had said he understood why she postponed the wedding, but he'd never said he agreed with her. What if, when it was all over, he decided he didn't want her after all? What if, in the end, she lost what she was so desperately trying to hold on to?

She shook her head, not willing to let her thoughts

go there. Not today. It might not be her wedding, but it was still a celebration. She was Roman Sonntag's fiancée. He loved her. And she intended to revel in that.

She realized with a start that the music had stopped, and that she and Roman were standing in front of the arbor where they'd intended to take their vows. She also realized that everyone at the party had turned to face them. Even her bridesmaids were standing in the background, not yet decked out in Vera Wang splendor.

What was going on?

"Julia, sweetheart, there's something I need to say."

Oh dear. She'd made her decision. They needed this. Surely he wasn't going to challenge her in front of all these people? Was he?

"Roman, we—"

He pressed a gentle finger to her lips. "No. Please. I need to say this."

She exhaled, then nodded. Apparently, yes. He was going to challenge her. So much for celebration. Now she got to add "fight with fiancé" to the list of things she did on her non-wedding day.

"Everyone," Roman said, turning to face the crowd of over three hundred people. "Can everyone hear me?"

The crowd answered back in the negative, and one of the guys from the band supplied Roman with a microphone. Julia looked on, amusement warring with mortification.

"Better," Roman said, his voice reverberating loud enough for the crowd, and probably for everyone still in town, too.

"Yesterday, Julia told you that we agreed to wait on the wedding. That this was going to be an engagement party, and that in time we'd get married in front of a JP or in Vegas or something.

"But that was last night," he continued. "Today, I've got a different perspective."

"Roman!" She tried to get a word in, but he just talked over her.

"You see, we hit a rough patch in our relationship because I was a total jerk." The audience snickered at that, and Julia decided that maybe she should quit trying to interrupt. Even the camera crews, she saw, had their lenses aimed at Roman. And Kiki, amazingly, hadn't even noticed.

"I was trying so hard to keep a grip on both my relationship and my business, that in the end, they both spun completely out of control. And all because I was an idiot. It's not something I admit easily, so listen up. Because the odds of me repeating this again are pretty slim. But I want everyone here to know. It's important that I lay it all out on the line for you—and for Julia."

He squeezed her hand, then, and she squeezed back, the lead weight that had settled on her chest lifting a little bit. She wanted to say something, but she didn't know what. And so she just listened as Roman continued.

"There's a couple of things y'all should know. First

off, I'm busted flat financially. Now, I've got a solid product in the winery, and I expect it's going to take off soon, so I won't be broke for long. But in the meantime, I know that I can get out from under this debt a lot faster with Julia's help than without it. The woman's got a head for business and—as an added bonus—she's got the bank account to back it up."

The audience tittered at that, and Julia knew he had them eating out of the palm of his hand. Roman, who'd been so afraid the town would look down on him if he admitted he was broke, had just won these people completely over.

And, she had to admit, he'd won her over, too.

But he wasn't finished yet.

"The other night, she suggested a business partnership. I didn't say no, exactly, but I didn't say yes, either. And I realize now that I should have. I was so busy trying to make sure that Julia saw only the man she fell in love with—the competent businessman—that I ended up doing something totally *in*competent. I didn't take a good deal when it was offered to me. That's a mistake I hope to rectify, because if Julia will have me, there's nobody else I'd like as much for a partner. In business or in life."

She blinked at that, her heart skipping in her chest. She knew how much Roman valued his reputation in the town. Admitting that he'd made a mistake where business was concerned—heck, admitting that he needed money—was a huge sacrifice for him. A sacrifice he was making for her.

"The other thing is that Julia told y'all last night

that we were going to take some time to get to know each other." He turned to her. "Well, sweetheart, I don't think we need any more time. Sure, there are things we don't know. But I know all the important things."

She cocked her head, started to open her mouth, but he pressed a finger to her lips.

"Hear me out," he said. "For the record, I know that this woman likes to wear cheap underwear imprinted with cartoon characters."

"Roman!"

"*And* she likes peanut butter M&M's."

"This is *so* not winning you points!"

"I don't know what kind of shampoo she uses because I never paid attention, but I know it smells good. And I know that she bites her lip when she's nervous—like she is now—and she blushes when I talk about her. Looks cute, doesn't it?"

Another roar of approval from the crowd, and her face burned even hotter.

"I know she's got a knack for marketing and a head for business. I know she hasn't got the faintest clue how to fix a clogged drain, and she'd rather call 9-1-1 than squash a cockroach. I know she loves her mom and her dad and her sister. And I even know she loves me."

A tear trickled down Julia's cheek, and she nodded.

"And I know one other thing." He took her hand and pulled off the new engagement ring. "I know that I want this ring back."

As Julia watched, Roman pocketed the ring. The crowd tittered nervously, then became silent as Roman withdrew another ring box. He got down on one knee, then held it out to her, the lid still closed. "I also know that the one thing Julia Spinelli has wanted for her whole life is a big, fancy, formal wedding." He reached out with his other hand and flipped the top. Olga's ring, still with its fake stone, winked at her in the sunlight. "Julia Spinelli," Roman said, "will you marry me? Right here. Right now. Because I love you. And I don't need any more time to think about that."

She couldn't speak. She really and truly couldn't speak. She opened her mouth, but words didn't come out. Inside her head a voice was screaming *Yes! Yes!* But the voice was staying in there.

In desperation, she did the only thing she could do. She slipped the ring on her finger, threw herself into his arms, and kissed him.

When they broke the kiss, the guests were still applauding.

"Is that a yes?" Roman asked.

Julia nodded, tears streaming down her face. "Oh, yeah. That's very much a yes."

Roman may have said he wanted to get married "right here, right now," but that really wasn't possible. Too many people were rushing the couple, tossing out kisses and congratulations.

Not that Roman minded. Heck, at the moment, he wouldn't have minded if a plane swooped down to pick them up and dump them in Las Vegas. All Roman cared about, in fact, was that Julia had said yes. She loved him. She'd forgiven him. And she was going to marry him.

How he got so lucky in life, he'd probably never know, but he'd never stop being thankful. That much he *did* know.

Right then, Julia stood only a few feet away from him, having been immediately mobbed by the girls from the book group. He caught Ann Marie's eye, and she winked at him. "You done good," she mouthed, over the heads of her friends.

Roman smiled back. Coming from Ann Marie, that was a heck of a compliment.

Wesley and Arvin came up, tailed by Viv and Syd, who each gave him a quick hug before trotting over to throw their arms around Julia. "Damn good speech," Wesley said. "And this party's got some good food, too."

Roman laughed. "We aim to please."

He was still laughing when his parents came up to hug him, telling him how proud they were of him and how happy they were he was marrying such a nice girl.

They froze in place when Marv approached, and Roman held his breath, wondering if there would be fireworks. But no explosions came. Marv held out his hand, and Robert took it. The two men nodded briefly at each other, and then the Sonntags departed, leaving Roman alone with his father-in-law-to-be.

"You done good, boy," Marv said.

"Thank you, sir. I've done a little more, too."

Marv squinted at him. "What are you talking about?"

"Julia's always wanted a big, formal wedding. We got a little sidetracked, but I'm still hoping we can make that dream come true." He let his gaze drift over Marv's outfit of polyester pants and a hideous ruffled cowboy shirt. "Your tux is in the house, sir. I took a few liberties this morning. With Syd's help, of course."

"And mine," Breckin said, moving up to them with quick, efficient paces. "Go now," he said, waving Marv toward the house. "Shoo! Shoo!"

Roman watched, amused, as Marv did just that. Then he watched as Breckin proceeded to crash Julia's little circle, shooing Syd and Viv away with just as much efficiency.

"Roman?" Julia asked, making her escape and coming to stand by him. "What's going on?"

A few feet away, Breckin whistled and signaled for a workman to roll a metal cage across the lawn. It came to rest behind the arbor, tastefully covered with a white cloth.

"Doves?" Julia asked.

"For after the ceremony. I took a chance. I called Breckin last night and, well, here you go."

"Thank you," she said, and the love he saw in her eyes told him that he'd done exactly the right thing.

"Breckin and I were able to get pretty much everything put back together. It won't be quite as organized a wedding, and the guests aren't in formal attire, but—"

"It's perfect. It's more than perfect." She pressed a kiss to his lips. "It's not the wedding that matters, you know. All that matters is us."

"And the dress," he added with a grin.

Her eyes twinkled. "Well, yeah. That goes without saying."

"It's in the guest bedroom," Roman said. "Breckin brought it over this morning. All you have to do is change."

She nodded, but she didn't move immediately toward the house. Instead, her eyes searched the crowd, stopping only when they landed on his mother. "About the dress," she said, her mouth curved into the tiniest of smiles. "I've got something else in mind."

Weddings weren't about fairy tales or fashion, Julia realized. They weren't even about just two people. Not really.

In the end, a wedding was all about family.

And that's why she didn't wear the princess dress with the hand-beading and the train and the flattering neckline. It was, after all, just a dress like so many others.

Sarah's dress had a family history. *Her* family's history.

And, really, the dress wasn't so bad. After all, she was a bride. She glowed. And Vera Wang made anyone look good—even a bride *not* wearing Vera, but who was surrounded by bridesmaids resplendent in the designer's best.

And, of course, standing next to Marv's tacky blue tux, any dress would have seemed stunning.

Mostly, though, she knew she was beautiful by the look in Roman's eyes as she walked down the aisle.

All the rule books instruct the bride to walk slowly, regally. And Julia tried, really she did. But she couldn't seem to manage. Instead, she hurried down the aisle, her father at her side and her groom ahead of her.

She hurried, because she couldn't wait to say "I do."

All right, girls, listen up. Your wedding is your big day, right? The be-all and end-all? The culmination of everything that you've hoped for and dreamed about? Right? Right?

Wrong. Your wedding is important, sure. But it's the life with your husband that counts. The man you love is putting a ring on your finger. Savor it, girls. And savor every day from the wedding on. The wedding may be big, but your life is even bigger. You've found a man to share your days and nights, your hopes and dreams. And that, my friends, is the biggest coup of all.

—Julia Spinelli

Dear Reader,

If we haven't met, let me introduce myself: I'm Jersey girl Sydney Spinelli, Julia's older sister and self-appointed protector. I still can't believe my baby sis is getting married before me, and to a guy she's only know a few short weeks!

But as I discovered when I met Alex, the best man, you can't really plan when or where or with whom you fall in love. It certainly wasn't convenient for me to flip over Alex, when my whole reason for flying down to Fredericksburg, Texas, was to stop Julia's wedding and convince her that she didn't know Roman well enough to love him.

Truth to tell, falling for Alex was highly embarassing for me. And unnerving. All of our lives, Julia's been the beauty and I've been the brain. So I couldn't believe it when Alex went after *me*, of all people, since he's so hot himself. I mean, Kiki, his high school girlfriend (and the groom's sister) was a runner up to Miss Texas! Ugh. I couldn't compete with that.

And it's not like Alex was under the illusion that I was a saint. He came right out and accused me of meddling. Can you believe that? I was *not* meddling, just trying to help.

Anyway. Alex is starting to get that look in his eye and I have a feeling that he's going to pop the question any day now. Shhhhh, don't tell anyone—since Julia will give me such a hard time—but I've even started to look at wedding gowns, which *is* so unlike me.

I'll let you know what happens! And if you want to know how Alex and I got together, pick up a copy of *First Date*, where you can read our whole story. You can find it at your local bookstore, or find out how to order it at www.KarenKendall.com.

Talk to you soon, Syd

Dear Reader,

I adore Julia and Roman's story, don't you? And not just because he's my brother, and she's now a sister by marriage. Well, maybe that is the reason. But I had to say something sweet before putting in a shameless plug for *my* book—*First Kiss*. You know the old saying: The *real* romance at a wedding can be found with the prettiest bridesmaid, preferably one who happened to be a runner-up for Miss America 1995. Okay, that's not really an old saying. I just made it up. But it's true!

Pick up my book (it's called *First Kiss*—did I mention that?), and you'll find out all about me and Fab. I know. How hot is that name? It's short for Fabrizio, and it's just so cool—the way it sounds tripping off your tongue, the way it looks when you write it down. *Fab*.

So here's the deal. One day I was plastered on the front page of every New York tabloid for something I *didn't* do (long story). Anyway, I'm on the run from the paparazzi (most of them ugly men with bad manners), and I dash inside Affair. It's *the* hottest boutique hotel in Manhattan, a place where stylish people go for, well, *affairs*. And that's when I met the owner, Fab Tomba.

Oh, my God—it was one of those unforgettable electrical connections. You know, when something inside you just clicks and you *know* that this man could turn your life completely upside down. It's like back in the 70s when Ali MacGraw met Steve McQueen (FYI—I use celebrity as a point of reference for everything). She saw him from two thousand feet away and almost passed out. My thing with Fab—practically the same! Well, sort of. Actually, I saw him for the first time from a much closer distance, I wasn't married at the time and we weren't on a movie set. But other than that—totally similar.

Okay, I'm not telling any more. You have to read the book!

Air Kisses,

Kiki Douglas,
Actress (mainly daytime soaps but would one day like my own sitcom)
Motivational Writer (tip for quick ego boost: send yourself a glorious floral arragement and have the card read something like, *I can't wait to get home to you . . . Matthew McConaughey*)

Dear Reader,

Have we met? I'm Julia Spinelli's best friend from school, Vivien Shelton. If you ever need legal advice regarding family law, just let me know—because I'm one of Manhattan's top divorce attorneys.

Since that's the case, let me tell you that it was the height of irony that Julia drafted me as a bridesmaid in her wedding! I honestly didn't know what to say, except to advise her to register for a pre-nup along with that silver punch bowl.

As you might imagine, that ticked off our Julia and she wouldn't even discuss the matter of a pre-nup with me. She's a romantic, and she was head over heels for this Texas winemaker, Roman Sonntag. It set all my inner alarm bells off, and I decided that it was my duty to bring up the pre-nup with Roman's attorney, J.B. Anglin.

Did I mention that the last time I'd seen J.B., I was, ah, somewhat naked? And he was rather annoyed since I'd just apparently used him and tossed him out of my hotel room? So our first meeting in Fredericksburg was a little awkward, especially since he felt compelled to bring up that topic.

We never did get either Julia or Roman to sign a pre-nup, but while we argued about it, J.B. and I fell in love, despite his ex-wife and my cynicism and utterly dysfunctional family life. Believe it or not, my five rescued greyhounds and I are considering a move to Texas. If you want to read the full story, I filed the briefs in *First Dance*. Get a copy at your nearest bookseller or go to www.Karen Kendall.com.

Keep in touch, okay? All best, Viv